HOLD BACK THE NIGHT

EMILIE RICHARDS

1

Sometime during the night, gang graffiti bled through the three coats of white paint the Reverend Thomas Stonehill and his ragtag congregation had slathered over the sanctuary walls. Sometime during the night, a homeless man picked the lock and made himself a bed under the unorthodox picture of Jesus that graced the front of the church. Sometime during the night, urban phantoms dumped trash on the steps, dug up the last chrysanthemum plant in the narrow flower bed and left a note in the mail slot complaining about the dessert at the Wednesday night sharing supper.

"More ice cream. Less talk." Thomas crumpled the two sentences in his hand and stared somberly at the old man who was gathering his belongings into a utilitarian stack honed by years of living on the street. Once he finished Thomas held out the note. "Did you write this?"

The old man shook his head.

"Do you know about our Wednesday night sharing suppers?"

The old man just stared at him.

"Every Wednesday night at six we serve a meal here for anybody who's hungry. You're always welcome. And next time you need a place to stay, ring the bell. I'll open the door for you. No need to break in."

"Churches ain't supposed to be locked," the old man mumbled.

"And kids aren't supposed to get their kicks out of spray painting walls and smashing furniture, but sometimes they do."

The old man inclined his head toward the picture that had watched over him as he slept. "Person who painted that must have taken a kick to the head."

The grim line of Thomas's mouth relaxed a little. "Think so?"

"Jesus with four different faces." The old man shrugged. "Who'd think like that?"

"How do you know it's Jesus?"

"That face looks like him." The old man pointed to one of the four images superimposed over the edges of the others.

"The white one, you mean? Maybe if you were black, the one beside it would look like Jesus."

"What kind of church is this? What call you got to come down here to the Corners and mess with people's religion?"

"What call you got to drink yourself blind every night and wake up in a strange place every morning?" Thomas asked the question without a trace of condescension in his voice. He knew he had no right to judge. He was no better than the man in the cast-off clothing, no better than anyone.

"Ain't got much pity in your soul for a sick old man, do you? What kind of preacher are you, anyway?"

"The kind who thinks pity's a waste of time."

Thomas looked at his watch. It was gold, twenty-four carats, with a new imitation leather band that was already cracking. "We'll be having church here in less than an hour. You're welcome to stay."

"Nah." The old man scratched himself, starting at his sparsely forested head and progressing steadily downward to places that most men didn't scratch in public. "I'll be moving on."

Thomas reached for his wallet. He pulled out three dollar bills and handed them over. "Will we see you on Wednesday?"

The man stuffed the bills in his pocket. "Don't take charity."

"Then think of it as supper with friends."

"Don't want no friends." The man strapped his belongings together with a belt and lifted the bundle to his shoulder. Without another word, he limped across the room and disappeared out the door.

The door slammed again a few seconds later behind a young woman herding two sleepy-eyed children in front of her. Her eyes were red, and her dark hair was uncombed. Her thin body seemed to fold in on itself, as if to protect the children with her shadow. Thomas didn't smile. "You're early, Ema. I haven't even set up the chairs yet."

"I'll help." She attempted a smile. It was hard, since her lip was badly swollen. "I don't mind."

"Have you had breakfast?"

"Sure."

"The kids, too?"

"They don't eat this early."

"There's cereal out on the kitchen table upstairs. Milk and juice in the refrigerator."

"I couldn't-"

"You will." Thomas hiked his thumb toward the hall and the stairs leading to his apartment. "And there's ice for your lip."

"Oh, my lip's fine. I just bumped into—"

"Wrap the ice in a dish towel. Twenty minutes on, twenty minutes off, until church starts."

She nodded. In moments she and the children had closed his apartment door behind them.

And Thomas Stonehill was alone with a painting of Jesus and his own thoughts.

He was comfortable with neither. The picture was new and

disturbing in its intensity. His thoughts were old and tormented him constantly.

He stared at the picture and filled the silence with the voice that had once held a congregation of thousands of souls enthralled.

"So, J.C., there go some of your little lambs, starting Sunday morning with the wolf right behind them."

He didn't expect an answer. He had given up believing in answers the same day he resigned from one of the most prestigious Protestant churches in the Midwest.

He moved closer. The four images seemed to merge, but he hardly saw them anyway. His vision was turned inward. "One homeless lamb, one battered, and two little ones so hungry and scared they don't know how to laugh. Imagine that, J.C., kids who've forgotten how to laugh—if they ever learned how in the first place."

He stared at the picture, but in his mind he saw the front of another church. He saw an altar spread with snow-white linen, a starkly simple golden cross and polished silver cornucopias overflowing with chrysanthemums, dahlias and the fruits of the autumn harvest. All the blessings of God's good earth on God's good table. For God's good people.

"One homeless, one battered, two hungry and scared," he said softly. "And one who talks to a God he doesn't even believe in anymore. That's what passes for God's kingdom around here, J.C. Welcome to the Corners. Welcome to the Church of the Samaritan."

The silence stretched into an eternity Thomas didn't believe in, either. Then, from St. Michael's Catholic church, three blocks away, bells chimed a Sunday morning welcome.

"Sorry, J.C, but nothing doing," Thomas said, turning away. "You can't fool me. I know you too well by now. If you had a voice, it would sound like tears."

Garnet Anthony was awakened by church bells in the distance. The bells blended into the symphony of car engines, rap from somebody's stereo, and the screams of a neighbor's child.

She opened one eye and saw that it was later than it should have been. She opened the other and saw that in stumbling to bed in the dark last night she had paired a magenta satin sleep shirt with chartreuse boxer shorts.

It was the best rationale for sleeping nude that she could think of. She was just glad she didn't have company in her bed this morning to witness the mismatch.

Not that she'd had company there for a long, long time.

Garnet slowly sat up and shook the scramble of dark hair that was constant visual proof the stereotypes people held about nurses were simply that. Her hair was long, thick and insolent—and she liked it that way. Even when it was tied back from her face, tendrils found their way into her eyes and ears, and curls bounced against her neck.

As she scrubbed sleep from her eyes, the mirror beside her bed reminded her that nothing about her called forth images of soothing voices or healing hands. She owed her outrageous face to generations of immigrant ancestors who had made the Corners their first stop in the U.S. of A. Some—the luckiest—had moved on to other, healthier places, but not before they had flooded the Corners' gene pool with a splash of this and a shower of that.

She had wide Slavic cheekbones and tilted almond eyes that she owed to a mystery country in the east—of a color green that brought to mind the hills of Ireland. Her tawny skin had been a gift from her father, who was half Egyptian, and her mother, who claimed Comanche blood. An infusion of Puerto Rican sunshine and Nordic frost had given her both a generous smile and enough caution not to use it very often. On the rare occasions when teachers had praised her during her school years, they had told her she was "striking" or "interesting." "Pretty" had been reserved for girls from more conventional backgrounds.

Garnet fought her way out of bed and crossed to the refrigerator for a long drink of milk straight out of the carton. She drank milk on waking and coffee at bedtime. She ate pasta for breakfast and pancakes at supper, and indulged in desserts any time the law allowed. She had never lived her life the way the world expected, and most of the time she didn't give the world's opinion more than a passing thought.

Except that today, considering what lay ahead of her, the world was probably right, and she was probably *loco*.

A quick shower later, and nearly dressed, Garnet noted that the child in the tiny apartment next door was still screaming.

Thirteen-month-old Chantelle probably wanted her breakfast. Her mother, Serena, no different from most sixteen-year-old girls, liked to sleep late. Of all the young mothers Garnet knew, Serena was the finest. But that didn't mean she had magically matured during childbirth into a woman who could willingly sacrifice all her own pleasures and desires for the sake of the bawling six-pound bundle of trouble that, in one supremely painful moment, had become her lifetime commitment.

In the hallway, Garnet buttoned the sleeve of her white blouse with one hand and knocked on Serena's door with the other.

"Hey, Serena, your kid's hungry. Either get up and open the door so I can feed her or get up and feed her yourself."

"Go 'way."

Garnet switched hands to button her other sleeve and continued to pound. "I'm not going anywhere," she said. "Open up."

The door gave way under her fist. On the other side of the doorway Serena pulled her T-shirt down so that it almost covered her panties. "You know, you oughta be somebody's mother."

"What? And be so busy with my own kids I'd miss chances to order you around?" Garnet squatted and held out her arms. Chantelle, tears dripping down her chin, came into them and wiped her face on Garnet's blouse.

Garnet rose, clutching Chantelle against her. "Thanks, runny nose," Garnet said wryly. "I probably have another clean blouse."

Serena yawned. "If you'd left us alone..."

"This was the best of two alternatives. If she'd kept on crying, I would have come over here and murdered you in your bed."

"At least I wouldn't have to get up."

"You are one lazy woman." Garnet reached out to rumple Serena's curls to take any sting out of her words. "Want me to feed her while you take a shower?"

"Nah. You feed her junk."

"Peanut butter and pancake sandwiches are not junk."

"I bought her favorite cereal yesterday." Serena held up her hands to stave off Garnet's next words. "And juice. I bought juice, too."

"You've been listening to my lectures."

"I just got a talent for self-preservation." Serena dragged Chantelle from Garnet's arms. "It's Sunday. Why are you dressed like a nurse? Don't you get a day off?"

Garnet was the administrator of Mother and Child, a unique maternal health project that struggled to provide both health care and social services to the women and children of the Corners. Garnet had carved the program and the job out of nothing, bantering and begging and threatening her way to obtaining grants from private charities and public programs so that no one in the community would have to suffer the way she once had.

She was administrator and nurse practitioner, secretary and janitor. She loved the variety, the constant challenge, the smiles on the faces of children who might not be alive if Mother and Child didn't exist.

And she despised everything and everybody who interfered with helping those children.

"I've got to go see somebody," she said.

Serena bounced her daughter on her hip, and Chantelle quieted. "Where?"

Garnet looked past Serena to the one-room apartment that was probably the nicest home the young woman had ever known. It was almost painfully clean, but Chantelle's toys cluttered the floor in colorful disarray. Garnet approved of the combination. "Wilford Heights."

"Uh-uh. That's Coroner territory."

"*People* territory."

"You're crazy, girl."

"Just doing my job." Garnet crossed her arms and prepared for battle. It would be good practice for the day to come. "And I'm not going to let a bunch of punk-ass kids keep me from doing it just because they think the dirt outside some housing project is worth dying for."

"You'd be the one dying."

"Better not be. These kids know me. I've delivered their girlfriends' babies, held their mamas' hands while they tried to come down off drugs. They aren't going to shoot me."

"It's Candy you're going to see, isn't it?"

Garnet turned her gaze to Serena. "She's been having cramps and she's afraid to come to the clinic tomorrow."

"It's not the Coroners you'll have to worry about, then. It's the Knights who'll shoot you. They see you going over there, they'll guess who you're going to visit."

"Let them."

"You're crazy."

"No. Sane. Somebody's got to be sane in this place. Otherwise those kids aren't going to know there's a better way to live than shooting each other over street signs and hand signs and colors."

"Candy knew what she was doing when she started kicking

with Francis and his friends. She knew Demon wouldn't let her get away with it." Serena poked Garnet's chest with an index finger to make her point.

"Francis is a good man."

"That's got nothing to do with it."

Garnet was glad to see Serena was worried about her. It was always a good sign when a kid like Serena, who already had the world on her shoulders, could still worry about somebody else. "I'll be careful," she promised.

"Listen, if Hell has a zip code, it's the same as ours. You can't change that, Garnet. The Corners has been here for a hundred years, and it'll be here another hundred. Everything'll be exactly the same when Chantelle's grandkids are out playing on the sidewalk."

"If Chantelle's grandkids are *able* to play on the sidewalks, then it *won't* be the same Corners. It'll be a better place."

"I still don't think you should go."

"It could be you over there, needing me."

Serena's response wasn't fit for the baby's ears.

"You'd better hope that's not Chantelle's first word," Garnet said.

"Let me know when you get home."

"Just don't go back to bed. I don't want to have to wake you up again." Garnet leaned over and kissed Chantelle's cheek.

Half an hour later Serena's door was cracked when Garnet strode down the hall—in a fresh white blouse. As she passed she heard the clang and screech of cartoons. She wondered if Chantelle was watching them, too.

Thomas had to set up chairs and install the pulpit under the picture. With three chairs under each arm, he made his way to the front of the church. The graffiti gleamed at him as he unfolded the chairs.

There was nothing to be done about the graffiti this morning. Another coat of paint might subdue it. Then again, it might not. The MidKnights had wanted their message to last through eternity. It had been painted a deep royal blue and outlined in black enamel. The artist had talent. Their symbol, a sword, had been rendered in loving detail. The profane, mysterious message accompanying it had been carefully stroked, layer upon layer, until it seemed to leap off the wall—right through three coats of white paint.

The victorious graffiti seemed to point out the futility of everything Thomas was trying to do. But over the past year he had grown to accept the feeling that little he was doing would make a difference, anyway. He had spent two years doing nothing at all before he moved to the Corners to start the Church of the Samaritan. That had been far worse. Here, at least, he was struggling, not drifting. If he and the people of the Corners were going to drown, they were going to go down fighting. Together.

A woman's voice interrupted his thoughts.

"You could get the boy who did that, you know, get him and his friends and tell them to paint you a mural over that mess. Jesus at Gethsemane or the Last Supper. Only way it's ever gonna get covered up."

Thomas turned. For the first time that morning he smiled. "You're early, Dorothy. Did you come to give me advice or help set up the chairs?"

"I'm on my way to Mass at St. Michael's." Dorothy Brown joined him in front of the graffiti. She was a tiny woman of indeterminate age, dark-skinned and silver-haired. This morning she was dressed in a perfectly preserved green rayon suit with padded shoulders and a pillbox hat with a short green veil. Dorothy had lived in the Corners as long as anyone could remember. She had taught in the Corners' schools, served in local government and chaired any board worth chairing. Her ruling passion was to create a community in this place that some people called a ghetto.

"Can't say those boys of ours got no talent." She cocked her head. "I'm betting Ferdinand Sanchez did that one. His mother taught him to draw like that. She was a pretty little thing. Used to spend hours with him teaching him to do stuff. Then one morning she just up and left. His father's no good."

"I've crossed Mr. Sanchez's path a time or two."

"Old Testament on this side—" Dorothy pointed to the opposite wall "—New Testament on that. Ferdinand could do it."

"Last time I saw Ferdinand, he was urinating on the front steps."

"Trying to get your attention."

"He succeeded." Thomas folded his arms. "So it's Mass this morning?"

"Your turn next week." Dorothy hiked her purse to her shoulder. "I spread myself around."

"Like icing on a cake."

"What am I missing here this morning? You gonna preach on something interesting for a change?"

"The miracle of the loaves and fishes."

"Just don't go getting down on folks like you usually do. They need some God on Sunday mornings. Get tired of hearing about how they're supposed to change the world. Most of them just sitting here wishing they'd got a little sleep last night or had something to eat for breakfast."

"And God's supposed to fill their stomachs?"

"He got a better chance at doing it than you got."

"I'll give them some God."

"Give yourself a little, too, while you're at it." She patted his arm. Before he could think of an adequate response she was gone.

Thomas stared out the window, watching Dorothy's small figure disappear into the fog of a Corners' autumn morning.

Three young men materialized out of the same fog. Two wore black hoodies left open to the elements, the other had chopped the sleeves off a denim jacket and covered it with custom patches. Underneath they wore muddy-hued plaid shirts buttoned just at the collar over black T-shirts and sagging khaki work pants. He knew that when they got closer, he would also see an array of piercings and tattoos, including the required knight's sword, tattooed on the inside of the right forearm.

Along with similarities there were differences. One wore a black watch cap pulled low over his ears, one a generic cap with the bill turned up. One wore nothing on his head except a folded bandanna tied to one side over cornrows divided and braided with military precision. Thomas knew the boys well enough to realize that the one with the watch cap was the one to worry about.

They weren't walking fast, and they weren't walking slow. They strutted as if they owned the sidewalk, the street and the neighborhood. If they had been on the other side of the street, their stride would have been jumpy and defiant. They were members of the MidKnights, often just referred to as the Knights, and the other side of the street, where the Wilford Heights housing project began, belonged to the Coroners.

And this place, where Thomas stood, where his small congregation would soon gather to try to find meaning in their existence, belonged to a God that Thomas wasn't even sure he believed in anymore.

As the young men approached the sidewalk in front of the church, Thomas watched closely. The church was nothing more than a converted storefront, the congregation nothing more than a few souls who, in giving voice to the despair that plagued their lives, spoke for a whole community. But the church and this congregation were Thomas's life.

He would be no less ruthless than any MidKnight in protecting what was his.

~

Despite her reassuring words to Serena, Garnet had expected trouble from the moment she promised Candy Tremira that she would go to Wilford Heights to examine her.

Garnet always expected trouble, and she was rarely disappointed. Optimism was a waste of time and pessimism a waste of energy. She was a realist, and by expecting the worst, she could always be pleasantly surprised if it didn't occur.

Today there were going to be no surprises.

"Where're you going, babe?" Andre Rollins asked as she waited for the walk sign at the corner of Twelfth and Wilford.

She turned slowly and raked him with her gaze. "Who's the babe here, Andre? I was changing your diapers when I was eight."

"I asked where you was going."

"I'm going across the street."

Andre moved in front of her, and two other young men flanked her. She sighed. "Come on. You boys got nothing better to do than hassle me this morning?"

"Don't go dissing us, babe," Andre said. "You show respect, or we'll teach you how."

"I respect you," Garnet said. "Only not as much as I used to." She felt a hand on her arm and fingers making bruises. She forced herself not to turn her head or wince. "See, I used to think you *were* somebody," she went on. "Back when you didn't need your enforcers to make you feel like a big man."

Andre barely inclined his head, and the fingers no longer squeezed her arm. "What call you got crossing that street?"

"My job, Andre." She moved a little closer to him.

"There's no clinic 'cross the street."

"There's a woman across that street who's afraid to come to the clinic because she knows you boys are waiting for her to show her face over here."

"Candy?"

She turned to the young man who had spoken, the same young man who had probably left fingerprints on her arm. He wore a dark watch cap pulled over his ears and rolled just to his eyebrows. The pale face that leered at her was one she never wanted to glimpse on a night when she was out on the streets alone.

"Demon, let it go," she said. "So maybe Candy took off with another guy. You think you're the first man that's happened to? It doesn't matter. You've got another woman now."

Sadly, that was true. Another young woman had replaced Candy Tremira in Demon's life. Another young woman who would learn that macho posturing and smoldering good looks meant nothing next to the reality of living with his erratic temper.

He smiled, and she was chilled by it. "Candy and I are going to have a conversation," he said.

"Andre." She turned to appeal to him. "I've got a job to do. You show me where it says a nurse or doctor can only help patients who wear the right colors. Show me where it says this stupid war between you and the Coroners is going to do anything for the Corners besides make life harder here."

Andre put his fist under her chin. She didn't flinch. She felt Demon and Ferdinand, the third MidKnight, close ranks around her.

"You go on over to Wilford Place," Andre said, "and you walking into trouble."

She looked straight into his eyes. They were the color of his skin, a deep, rich brown. "Look, I've watched you grow up. I know what you can do and who you can be. I know who you *are.* Don't do this, Andre."

There was always something flickering, simmering in Andre's

eyes. Some of the kids who patrolled these blocks had eyes that were as empty as the futures they had been bequeathed. Andre's weren't. She stared into them, willing him to face the struggle going on inside himself, willing him to make the right decision.

"Get your hands off the lady."

A man's voice cut through the tension and splintered it into a thousand evil pieces. Garnet felt a hand on her shoulder, and before she could do anything, she had been flung to one side. In an instant a man's large body was wedged protectively between her and the MidKnights.

"What do you think you're doing?" the man asked.

For one confusing moment Garnet didn't know to whom the question had been addressed. Then she saw the sneer on Andre's face and knew it hadn't been addressed to her. She had been cast aside as if she no longer had a part in the confrontation. A man in a plain gray suit was facing the MidKnights for her.

"Nobody's talking to you, Padre." Andre stood taller than he had with Garnet. He and the man, who easily topped six feet, were staring eye to eye. "Don't get yourself involved in things got nothing to do with you."

"Anything that happens in this neighborhood's got something to do with me. You're standing in front of my church. I live here."

"That what you call it?" Andre reached into his T-shirt pocket for a cigarette. His gaze didn't waver. He snapped his fingers, and Ferdinand moved around Thomas to light it for him.

"Who are you?" Garnet demanded. She tried to move, but the man continued to shield her.

"Thomas Stonehill," he said shortly.

"Padre," Andre said. He blew a puff of smoke in Thomas's face. "Got himself a real important church right over there, with at least two, three people coming of a Sunday. Got himself an idea he's gonna save the world. Starting right here on this spot."

Shock began to recede, and anger seeped into its place. Garnet couldn't fault the man, this Thomas Stonehill, for trying to protect her. Every time she had an audience she preached the gospel of people in the neighborhood watching out for each other.

But she could fault him for thrusting her aside when she had been in the midst of working out her problem with Andre. The good reverend had committed two unpardonable sins, and *she* was probably going to pay for them.

"This is between me and Andre," she said, trying to step in front of Thomas. "Thank you, but we can finish this ourselves."

Thomas hardly seemed to do more than shift his weight, but he cut off her path to Andre anyway. "I don't think the young man's intentions are the best."

"That's for me to decide."

Thomas acted as if he hadn't heard her. "The lady has a right to walk these sidewalks without you kids bothering her. Everybody has that right."

"Think so?" Andre tossed his cigarette at Thomas's feet. It bounced off his shoe. "Well, I think she don't. I think she crosses that street today, she gonna wish she never did walk these sidewalks, 'cause we be walking them right behind her."

Garnet's heart sank. Andre had committed himself now. If she ignored his warning, she would pay. She wasn't afraid; she was only sorry the chance to change things had been taken out of her hands.

Futilely, from Thomas's side, she made one last attempt to bring Andre to his senses. "Andre, taking care of Candy's my job. Even warring nations let the Red Cross come on to their battlefields to care for the wounded."

"Candy flipped sides. She hang with the Knights first, and now she be hanging with the Coroners. She not wounded," Andre said. "Yet."

"She's dead," Demon said, with a smirk. "You're dead if you help her."

"Don't make threats, son," Thomas said. The words were mild; the tone was steel.

"You gonna stop me, Padre?" Demon stepped right up to him. He wasn't as tall as Thomas, but his adolescent body had been fired in the furnace of hot city streets. His chest was broad, and under the stretched-out hoodie, Garnet knew that his shirt bulged with muscle. And quite likely something even more sinister.

"If I have to."

Demon took a step backward and looked away, as if his bluff had been called. Then he sprang.

Garnet leaped back in horror as Thomas Stonehill came crashing toward her. It took her a second to realize that he had not been taken unaware. As she watched he twisted, using his weight to take Demon down with him. In moments Demon was pinned underneath him. Thomas had the side of one hand against Demon's Adam's apple and a knee in Demon's groin.

Demon seemed to be in shock; then he raised a fist.

Thomas slammed Demon's arm to the ground with his free hand. "Hit me, son, and I'll have to choose between cutting off your air or your chance to make babies."

Andre and Ferdinand had just looked on, used—Garnet guessed—to Demon fighting and winning his own battles. Now they started toward Thomas.

"Leave him alone!" Garnet kicked off her shoe, a pump with a sizable heel. She grabbed it to use as a weapon.

Andre glanced at her, but he kept coming. Ferdinand backed off, not from fear, she guessed, but from a deep-seated belief that fighting with women was not masculine.

Garnet moved forward as Andre closed in, but before she could attempt to strike, Thomas's foot shot out and connected with Andre's ankle. The kick had just enough force to make him stumble backward.

A siren sounded. For a moment Garnet couldn't believe it. The Corners had inadequate police protection, as well as every other type of public service. Response time on direct calls was often longer than it took to dismantle a building brick by brick, and police patrols were few and far between. Now, for the first time in her memory, a police car was *where* it was supposed to be, *when* it was supposed to be.

She wondered if the Reverend Thomas Stonehill had somehow found time to pray for intercession.

Before her eyes, Ferdinand melted into the fog and disappeared down an alleyway. Andre started toward Thomas and Demon again, but Thomas had already rolled to the side. Demon was suddenly free. He sat up and looked around wildly, as if considering whether to go for Thomas, a gun, or to escape before the police got out of their car. Andre jerked him upright and made his decision by grasping his arm and pulling him toward the alley where Ferdinand had vanished.

The police car door opened, but for a moment Garnet and Thomas were the only ones on the sidewalk.

Thomas got easily to his feet. "Are you all right?"

Garnet stared at him. She was filled with confusing emotions. His black hair was ruffled, and his suit was dusty, but otherwise he looked as if his fight with the MidKnights had been no more taxing than a Sunday school class.

"Who in the hell do you think you are?" she exploded.

He stared at her as if she were crazy.

"You come here and think you can change this place, but you don't know a thing about it," she said. "You've just made sure that the Knights will stay on my case. Well, Reverend Stonehill, you'd better say your prayers loud and clear tonight. Because the next time those boys come looking for me, they might well *use* the guns they had tucked away today!"

2

Thomas Stonehill had committed two unpardonable sins.

First, he had made Garnet lose face with the MidKnights. She had few pluses on her side when she negotiated with either the MidKnights or the Coroners, but she had always commanded their grudging respect. She had never showed them she was afraid; she had never avoided them. Now, by coming to her rescue, Thomas Stonehill had given Andre and his friends the idea that she couldn't take care of herself. And since they preyed on weakness, that was a dangerous idea for them to have.

The second sin was even more serious. By confronting Andre head-on, adult to child, Thomas Stonehill had made it impossible for Andre to compromise. There was no way that Andre could back down without appearing weak. And weakness was worse than death for kids like Andre. They had nothing except their pride. They would die for it.

They would kill for it.

On Monday afternoon Garnet sat alone in her office, shooting rubber bands into a wastepaper basket. The score was seven to three. Not bad, considering that her mind was somewhere else.

The morning had been busy. On Monday and Thursday mornings Mother and Child held prenatal health clinics. Garnet and Tex, her assistant, weighed and took blood pressures and did nutritional counseling and urine checks in preparation for Wednesday and Friday afternoons, when a rotating staff of volunteer physicians saw patients.

The system worked most of the time. The nurse practitioners handled routine care, and the physicians handled problem pregnancies or patients close to their due dates. It didn't work when a doctor's Wednesday afternoon golf game took precedence over his commitment to the clinic, or when a patient's fears or disinterest kept her from keeping an appointment.

The same was true of the pediatric clinic on Tuesdays. Most of the time the residents from a local hospital, who served a portion of their pediatric rotation at Mother and Child, were excellent, reliable physicians. But sometimes their middle-class disdain for what they saw in the Corners was so obvious that embarrassed or angry parents never returned with their children.

Garnet's job was to make sure everything ran smoothly. She trained residents to work effectively with the poor and pleaded with practicing physicians to do their part. She knocked on doors and persuaded mothers-to-be and mothers-who-were to use the clinic's resources. She spoke at suburban club meetings, wrote grant proposals, organized fund-raisers and started new programs the moment more money arrived.

And sometimes, like now, she shot rubber bands into wastebaskets simply because she had to sit and think.

After her accusations yesterday Thomas Stonehill had been taciturn and cold. The police had come and gone quickly, and they had been left alone together.

He was a man anyone would take note of. His hair was coal black and his deep-set eyes a soul-piercing blue. His brow was wide; his nose and square jaw would have looked at home on a Roman centurion. There were no smile lines at the corners of his narrow lips, no crinkles around his eyes to soften his face. The frown lines in his tanned skin had been put there by dogged concentration, by brows drawn together as he stared at a world that was less than he wanted it to be.

Until that moment she had never met Thomas Stonehill, but she guessed that he was a man who not only never stopped to smell the roses, he probably trampled them underfoot on his way to his next mission.

Unfortunately, this time his mission had been one Garnet Anthony.

Between one rubber band and the next she was transported back to the corner of Wilford and Twelfth.

"Do you want me to walk you somewhere?" he had finally asked.

She shook her head. "You don't get it, do you? The only reason I've been allowed to walk these streets at all is because these kids think I'm not afraid of them. I listen when they talk, and as often as possible, I do what I can for them. But when it comes right down to the nitty-gritty, I've just gone on and done what I had to, no matter what they think. And until today, they've let me. I can't show them I'm afraid now, or I'll never walk these streets again."

"That kid had his hand at your throat."

"Andre." She realized how angry she sounded, and she lowered her voice. " 'The kid' has a name. And he's bright and perceptive, a natural-born leader. He's also not above throwing his weight around if he gets pushed into a corner."

"That's what you think I did?"

She told herself to try for patience. She couldn't really blame Thomas Stonehill. In his world men rushed to the rescue of women. He just didn't realize yet that the Corners wasn't his world.

"He wouldn't have hurt me," she explained, lowering her voice. "We have a relationship. I've known him since he was a baby. He had to threaten me like that to save face with his friends. And then, since I was asking him nice, he would have let me go on to do what I had to."

"You're sure?" His voice indicated that he thought she was wrong.

"I'm never sure about people. Good-looking, clean-cut kids in their daddy's BMWs and Porsches show up on this corner on Friday nights looking for cheap dope and fifty-dollar women. Kids like Ferdinand, with his tattoos and scars, rescue kittens from trees and organize parties to clean up vacant lots so little kids will have a place to play baseball in the summers."

"What are you going to do now?"

"I'm going to do what I started out to do. I'm going over to Wilford Heights, and I'm going to see a patient."

"A patient?" He frowned.

"That's what this was all about. I'm a nurse. I'm on my way to see a patient."

She could tell by his expression that he was adjusting his evaluation of her. "What did you think?" she asked. "That I was one of those fifty-dollar soul-sellers doing an early morning shift?"

"I didn't have a lot of time to think anything."

"But I don't fit your impression of a nurse, do I?" She glanced down at her clothes. Conservative to her meant a skirt that covered the essentials and a blouse that didn't call more than modest attention to her breasts. In her opinion, today's attire met those standards.

She looked up again. "You'll find that we're a lot less worried about impressions around here than we are about survival." She realized he was assessing her legs, as if he wondered how Florence Nightingale had sunk to this. "Hey, Reverend, are you ogling, condemning or repenting?"

She didn't wait for an answer. An eon had passed since she first waited for the walk light, but now it was green and no

MidKnights were in sight. She turned away from Thomas Stonehill and crossed the street. And when she stood at the entrance to Wilford Heights, she looked across Wilford Avenue and saw he was gone.

And because of him, now she was going to have to find a way to protect herself from the MidKnights. If she didn't, her effectiveness at Mother and Child was finished.

She was pulled back to the present when the office door opened, and her colleague Tex stood in the doorway and counted rubber band wins and losses, whistling at three misses in a row. "Bad day, huh?"

Tex had never been to Texas. Her father and mother were Polish immigrants, and Tex had been born just two weeks after their arrival in America. The doctor who had delivered her had tugged and tugged as inch after inch of slippery baby girl emerged, and when all of her had finally been delivered his first words had been, "Lord, this one's as big as Texas and just as sure of herself." Her mother, whose grasp of the English language had been minimal, named her daughter after this Texas that the baby so apparently resembled.

Tex always said she was grateful that the doctor's delivery-room chatter hadn't run to four-letter words.

Garnet swept the remainder of her rubber band supply into her desk drawer. "I guess things went okay."

"I guess you almost threw Mary Ann out the clinic door."

"I guess sweet little old Mary Ann is using as well as dealing."

"And if she doesn't come back here, then we don't have a chance with her at all, do we?"

Garnet didn't have the delivery room doctor's self-control. She rattled off a list of expletives.

"Now put them in alphabetical order," Tex said, unruffled.

Tex was never ruffled, and that was why Garnet had hired her. She was six feet of blond composure. She didn't judge and she didn't lecture. When she had a mother-to-be like Mary Ann, who was slinging drugs to support herself and probably using them, as well, she calmly outlined the realities of living with a child who had been prenatally damaged. She showed photos, explained what it was like to have a child who cried constantly and couldn't be comforted, to have a child who might never be capable of showing affection or whose problems in school might mean that he would always be dependent on his mother to meet his basic needs.

And occasionally, when a mother wasn't too far gone, she listened to Tex. Sometimes she even changed her life-style. But no mother ever changed because someone had gotten angry at her, the way Garnet had gotten angry at Mary Ann today.

"So what's really bothering you?" Tex asked.

Garnet looked up and saw the real source of her tension walking forward to stand behind Tex in the doorway. She tapped her fingers on her desk and stared at Thomas Stonehill. Then she stood.

"I'll tell you later," she said.

Tex turned as Garnet's gaze flicked past her. She examined the newcomer almost as thoroughly as she examined her pregnant patients. Then she turned to Garnet. "I can see why you want to wait," she said. She flashed a big, toothy smile before she edged out of Thomas's way and did a sassy stroll down the hallway.

Thomas stayed in the doorway. He took in the room in one glance. This was a medical clinic, and he had expected institutional green walls and cheap, soothing prints. Instead he had been blasted with color from the moment he entered the door. Two of the walls in the reception area had health and safety messages heralded in gaudy gang-style graffiti. The other two had a mural of children of different races playing on emerald green grass against a royal blue sky. The chairs were shiny plastic in primary colors. Even the flyers and brochures littering every available surface had been designed to scream for attention.

The director's office, decorated in splashes of yellow and red, had obviously been designed with the same goal in mind. And the woman standing at the director's desk was no different.

Garnet Anthony was not a fan of subtlety. He had never known a woman who could make such a blatant, sensual statement wearing white. Her scoop-necked T-shirt was a soft knit that hugged generous breasts; her skirt and wide white belt called attention to a small waist and sleek, womanly hips. She was standing behind her desk, but if the skirt was similar to the one she had worn yesterday, he supposed it stopped above her knees.

It wasn't only her provocative display of assets that proclaimed a sensual nature. She wore costume jewelry suitable for a cocktail dress and cosmetics designed to emphasize her unusual features. Her dark hair writhed with life. Medusa's snakes came to mind. Individual locks twisted and curved over her shoulders, despite being tied back from her face. And the face itself was exotic enough to draw notice anywhere in the world. It was an earthy, recalcitrant face. Eve's face. The face of Mary Magdalene.

"Come in," Garnet said. "I won't tell you to make yourself at home, since I doubt you'd *ever* be at home here. But have a seat."

She sat down and turned her desk chair toward a sofa and two comfortable armchairs that she was storing for a patient who had been evicted from her apartment. Garnet never talked to anyone from behind a desk. It went against her basic nature to pretend that she was better than anybody else.

"Coffee?" she asked, waving her hand toward the pot on a table by the window.

"No, thanks." Thomas lowered himself to one of the chairs.

Garnet had expected him to sit carefully. He wasn't a prissy man. No one could look at a man of his size and say such a thing with a straight face, despite his profession. But he was a serious man, as serious as they came. She had expected him to sit tall, feet flat on the floor, perhaps to lean forward when he spoke, as if the world's fate hinged on the words they exchanged.

Instead, he sprawled, as if his family had owned that chair for centuries, as if he had lounged there since the clinic's opening, and irradiated her with his electric blue stare as she worked at her desk.

And Thomas Stonehill lounging was an impressive sight.

"If you've come about yesterday, let's just forget it." Garnet folded her arms.

He watched the movement pull the fabric of her shirt tighter against her breasts. He watched a necklace of red and purple beads dip under the neckline of her shirt, but he didn't say anything.

"You were trying to help," Garnet conceded.

"I've come about your sister."

She was caught off guard. She had expected an apology, or at least an argument. She took a second to silently laugh at herself for thinking her opinion was important enough that he—or anyone—would come for either.

"Which one?" she asked at last.

"Ema."

"How did you know she was my sister?"

"She's mentioned you several times before, but it only clicked this morning, when she was talking about your job."

"I thought maybe you'd been overwhelmed by the family resemblance."

He thought of Ema, whose short, poorly cut dark hair was the same mahogany as Garnet's. Hair color was the only similarity he could detect. Ema never looked anyone in the eye, but whatever color her eyes were, he knew they were not the steamy rain-forest green of Garnet's. And although Ema might be pretty if she was well-nourished and confident, she was now, at the very best, pleasant to look at. No one would ever call Garnet's appearance pleasant.

Never pleasant.

"Do you know her husband beats her?" he asked.

"Do you know I have two eyes in my head and a brain residing behind them?"

He studied her. She didn't look angry. In fact, she showed no emotion. Her face had lacked expression yesterday, when she was dealing with the MidKnights, too.

"Then, if you know, do you have any idea what can be done about it?" he asked.

"She can leave Ron. She chooses not to. Most of the time she even refuses to admit he beats her. But I suspect you already know that much, Reverend."

"Thomas."

She tilted her head. "Really? Won't you feel naked without a title?"

"No."

She shrugged.

"She needs encouragement," he said.

"She needs a signed affidavit from God assuring her that if she leaves Ron Celabraze, he won't come after her with a gun and kill her in front of the kids. Can you offer her that?"

He heard emotion. For a moment he wondered if he had imagined it, her words were so flip. "You're frustrated because you don't see any way out for her, either."

"You're pretty good at this. Most preachers wouldn't be listening so hard."

"Am I right?"

"Close enough." Garnet wished she could open her drawer and pull out her rubber bands. Instead she began a necklace of giant paper clips. "Ema's married to a maniac. Ron's close to tolerable when he isn't drinking. But that's about one waking hour out of every day."

"Ema says he hasn't always been that way."

"Ema thinks Lucifer fries people in hell because he was the product of a broken heavenly home."

"And she stays with her husband out of pity? Out of fear?"

"Yeah. And out of some perverted moral teaching forced down her throat by every church she's tried to be part of. The last preacher she talked to told her it was God's wish she stay married. St. Paul and death do us part and all that. But I'm sure you know the Bible better than I do."

"I don't know that part of the Bible at all."

"Well, you folks have always been good at using what you like and tossing out what you don't."

He ignored the jab. "If she had a place to go, would she leave?"

"She can come to my place and live with me any time she wants."

"You know she wouldn't put you in danger."

Garnet looked up from a paper clip chain that was growing long enough to stretch across the space between them. "Did she tell you that?"

"You did."

"Not exactly." She added three more clips. "But you're right. She'd die willingly before she endangered anyone she loved. In fact, if I could convince her that Ron might harm the kids, she'd leave him. But he's never lifted a finger to either of the girls. Ema never gives him a chance, of course. She drains off his anger singlehandedly. He can beat her anytime he wants, so he doesn't have to take out his temper on his babies."

"But you think he might."

"It's just a matter of time. Some day if Lisa cries too loudly or Jody asks for more milk when Ema isn't on the spot to deflect his anger, Ron will beat them."

Thomas made a tent of his fingers. It was something he used to do in the pulpit, a calculated, thoughtful gesture.

Here's the church, and here's the steeple. Open the doors and see all the people.

Except that the people weren't there anymore. Not to hear him, anyway.

"What can I do?" he asked.

There really was no purpose Garnet could think of for a two-foot paper clip chain. Reluctantly she tossed it to her desk. "One preacher prayed with her, another prayed for her. One went looking for Ron and asked if Ema was telling the truth. That one probably didn't have any doubts the next day when she came to church black-and-blue."

"What can I do?"

Reluctantly she gave him a bonus point for asking. "She's had all the courage beaten out of her. She was a spunky kid, and she's plenty bright. She can make it on her own if she just starts to believe in herself again. If you can help her do that, then maybe she'll still have a chance to get away from Ron and make a life for herself and the kids."

"Will he come after her?"

"Not if she's two thousand miles away, or even a thousand. I don't think he's capable of drying out long enough to mount an intelligent search. And he doesn't have any resources. Our family's not exactly the Brady Bunch, but we could help her escape and start over." She stared at him. "Would you help, Reverend? Or would your religion stand in the way?"

"Thomas."

"No one ever called you Tommy, did they?"

He didn't smile, but he was surprisingly tempted. "No one did."

"They should have. But it's much too late now." She stood.

He didn't. "Do you have time to show me around?" he asked.

"Why?"

"Because I'm a good source for referrals."

She considered that—and the fact that he was watching her

from his chair like a zoologist collecting data on an unknown species. "I'm about to eat lunch," she said. "Join me?"

"Here?"

"I've got enough in the refrigerator for two."

"Then you'll show me around?"

"I'll show you around before we eat, or *while* we eat, if it makes you feel better about not wasting time."

He rose. "What can I do to help?"

"You can make your own sandwich."

The tour went swiftly because there wasn't much to see. Mother and Child was a shoestring operation. "Clinic" was almost a misnomer. The space had once belonged to a men's clothing store, but when it had become clear that men's suits weren't in big demand in the Corners, it had become one of a string of vacant buildings.

When Garnet and a committee of community leaders approached the landlord about renovating and leasing the space to them, he had been enthusiastic. Since he owned several other properties on the block, he gambled that Mother and Child would bring business back into the area. The gamble had paid off. Now the mothers who visited the clinic shopped for groceries at a corner store and bought clothes and household goods at a discount center two doors away. There were still vacancies, but as foot traffic increased, interest in the remaining property increased, too.

Garnet showed Thomas the tiny examining rooms, the clinic office, the workroom. She explained about the parenting groups who met in a cozy meeting room that doubled as a drop-in day-care center two afternoons a week.

After ten minutes they made their way to the kitchen. There was enough food in the refrigerator for a dozen sandwiches. Mother and Child didn't have the resources to offer regular meals; they couldn't do everything—not yet, anyway. But Garnet always made sure there was plenty of extra sandwich meat and cheese in the refrigerator. She bought bakery outlet whole wheat bread and food service containers of peanut butter and honey. Any patient who was hungry on arrival was not hungry when she left.

Now, in the small kitchen off her office, Garnet set cold cuts on a tiny metal table for Thomas to choose from. While he made his sandwich, she washed a tomato and lettuce to go with it.

He wasn't a man who needed talk for talk's sake. She had to give him that. He was neither a glad-handing preacher nor a pious priestly type. At least, she didn't think so. He had come to her rescue in a potentially dangerous situation. And even if his intervention had made things worse, at least he had tried to intervene.

Why?

It wasn't a question she could ask out loud. She would get an answer, but not the real one. His motivation for being in the Corners at all made for interesting speculation. His motivation for putting his body on the line yesterday was even more interesting. But not interesting enough to pursue. She imagined that getting the real story about Thomas Stonehill *from* Thomas Stonehill would take time, patience and a certain amount of absorption in the subject. She had none of the above.

"Would you like me to make you one, too?" he asked.

She paused in the middle of slicing the tomato. "Sure. Just mix everything up. I like surprises." She turned and saw the excuse that passed for his own sandwich. One slice of ham and a layer of mayonnaise so thin not a pore in the bread was clogged.

"Is that all you're going to put on it?" She grimaced. "I'll bet you don't eat gravy on your meat, and vegetables never touch on your plate."

His smile was rusty with disuse.

She blinked in surprise, then turned to her tomato. "Well, don't short me the same way."

Two sandwiches were nearly finished when she brought the

tomato and lettuce to the table. He had added a slice of cheese to his, but hers was a masterpiece.

"One of everything? Not much imagination, but it looks delicious." She sat, waving in the direction of the refrigerator. "Get yourself a drink. There's a little of everything in there."

He came back with club soda and two glasses. She nodded when he lifted the can in question and accepted one of the glasses after he had poured her share.

Thomas observed Garnet as he ate. She ate as if food were her whole world, as if the sensations against her tongue and throat were the reasons for existence. Halfway through his own sandwich Thomas watched her press the crumbs on her plate against her index finger and lick them off with a flourish.

"You didn't have breakfast," he said.

"Sure I did. Last night's fried chicken and biscuits with cream gravy." She thought a moment. "And pineapple upside-down cake."

He wondered where she put all the food. Her figure was lush, but by no one's standards was she overweight.

"I burn it off," she said, as if in answer. "The best thing about working here."

"What's the worst?"

He was approaching her psyche through a back door. She had to admire his ability to ask leading questions.

She wondered what else he was that good at. She watched him take a bite of his sandwich as he waited for her answer. He ate as if the food wasn't even there. A means to an end. Someone had told him he was supposed to eat three times a day, and he didn't question authority.

Did that attitude pervade his life? Did he meet his other needs with the same disregard for his own pleasure? For a moment she imagined Thomas Stonehill in bed. It wasn't a large leap into fantasy. She told herself he was just the type of man who provoked those thoughts in women. There was something about his brooding eyes and a body that, unclothed, probably qualified as a miracle.

He must have a wife. All preachers had to have wives, didn't they? Who played the organ or taught Sunday school if the preacher wasn't married? Did Thomas and his wife make love on Wednesdays and Saturdays because someone had told him that was the expected thing? Did he partake of the pleasures of love without tasting those, too?

"There is no worst?" he asked, when she still hadn't answered.

She hauled her attention back to the conversation. "The worst is that time, by definition, is limited. I work too hard. There's only so much I can do, and everywhere I look there's more that needs doing."

"I know that feeling."

"Do you?" She sat back and sipped her soda.

"That surprises you?"

"I thought the passing of time thrilled you minister types. Doesn't it take you closer to your heavenly home or something?"

Emotion flickered behind his steady gaze. She saw it as surely as she didn't understand it.

"No," he said. "It doesn't thrill this minister. All you have to do is look around to see how much needs to be done on earth."

"Well, you can't do it all. I can't do it all." She reached for an apple in a fruit bowl on the table. Mr. Loo, who ran the vegetable market two streets over, saved damaged and overripe fruit for her. She had hauled in two bushel baskets of spotted apples and given them away this morning. One of her young mothers was going to make apple pies with her share.

"Are you really that offhanded about what you can't do?" he asked.

"Really?" She crunched a large bite. Juice spurted across her tongue, and she savored it before speaking again. "Yeah."

"Then you can turn off what you see here every day?"

"If I believed that worrying all the time was going to help

somebody, I could work myself up. But it won't help." She nearly echoed Serena's words of yesterday. "The Corners will be The Corners when I'm gone. I was born here, and I'll probably die here. Maybe even sooner than later. In between, I'll do what I can."

Thomas had checked up on Garnet before seeking her out. He had discovered that Mother and Child was her own creation, that it was the only social service project in the community that had been started right here and not by an outside charitable organization. He knew, from a conversation with Dorothy Brown, that even though she was only somewhere in her mid to late twenties, Garnet had single-handedly whipped up interest, grubbed for funding and orchestrated every aspect of the fledgling clinic.

Dorothy had nothing but respect for Garnet, but Thomas himself wasn't so sure. Her attitude irritated and simultaneously intrigued him. Now only the irritation showed. The intrigued portion was more dangerous. "Why do you work so hard if you don't care whether things change?"

With practiced expertise she tossed her apple core in the garbage pail across the room. She sat for a moment, studying the wall behind it. When she turned to him, her eyes were a smoldering fire. "At any point along the way did I say I didn't care?"

"Close."

"I said I know I can't change the world. I'm from here. Maybe that gives me perspective. Your perspective comes from somewhere else. From the accent and the manners, I'd say Eastern seaboard. Private schools, upper middle-class family?" She watched his face. He was very good. His expression hardly changed. But she saw—because she had trained herself to be perceptive in order to survive—that she was right.

She went on before he could respond. "You're here because for some reason your social conscience is as big as the potholes in Wilford Avenue. Maybe you grew up with everything and one day it hit you that some of us grew up with nothing. So you're here, in the Corners, serving out your own personal version of the Peace Corps. And you're so damned sure you're doing what's right that you don't think anybody else could be doing anything right, too."

"From what I've seen of this place, it looks like you're doing some things right."

"But not for the right reasons, huh, Padre? Not because God came down and told me to. Not because I think I'm so important I can change hell into heaven. I'm doing it because it needs to be done. And I'm doing everything I can to make it fun along the way. That's what bothers you. Joy bothers you and your kind. I'm not serious enough for you. And I'm not pompous enough."

"Not *pompous* enough?"

She stood. "Get off your high horse, Padre. The world's going to keep right on spinning when you're wearing angel wings. Whatever we can do here isn't even a drop in the bucket. It's less than vapor. It's nothing. *Nada.* So lighten up. If you're going to subject yourself to living here, at least be realistic about it. Don't kill yourself trying to make a difference. Soon enough this place will kill you anyway."

"You were angry that I tried to protect you yesterday. You were angry today because I want to help your sister. Now you're angry just because I'm here?"

"Angry?" She shrugged. "Nothing so important. I've just seen your kind come and go until I'm tired of turning my head. You want to change things. One day you wake up and find out how little you can do. So you leave. And all the people who were starting to count on you feel a little worse than they did before you came. When you've served your time, you'll go back to some pretty little rose-covered church with a steeple pointing the way to heaven, and we'll still be right here. Just trying to make it one day at a time and finding what joy we can in little things."

"There's no little rose-covered church in my future."

"No? The evangelism circuit, then? A worldwide television ministry? Politics? What? Don't tell me we're not just a stopping place on your way to somewhere."

He stood, too. Face-to-face, she was all too aware how much taller and altogether larger he was. His shoulders were broad enough to take on the Corners' problems—if he stayed long enough to try.

"This is the first time I've been *anywhere* in a long, long time," he said. "I intend to stay. But not to prove anything to you or even to myself. I'm going to stay because there's no place else to go."

Before she could answer him, he gave a curt nod. "Thanks for lunch. I think."

Then he was gone, and she was left to wonder why every time she was in the presence of Thomas Stonehill she sounded as if she cared far more than she did. About everything.

3

Thomas stood outside the entrance of the Church of the Samaritan and looked at the bleak stretch of land directly across from the church on Twelfth Street. Once Kensington Park had been a green jewel, but once the Corners had been a community to be proud of, too. Now the park was a squalid wasteland of litter. The worn, damaged benches had been removed by the city and never replaced. The water fountains hadn't been turned on for the summer because of a leak underground. No flowers had been planted in the expansive beds surrounding the graffiti-adorned statue of Carroll Kensington, one of the Corners' founding fathers.

Once the park had been a playground for laughing children. Now it was a business center for drug dealers and hookers.

Thomas hadn't lived here long enough to know exactly when the changes had begun. The Corners was just a small section of a Great Lakes industrial city. The city itself was irrelevant, since it had washed its hands of the Corners long ago. The Corners could have been lifted intact and deposited in Detroit or Chicago, and no one would have been surprised to find it there. Its history was one of immigrant groups who, one after the other, replaced the original settlers who had built solid stone and brick buildings and wide, tree-lined streets.

The new residents had made what improvements they could; then they had moved on to wealthier, more congenial neighborhoods with better schools and more political clout. For one reason or another, those left behind had never realized the American dream. Tenaciously they had hung on to what they had. The Corners was better, oh, so much better, than inner-city this or inner-city that. There had always been hope here.

Until recently.

Thomas watched a man and a woman with two children skirt the edges of Kensington Park, protective hands on the children's shoulders. It might be Sunday morning, but as usual business was being conducted at the park and in front of the Kensington Hotel, a temporary stop for the homeless across from the park's eastern corner.

Others passed by as Thomas waited outside the church, and he found the array of skin colors beautiful. The Corners might be like a hundred other communities throughout the Northeast and Great Lakes region, but it was fairly unique in its mixture of races. People had moved out and people had moved in. But those who had stayed had made room for everyone.

As a student of human nature, he doubted that this unusual kind of coexistence was due to a deep-seated commitment to equality. People who couldn't move to the suburbs had simply dug in rather than leave for something potentially worse. And because people had stayed right where they were, there were no divided streets in the Corners. Blacks lived next door to whites, who lived next door to Asians or Hispanics. Central Americans, Filipinos and Chinese, the newest immigrant groups to flock to the Corners, had moved into a house here, an apartment there. Wilford Heights, the only housing project in the community, was a model of integration, if not of anything else.

The divisions in the Corners were rarely along racial lines.

The congregation of the Church of the Samaritan was mixed. The youth gangs that had formed weren't even divided. They were devoted to turf, and since the turf was integrated, so were the gangs, which made them less likely to be infiltrated and controlled by the larger criminal gangs that were stretching their tentacles across the nation.

From a sociologist's standpoint, all that might be worth studying, but from Thomas's standpoint the differences didn't mean a whole lot. The MidKnights and the Coroners might be rainbow colored, but they were still gangs, increasingly devoting their energies to violence and crimes against property. The community had to do something about them.

"Morning, Reverend Stonehill."

Thomas held out his hand to the couple with the two children. They had braved the park and crossed the street to come to church. It was the equivalent of running the gauntlet.

"How are you, Sarah? Jack?" he asked.

He listened to their polite replies before he squatted to say hello to the children. "Kimmy? Who's your friend?"

The little girl smiled shyly and held out her teddy bear for him to see.

"Does he keep you company at night?" Thomas asked.

She nodded.

"Frankie." Thomas held out his hand to the little boy. Frankie rested his hand in Thomas's, and Thomas shook solemnly. "I've been told there's a special treat after Sunday school," Thomas said.

"Doughnuts?"

"I promised I wouldn't tell."

Frankie's eyes sparkled. "I bet it's doughnuts!"

Thomas stood, and the family went inside to settle the children upstairs in Thomas's apartment, which served as the Sunday school wing. For the next ten minutes he was busy greeting his parishioners. Then, when the small stream trickled away, he went inside, too. At his appearance the pianist struck up a bluesy medley of hymns as Thomas walked up to the front of the church.

The pianist, Greg, a young man with shoulder-length blond hair and inch-thick glasses, made his living performing in a jazz club uptown. The congregation was blessed to have him. Greg had wandered in one day, seemingly out of nowhere, and volunteered. He could play anything in his own style, and although there had been raised eyebrows when he played his first service, now there were only tapping feet.

For a moment, listening to Greg's splashy finale, Thomas thought of Garnet. She had spoken of the need for grabbing a little joy. There was joy in Greg's music. Thomas suspected that some of the people sitting in the fold-up chairs were here just to listen to Greg.

He didn't care why they were here. He was just glad they were.

The first part of the service went off without a hitch. There were announcements, prayers, hymns and readings. He used eclectic sources for his readings. Truth and meaning were found everywhere. It was his job to share what he found with his congregation. Sometimes he saw understanding and even enlightenment in their eyes when he hit upon something that had special meaning to their lives. Sometimes he saw irritation. But he never saw boredom. There were many things that could be said about Thomas's ministry, but never that it was boring.

The choir of eight came up to stand in front of the picture of Jesus. They wore the cast-off green robes of another church, but as few as they were, they sang like angels. That was Greg's doing, too. He worked with them on Wednesday and Sunday nights, his two nights off. Today their anthem was a gospel standard. They swayed in rhythm and featured Cretia Barnes, a large woman with more than her share of soul. When they sat down, the church was appropriately silent and awed.

Thomas stood and walked to the pulpit.

"The text this morning comes from Isaiah 35, verse 7. 'And the parched ground shall become a pool, and the thirsty land springs of water: in the habitation of dragons, where each lay, shall be grass with reeds and rushes.'"

Thomas set aside his Bible. He looked over the small group gathered to hear his words of wisdom. For a moment something very much like fear clutched at him. What right did he have to be standing here? How could he possibly think that anything he had to say was worth these good people's time?

He couldn't talk to them with God's voice. He and God weren't on speaking terms anymore. He couldn't tell them about his life. What part of it could he hold up as a model? And what sins had he committed that he would willingly share?

He looked at faces and saw Ema, not visibly bruised today, but bruised and aching inside. He saw Cretia, who despite her rich, booming voice was fighting an illness that threatened to take her life. He saw Sarah and Jack, Kimmy and Frankie's parents, trying against terrible odds to raise their children to be good citizens despite Jack's recent unemployment.

They were all looking to him for comfort, for sustenance, for something they could take away that day to nurture them in the coming week.

And what could he give them?

The door creaked, and a woman slid through the narrow opening, spilling sunlight across the floor before the door shut once more. Dressed in white as always, Garnet met his eyes. Then, as he waited to begin, she moved across the room to take the nearest empty seat.

His greatest critic had arrived. When she spoke to him of his fallibility, she spoke with his own voice. He was nothing, and he had no right to be here. She had seen through him from the start.

He looked away and saw the other faces again. Pleading, yearning faces. He was nothing. He had nothing to say. And still he had no choice but to offer them what he could.

"The habitation of dragons," he said. "We live in the habitation of dragons, don't we? All we have to do is open that door and look outside. Look at the streets. Look at Kensington Park. Stare at the sidewalks in front of Wilford Heights long enough and you'll watch a crime being committed.

"This is the Corners. Dragons abide here. And the ground is parched and aching with thirst."

He moved away from the pulpit. Most of the time he just used it as a place to leave his Bible. He had never liked to have anything separating him from the people to whom he spoke. The pulpit in his former church had been raised ten steps off the floor, like the ornate prow of a ship. He had climbed those steps because it had been expected of him. He had stood halfway to heaven and looked down at the congregation to see rapt, worshipful faces.

And he had spoken with the voice of God.

Now he spoke with his own voice. He walked to the front row. No one had to look up to see him now.

"Dragons breathe fire. They devour cities and families and landscapes. What they don't destroy, they taint with their smoke and their smell. Nothing in their vicinity is left untouched. You can't live where a dragon has been. Oh, you might be able to survive. You might be able to skulk around and scratch out a living when the dragon's head is turned. But that's different from living, isn't it?"

He saw heads nod. Sometimes in his former church his sermons had hovered on such a lofty plane that even he lost the point somewhere close to the middle. But not this sermon. This was something everyone understood.

They understood because they lived intimately with the dragon.

"The dragon has touched us, all of us, hasn't it?" More heads nodded. "His fire smolders on our streets and alleys, in the hallways of our apartments, in our schoolyards and classrooms.

Every time one of your children is offered drugs, every time someone is robbed or beaten, the dragon's fires burn a little brighter."

Someone said amen. In his former church no one would ever have dared interrupt Thomas's sermons. Now he found the man who had spoken and nodded to him. "Amen? Then you've seen the dragon, Seth?"

There were more amens. Thomas moved down the aisle restlessly. "There are dragons within us, too, aren't there?" His gaze settled on Garnet. Her face showed no emotion, but something about the way she sat, arms folded, fingers tapping against her own skin, told him she was listening carefully.

"I have my own dragons. Some people call those dragons sins. Some people call them neuroses or problems or even just feelings. But if they scare us, if they make us feel violated, frightened, alone, then dragon is just as good a word as any other."

He turned away from Garnet. "Isaiah says that in the habitation of dragons, where each lay, shall be grass with reeds and rushes."

He walked to the front so that he could see everyone. "So how do we get from parched ground, ground that dragons have destroyed, ground where dragons have eaten and slept and roared their fiery roars, to a place green with grass, fertile with reeds and rushes? Grass only grows where it can't be trampled, doesn't it? Reeds and rushes grow where calm water laps at their roots. How do we get to that place?"

The answer was harder than the question. He looked at the faces that were becoming so familiar to him. He wanted to tell them about redemption, about God's forgiveness and strength. But he could not say those things, because he could no longer feel their truth.

"I want to tell you it's easy," he said. "Believe the right things, say the right things, do the right things, and one day we'll all wake up and Kensington Park will be green again. Schools and streets will be safe again. We'll wake up and find that we have only joy inside us, love inside us, hope inside us."

He put his fist against his chest. "Would you believe me?"

He saw heads shaking. He sighed. The sigh was real. Once it might have been for show, but now it came from deep inside him.

"Would you believe me if I told you it's not going to be easy?" Heads nodded. "It's not. I can tell you that much for certain. Legend tells us that St. George slew his dragon. But I'm not St. George. I can't rise up with a mighty sword and make this a place of grass, a place of reeds and rushes. Neither can you. The dragon is too large, his fire too blistering for any one of us."

He walked away, as if to return to the pulpit. But at the pulpit's corner he stopped. "Could we do it together?" He let the question linger a moment. "If we band together, what can we become? If we band together.. .with God's help... what can we do?"

And will you help us, Lord? Or are you even there to hear this plea?

He moved to the pulpit and picked up his Bible. He didn't open it. He recited the quote from memory. " 'The parched ground shall become a pool, and the thirsty land springs of water: in the habitation of dragons, where each lay, shall be grass with reeds and rushes.'"

He spoke for another ten minutes. He hammered at the idea that, together, they could slay dragons. He spoke of strength in numbers and the way it was multiplied by good intent. He spoke specifically of projects they could accomplish. Together. With the help of the God he had to force himself to speak of. He ended with Isaiah's quote again.

Then he looked out over the tiny congregation. "It will take us all," he said. "All of us, and everyone else in this community who believes what we do. Do we want to slay the dragon? Do we long for a place free from fear? A green, fertile place? Or have we been so singed by the dragon's fire that we're afraid to live with only the sunshine of God's love to warm us?"

He set down his Bible and nodded to Greg. Then, as Greg

played the opening bars of the final hymn, Thomas motioned for the congregation to rise.

Garnet waited in the background as Thomas shook hands with each exiting parishioner. She chatted about nothing to Ema—because that was the only way Ema would have it— and hugged her two nieces, promising that they could come over to her apartment to play after school tomorrow. When Ema had protectively shepherded them out the door, she was alone with Thomas.

He didn't speak. She had already learned that he was a man who wasted little time on pleasantries. If she hadn't heard him preaching today, she would almost have said he was a man who believed that the fewer words, the better.

But she had heard him speak. He had opened his mouth, and words had poured forth, golden words, emotional words, words that had bored straight to the heart of the problems in this community. The community she had believed he didn't care an honest fig about. The community she had accused him of exploiting for his own selfish purposes. The community she had expected him to leave as soon as he tired of trying to help.

"Save any souls?" she asked.

"You tell me."

"Well, you made them believe change was possible. I saw it in their eyes."

"And you think I lied to them."

"I don't know." She honestly didn't. For moments during his sermon, despite every screaming voice to the contrary inside her, she had believed he was right. Change. Real change. Lasting change.

"You know, I think you and I are on the same side," he said.

She still wasn't sure; she still didn't trust him. She had seen too many do-gooders come and go. And now that she'd heard him speak, now that she'd heard the power of which he was capable and the way he could mesmerize even the harshest critic, she was that much more certain Thomas Stonehill would be gone from the Corners before another year had passed. Gone to bigger and better things and places.

She pushed her hair away from her face. She hadn't restrained it today. She liked it best when it was down, liked the feel of it moving over her shoulders and back. She saw Thomas's gaze flick to her hair, and she guessed that the preacher man disapproved of anything so free, so overtly rebellious.

"I need you to be on my side today," she said.

He waited.

"I have a patient. Her name is Candy Tremira. She's about to give birth, and she isn't married. I saw her a little while ago, and she's nearly hysterical. Her boyfriend is willing, but neither of them knows anyone who could perform a ceremony. They have a license, and they had planned to go down to City Hall this week. But it'll be too late if they wait that long."

"What does 'about to give birth' mean?"

She shrugged. "I saw her just before coming here. She's--"

"Is this the girl in Wilford Heights? The one the Knights warned you against visiting?"

"Your memory can't be faulted."

"Is she in labor?"

"She's about three centimeters dilated, and her contractions seem real enough."

"Where is she?"

"She's still at home. She's refusing to go to the hospital without getting married first. She says the nurses will look down on her. She says God will curse her baby."

"No God I'm familiar with."

"Women in labor don't necessarily make sense, Padre."

"I am no one's father."

She heard the irritation in his voice and she was momentarily ashamed. "Will you help, Thomas?"

He realized she had made a concession. "Would she like to come here? Is she able? Or do you want me to go there?"

"Here is the border of Knight's territory. She won't set foot here or in the clinic."

"Then she takes the gang talk seriously."

"It's not talk. Demon is perfectly capable of killing her. I think he's probably killed before."

Thomas listened to the matter-of-fact way Garnet made the announcement. It was almost as if she had said that the local library was closing for repairs, or the Wilford Heights residents had organized a block party.

"Will she go to the hospital?" he asked.

"There's one across town that's agreed to accept her. It's far enough from here that I don't think she'll have anything to worry about. I'm going to drive up to the back entrance of the Heights after the wedding and take her there myself."

"We'd better get going, then."

"You'll do it?"

"What did you expect?" He let his gaze travel over her. The outfit was familiar, but today she wore it with gold and crystal beads and earrings that dangled so low they almost touched her shoulders.

She tossed her head, and the earrings danced. "They worked up their nerve last week to ask another of our local clergy to help them. He refused, because their religious backgrounds are different. Francis is Catholic, and Candy doesn't know what she is. That pastor said that in good conscience, he couldn't bless their marriage."

"I'll get what I need. I'll be back in a minute."

As she waited for him, she stared at the multiple faces of Jesus in the front of the church. Her mother had never been much of one for religion; Garnet's acquaintance with Jesus was minimal. But as she stared, the four images seemed to blend into one integrated whole. She wondered what the picture said about Thomas's ministry. Or about the man himself.

No stranger would have been able to tell the difference between the Coroners and the MidKnights. There were only subtle variations in clothing. The Coroners usually wore red, the color of blood, somewhere on their bodies, accompanied by baseball caps with the letter "C." Ohio alone had given them the Cincinnati Reds and the Cleveland Indians to choose from. The MidKnights wore somber grays, blues and blacks, work boots with blue laces, dark bandannas or do-rags. The Coroners and the MidKnights might be fledglings in the gang world, but they were catching on.

Thomas had learned enough about gangs to realize what a dangerous time could lie ahead for the Corners. The Coroners and the MidKnights might be largely unorganized and unaffiliated now, but each day saw them closing ranks, assuming more and more of the traditional gang postures and traditions. Their graffiti showed less imagination and detailed more threats. Police officers he had spoken with claimed that they were seeing more devotion to "lit," the gang members' bible of rules and regulations. More members were "strapped"—carrying weapons. And more and more often, they were suspected of committing serious crimes.

There had been drive-by shootings, too. As Garnet led Thomas through the graffiti-tainted walls of the Wilford Heights housing project, she told him about one involving Candy and Francis.

"You know Candy used to be Demon Harris's girlfriend."

"Demon was the kid with the cap pulled over his forehead?"

"Remember that face. He didn't come by his name without

cause." Garnet stepped around a pile of old rags and newspapers that had been abandoned on the stairwell. "Candy's a good kid. She's never had much of a home life, and she developed early. The guys were all over her. She was flattered by Demon's attention. Without the hat he's a good-looking man, and he spends money lavishly on his women. Candy fell into his trap. Then she began to find out what he was really like."

"He abused her?" Thomas tried not to breathe more deeply than he had to. The stairwell was filthy, and the smell made him glad he hadn't just eaten. Something small and brown moved at the edge of his vision. It wasn't a cat.

"He beat her whenever possible. She knew Francis from her classes at school, and one day she ran into him again at a mall. They started seeing each other secretly. She knew if she left Demon and moved in with Francis, Demon would declare war on Francis and the Coroners."

"I gather that's what happened."

Garnet stopped climbing at the fourth floor and turned down a hallway. "Candy finally realized she had to make a choice. Francis was good to her and Demon wasn't. I think she really believes she loves Francis. So she left Demon and came here to live."

They passed a group of three young men, each wearing a baseball cap sporting a "C," bill turned to the back. Garnet spoke; only one mumbled in response.

Farther down the hallway she continued her story. "It might not have been so bad, but about the same time there was a drive-by shooting on Fourteenth Street. One of the Knights, a kid named Wolfman, was killed. Supposedly the gunman's car was dark gray or blue and banged up, like one that belonged to Francis's brother. It was late at night, and no one is sure who did it, of course, but a Knight who saw the whole thing swore Francis was driving."

"What do you think?"

"Francis says he wasn't anywhere near Fourteenth at the time. He has friends who say he was with them, so the cops had to let him go. But the word of these gangsters isn't worth an inch of this stinking hallway."

"You don't like Francis?"

"Actually, I do. He's a quiet kid, a little too macho and swaggering, like all the others. But he's smart, and he has good instincts. He reads. He finished school against impossible odds, and he wants to get a real job. When he found out Candy was pregnant, he wanted to marry her right away."

"Then why did they wait?"

"For one thing, she's been terrified that if she married Francis, Demon would be even angrier, and he'd work harder to find a way to hurt them. But there's more. The Knights are after her, and because she used to hang with them, the Coroners don't totally trust her, either. So she hasn't had anybody she could really talk to. She's been alone through this whole thing, except for Francis."

"And you."

Garnet was silent.

"Can they get out of here? Start a new life somewhere together?"

"They're going to have to. Or you're about to sanction the marriage of two dead kids." Garnet stopped in front of a door and banged twice, paused and banged twice again.

The door opened. The face of the young man on the other side was drained of all color. He looked pathetically grateful to see Garnet. "She's crying," he said. "My mother tried to get her to stop, but she can't."

"You go into labor sometime, Francis, and see if you get through it without a tear or two." Garnet stepped inside and motioned Thomas to follow. "This is Thomas Stonehill, minister of the Church of the Samaritan. He'll do the ceremony."

"I don't think Candy's going to wait long enough for any ceremony."

"Why not? She planning to go somewhere without the rest of us?"

Francis swallowed. Thomas realized he was seeing the young man without any of his macho posturing. He was just a good-looking, brown-eyed, brown-haired kid like a million other kids around the world. A scared kid—a scared kid who was about to become a father.

A scream split the fetid air of the small apartment.

"Well, that's more than a few tears," Garnet said. "I'd better check this out."

Thomas watched her disappear through the doorway. "Is your mother with Candy now?" he asked.

"She left. She and Candy don't get along."

"She knew you were going to get married this afternoon?"

"She don't care."

"Anyone else here?"

"My brothers are around the Heights somewhere."

Another scream made Francis turn even whiter. "I think she's dying."

"You should have called an ambulance."

"Candy wouldn't let me. Besides, they don't want to come into the Heights. The baby'd be a year old before they showed up."

Thomas heard the young man's bitterness. He couldn't blame him. City services were notoriously unavailable to anyone in the Corners, and especially to anyone unlucky enough to live in Wilford Heights.

Garnet came into the room. "Francis," she said calmly, "remember all those movies you've seen where somebody has to boil water because a baby's on the way?"

Instinctively Thomas reached for Francis's arm. The young man sagged appreciably.

"Well, kid, get some boiling," Garnet said. "And tell me you've got clean sheets and towels somewhere."

"You're going to deliver a baby here?" Thomas asked.

"Either that or it's going to deliver itself without me."

"But you said—"

"She was only three centimeters. I know. She was. And now she's a full ten and the head is crowning. In less than an hour. And she's only seventeen. Lucky thing I brought supplies with me this morning, just in case."

She paused a moment to judge the expression on Thomas's face. She expected to see disapproval. She hadn't anticipated this scenario. She was angry at herself for casually ruling it out. Candy was young and small-boned, and this was her first baby. She had claimed that she had been in labor all night, but when Garnet had examined her, Candy had only been slightly dilated. It would have been unlikely, nearly unheard of, for her labor to suddenly take off in the short time Garnet had been away.

But Garnet was a good enough nurse to know that the unheard of usually occurred when no one was looking. And she hadn't looked hard enough.

"What can I do?" Thomas asked.

There was no disapproval on his face. No blame. Just an obvious willingness to do whatever needed to be done to salvage the situation.

Garnet felt a peculiar relief. Almost as if someone, somewhere, had forgiven her for this mistake. "She wants that wedding. Do you think you're up to doing it between contractions while I deliver the baby? It might not be pretty."

"Are you up to being the groom?" Thomas asked Francis.

"Yeah, sure. I-"

"Go find two witnesses. They can stand outside the door. That will be legal enough. I'll boil the water." Thomas still had his hand on Francis's arm. He squeezed it. "And don't forget to come back, son."

Francis definitely looked as if that thought had entered his mind. Then he nodded. "I don't have to watch, do I?"

"You can stand up at her head," Garnet said. I'll cover her with a sheet."

"I'll get my brother and his girlfriend."

"You do that." Thomas released his grip on Francis's arm. The front door slammed behind him. "Is she going to be all right?" Thomas asked.

"I think so. The baby's in a good position, and Candy's been taking care of herself. But she's young and scared, so be prepared for anything. I've already called the ambulance, but you can be sure the baby will get here before they do."

"What about a doctor?"

"Do you know one who'd be willing to come to Wilford Heights?" When he didn't answer, she smiled a little. "Thank you, Thomas."

"For what?"

She didn't know how else to say it. "For being here," she said. "Now find me some clean towels and sheets and forget the water." Then she disappeared through the doorway again.

4

The baby was a boy, seven pounds six ounces and perfect in every way. The delivery had taken twenty minutes. Twenty-four hours later, the mother and father were probably still dazed.

Thomas hung up the phone in his study on Monday morning and stared at the blotter on his desk as he thought about Francis and Candy.

"Study" was an exaggeration, almost as much a one as referring to the room just beyond as a church. Like Mother and Child, the Church of the Samaritan had once been a store, in this case a hardware store. It had been vacated two years before Thomas saw the space, saw the for-rent sign tacked to a piece of the plywood covering the shattered front window and saw the potential.

The landlord had been willing to donate the use of the building. A tax deduction was better than no compensation at all, and Thomas had agreed to do the renovations necessary to open the doors. The landlord had even thrown in the small apartment on the second floor. He was tired of low-class tenants who forgot to pay their bills, he had told Thomas. It cost more to evict them than he realized in rent. This way, he could deduct the cost of the apartment, too.

Thomas had carted trash to the curb by himself for a week. The building had been a flophouse for derelicts, a place to score drugs, a home away from home for gang members. Refuse was hip-deep in places. Vermin of all sorts infested what was left of the walls. The storeroom in the back—now Thomas's study—had been gutted by a fire.

At the start of Thomas's second week of hauling trash, a man offered to help. The word was out, he said, that Thomas was a preacher. He didn't look like no preacher. Thomas agreed. He got cleaned up when he preached, he explained. But who wanted to haul garbage in a suit and tie? The next day there were two men, the next four.

It took three months to open the doors of the church for the first service. The handful of people who showed up were mostly just curious. A few of them had helped Thomas tear down walls and nail up new ones in their place. A few had shaken their heads along with Thomas when those new walls had been covered with gang graffiti. A few more had been with him when he slathered the graffiti with three coats of paint.

But a lot of his helpers had never yet set foot in the church for a service. Some claimed they had churches of their own; some wanted nothing to do with formal worship; some had simply disappeared into the stream of Corners life, and Thomas had never seen them again.

Now, six months after the doors had been flung wide, Thomas's congregation had tripled. That was the positive way to view the changes. The negative was that there were still fewer than thirty committed members of the Church of the Samaritan. And very little could be accomplished by thirty people.

But yesterday the Church of the Samaritan had added one more. Thomas relaxed in his chair and smiled as he thought of the baby Garnet had delivered into the world. The child's beauty had been a surprise. Thomas had never presided at a birth. The youngest babies he'd seen were the ones he'd baptized in his former church, pink and white perfection in white lace christening gowns. This baby had been as red as an apple, and his face had been screwed up in dismay at the world he'd been brought into. Still, his tiny features had been perfect, and after he'd been bathed and calmed and put to his mother's breast, he had seemed as much a miracle as the wealthiest, most pampered and protected child in the city.

Matthew Francis, to be called Matt.

At a knock on the study door, Thomas looked up. The door opened before he could respond, and Garnet poked her head inside.

He hadn't expected to see her. She had been outwardly grateful to him for support yesterday, but he wondered if cynicism still simmered just beneath her gratitude. He stood and made his way around the desk.

"Recovered yet?" he asked as she entered.

"Everyday stuff for me." She smiled a little. She'd never seen Thomas in casual clothes. Somehow, in jeans and a slightly tattered polo shirt, he was even more formidable. "But not for you," she added. "Ready to do it again?"

"You can't have another patient who needs a wedding."

"You're right."

She wasn't dressed in white today. She was wearing black stretch pants and a soft, brick red shirt tied at her waist with a multicolored scarf. Her hair was wild; today the inevitable necklace was made of ropes and ropes of brightly painted wooden beads and carved animal heads.

"I'm glad you came by," he said. He realized he meant it. And the moment he realized that, he wasn't glad to see her anymore.

"I thought you'd want to hear about Matty," she said.

"Of course."

She watched him fold his arms, as if to ward her away. She

had thought for a moment that he was genuinely pleased she had come by. Now she tested the theory that for some reason he had changed his mind. "Shouldn't I be here?" she asked. "Is it improper for me to be alone with you in here?"

"The door's open."

"Do you have a jealous wife?"

"I don't have a wife at all."

"Hot damn. I'll bet the deacon's daughters had designs on you."

He didn't know why he responded. "I had a wife. She died."

"I'm sorry." And she *was* sorry, though Thomas didn't look sad. His expression hadn't even changed, but she knew how easy it was to cover emotion. It was one of the first things anyone who wanted to survive the Corners had to learn.

She wondered if his wife's death had had anything to do with his decision to come here. Or had he been sent by a church hierarchy hoping to establish a religious presence, a mission in the ghetto? His arrival in the Corners was almost as mysterious as the man himself.

"What about the baby?" he asked.

"Candy and Matty were dismissed from the hospital this morning."

"That seems awfully soon."

"She was lucky they took her at all, since the baby was an hour old by the time the ambulance got there. Candy's got no insurance, and she's not on welfare. Francis has been supporting her with whatever he could make doing odd jobs."

"Is he a good worker?"

"Yes."

"Would he be willing to work construction?"

"What are they constructing around here, Thomas? Haven't you noticed? This is a destruction kind of place."

"Not here. In Deering Hills."

She frowned and wondered how Thomas could be so out of

touch with reality. Deering Hills was one of the most expensive suburbs of the city. It was green-landscaped hillsides, house prices starting in the high six figures, and high schools with television studios and high-tech computer laboratories.

"How could a kid like Francis get a job in Deering Hills?" she asked. "Don't you have to have a college education just to clean up litter on the streets? Hey, forget that, there *is* no litter in Deering Hills, is there?"

"I've called someone I know, a man named Stu Wilson. He's willing to give Francis a job."

"But Francis doesn't have a car. Could he take the bus that far? Isn't Deering Hills the kind of place that only schedules public transportation when housemaids from the city are coming and going?"

"You said yesterday that Candy and Francis can't stay here."

"Sure, I said that."

"Did you mean it?"

"Yeah, I meant it." Garnet fingered a cheap glass paperweight on his desk. It was the only decoration in the room. The study was as Spartan as the man. She looked at him. "There are a lot of people who stay here who shouldn't."

He supposed she thought he was one of them. "I've found Candy and Francis a place to live in Deering, if they're willing to move."

"Willing?" Garnet considered. "Candy's miserable where she is, and now she's terrified for Matty. Francis wants to do the right thing by her, though God knows where he picked up his morals. His father left his mother before Francis was born. His mother gave up on everything a couple of years ago and drinks herself numb every chance she gets."

"Deering Hills is a long way from home."

"In their case, that's for the best. Where would they be living?"

"A woman I know has a garage apartment in back of her

house. She says it's small, but I'll bet it's five times larger than Francis's bedroom at the Heights. Marcia's nearly seventy, but she refuses to have household help. If Candy was willing to do the daily cleaning and Francis was willing to do the yard work, it would help Marcia."

A smile crossed his face so quickly that Garnet wasn't sure she had seen it. "They'll have to pretend they're not helping, though," he added. "Candy can bring Matty to visit in the mornings, then just naturally offer to help with the dishes. She can dust when Marcia's not looking."

Garnet understood. "And Francis can mow the lawn in front of the garage, only he'll just forget and mow the whole yard."

"Exactly."

"Do you really think it will work?"

"Stu Wilson needs a new carpenter's assistant. Marcia Branthoover needs help. The kids need to get out of here."

"I've already given them some baby clothes and equipment Mother and Child had on hand, but they'll have to have money to help them get started." Garnet pulled her checkbook out of a bulky patchwork leather purse. She flipped to her check register. "I can spare some."

"I've already written them a check." He reached around the top of his desk and pulled the check out of his drawer.

She looked up. "Lord, does everything always come this easily to you?"

He handed it to her. "What makes you think any of this was easy?"

"You make it seem effortless, like you've got hundreds of people just waiting in the wings to help anybody you give a nod to."

He decided her face was as insolent as her hair. No eyes should see straight through everything and everyone. No nose should be lifted in such disdain. And her mouth... It was harder to think about her mouth, the mouth that spoke without thinking and regretted nothing. The mouth that curved in unrepentant smiles and world-weary frowns. The smooth, seductive red lips.

"Does it please you to think I might not have worked hard to make this happen?" he asked.

"It would please me more to think you had to slave. I don't know, Thomas. You just look like a man everything comes easily to. Though God knows why you'd have ended up here if that was true."

"I'm just slumming for a year or two. Remember?"

"Did I say that?" She smiled and thought she saw it register somewhere just behind his eyes. "Since you're keeping track, did I say thank you just now?"

"It's not necessary."

"Should I go down on my knees and thank anyone else?"

"Something tells me there aren't any calluses there."

"And yours are probably as tough as an armadillo shell." She turned to leave, then turned back. "Look, I almost forgot. Watch your back for a while. The Knights know about yesterday."

He took her arm before she could turn away again. Her flesh gave under the pressure of his fingers. "What have you heard?"

Pointedly, she looked down at his hand. He released her immediately. "Very forceful, Thomas. Andre would be impressed."

"What have you heard?"

She considered several versions of the truth, but finally settled on the one that didn't leave out strategic information. "It went something like this. 'Yo, girl. You done what we told you not to. Now you and the padre gonna be sorry.'"

"Andre?"

"That's Andre in front of his buddies. Andre by himself would have been more articulate and less threatening."

"You should get out of here."

She stared at him for a moment before she spoke. "No, I shouldn't."

"Then you don't think he means what he says?"

"He means it."

"Then he could hurt you?"

"Or worse. Yeah, I know. But I also know how to take care of myself. I'm not a fool. I grew up here. I'll be careful. But nobody's going to chase me out of the Corners. I'm staying here till the day I die."

His fingers itched to take her arm again, but he knew how little good that would do. There was something in her voice, something that went far beyond stubbornness. "I'll talk to him."

She shook her head, and her hair flew around her shoulders. "That's not a good idea. He'll have to be even more macho with you."

"I'll talk to him."

She grimaced. "Good luck, then. Just catch him when Demon's not around. Demon will be ready for you next time." In the doorway, she turned once more. "When should Candy and Francis be ready to leave?"

He didn't want to abandon the subject of Garnet's safety, but the choice wasn't his. He had nothing to say about her life or her decisions. "They can move in today, if Candy's feeling up to it."

"She'll feel better the sooner she gets out of Wilford Heights. I'll drive them myself this evening."

"I'll go over and tell them about Marcia's place now. I'll leave directions with them. The apartment is furnished. All they'll need to get started is their clothes and whatever things they have for Matthew."

"And a thousand prayers. Maybe they've hooked up with the right guy after all, huh?"

Thomas could hardly tell her no. He didn't advertise his belief that if he prayed a thousand prayers, ten hundred of them would be wasted.

Andre lived in a small frame house in a row of similar houses half a mile from the church. Once the neighborhood had existed solely to supply a local factory with workers. The houses had been as alike as the proverbial peas in the pod. Now, time and spotty maintenance had given them the individuality they had lacked. Some had been recently painted or covered with siding; some had been stripped by sun and rain down to bare wood. Some had porches, alive and green with hanging plants in the summer. Some porches had fallen away.

Andre's house was one of the nicer ones. The sidewalk was still lined with golden chrysanthemums and silver dusty miller, despite a frost or two. Some imaginative soul who favored yellow and pale blue had painted house and trim until it was storybook picturesque. Hardly a house for the self-proclaimed leader of the MidKnights.

Thomas had trailed Andre from a distance for most of the last hour until he could catch him alone. It was late now, but the porch light was on. Thomas waited until Andre was on the porch before he got out of his car.

"Andre?"

The young man turned. His hand slid inside the ever-present hoodie.

"I just want to talk to you," Thomas said. "If you have to hold a gun in your hand just to have a conversation, then we're in trouble already."

"Who's there?"

"Thomas Stonehill. Padre, to you."

"Yeah." Andre seemed to think about his decision. Then his hands fell to his sides. "What do you want?"

"I just want to talk."

"Yeah. Sure you do."

"Can we sit on your porch? Do you want to go somewhere for coffee?"

"Don't drink coffee." Andre looked around. "You can come on up. Just keep it down. My mama's sleeping."

Thomas walked up the sidewalk. There was a zigzagging ramp up to the porch instead of steps. He held his hands carefully away from his sides, in case Andre had some idea about being double-crossed. He saw Andre near the door, and the porch light went off. It took a moment for his eyes to adjust.

"What do you want?"

Thomas turned toward the sound of Andre's voice. Now he saw the young man's silhouette in the far corner. Thomas leaned against the railing beside the ramp. "I want to ask you to leave Garnet alone, Andre. She's just doing her job. For that matter, I'm just doing mine. We're trying to make this a better place. For us, for you, for your friends. And for that little kid who was born yesterday. A little kid who's never going to hurt you or the Knights."

"You don't know nothing about it."

"Then tell me about it."

There was silence from the corner. Finally Andre spoke. "What you come here for, Padre? You think we need you? You don't know nothing about nothing."

"I know killing people is wrong. Sometimes I'm not sure what I believe, but I know I believe that. And threatening to kill them's wrong, too. Threatening to hurt them, hurting them. All wrong. There's no good that can come from any of those things."

"Is that all you come to say? I gotta go in."

"This is a nice house." Thomas gazed above him. There were hooks lining the porch for plants. Someone here spent time growing things. He gambled that the person was Andre's mother. "Your mother keeps it painted nicely. Is she the gardener?"

"No."

"Someone here is."

"You done talking?"

Thomas realized Andre was standing in front of him. "If you

want me to be, I guess I am. But please, think about what I said. Garnet says you're a smart kid. She believes in you. Don't give her reason to question her own judgment."

"I'm nothing to her. Just because she grew up on this street..."

Thomas was interested. "Did she?"

The front door banged in answer. Thomas sighed and moved away from the railing, starting toward the ramp. He stopped when he heard a whirring noise, then the murmur of voices inside.

"You're late, Andre. I been waiting up for you."

"You shouldn't, Ma. I told you I'd be late."

"Who were you talking to? That Demon Harris again?"

"No, Ma. Nobody you know. Now you got to get to bed. I'll push you in."

A wheelchair. The sound connected with an image in Thomas's mind. A motorized wheelchair. Which explained the ramp. He wondered what kind of disability Andre's mother had. He wondered how it had affected Andre. One thing was clear, even from the snippet of conversation he had just heard. There was love here.

And wherever love existed, there was hope.

Candy and Francis's new apartment was luxury itself. There was a spacious, carpeted living room with tastefully upholstered furniture. There was a bedroom with a large double bed, and a small nook off it that was perfect for a nursery. The kitchen had all new appliances and a priceless view of Deering Hills out of the window over the sink.

Marcia Branthoover had explained to Garnet that her late husband had built the apartment just for something to do after his retirement. They'd planned to rent it so that someone would be on the premises when they traveled, but he had died soon after, and Marcia had never been that interested in traveling without him. Except for visits from her children and grandchildren, no one had ever stayed there.

Garnet had watched Francis and Candy wander through the three rooms, eyes like children's at Christmastime. Garnet had seen the softening of Marcia's prim expression, her evident interest in Matty—she'd raised four of her own, yes, she had, scattered all over the country now—her careful, tactful advice when Matty wouldn't stop crying. Garnet knew a miracle had truly been wrought here. Four human beings who needed each other had somehow been brought together in this unlikely place.

By the ministry of one man who was completely out of place in the Corners.

Garnet had left Candy and Francis with a hundred dollars in cash from her own bank account and with Thomas's check. She was sure they could manage until Francis got paid. Marcia had two cars—she had somehow never gotten around to selling her husband's—and she was happy to let Francis drive one of them to work.

There were few days in Garnet's memory that had turned out so well. The apartment in Deering Hills was only a partial solution to Candy and Francis's problems, but it was a step in the right direction. One small family had beaten the odds, at least temporarily.

Now there were only thousands of others left for Garnet to work with.

She parked her car in the tiny lot behind the clinic. She was tired, and the muscles in her neck ached. She shut her eyes, tucked her chin and slowly turned her head from side to side. She could feel the tension easing. She envisioned the claw-footed tub in her apartment filled to the top with hot water. She had just enough bath oil left for one last soak. Tonight would be the night.

The splintering of glass thrust her into the present. Reflexively her arm rose to protect her face, and she tucked her head lower. Shards of glass rained in on her. As she tried to make sense of it, her door was jerked open and she was hauled out of the car.

"We told you, Garnet babe, you were supposed to stay away from Candy!"

Fear told her to keep her eyes closed. The sound of shattering glass still filled her ears. She was terrified that her eyes had been damaged. She fought off the hands hauling her across the lot, kicking ferociously but ineffectively at her tormentor.

Something crashed into her midriff, and her eyelids flew open. She saw a fist coming toward her, and she doubled over in pain. Another fist to her head slammed her eyes shut again. She flailed her arms to stop her attackers until someone grabbed them and forced them behind her. The blows were coming from different directions. Somewhere it registered that more than one person was responsible.

"Stop!" she screamed. She ducked to keep her face from being hit again and rammed her head into someone's stomach. She felt a sharp blow against the back of her skull.

Then she felt nothing at all.

~

She awoke to the sound of sirens. She was immobilized. She couldn't move; she couldn't speak. There was something cool across her face. For a moment she panicked, afraid she couldn't breathe. She found that she couldn't open her eyes, either. Something seemed to be covering them. Then she felt the hand encasing hers.

"Easy." The voice was familiar, although at first, in her panic, she couldn't place it. "Easy, Garnet. You're all right. You're on your way to the hospital. Just take a deep breath. Good. Now take another. They're giving you oxygen, just to make breathing a little easier. They put in an IV and strapped you down because they were afraid you'd pull it out."

"I...I..."

"Don't try to talk."

"My.. .eyes."

"There's nothing to worry about. The paramedics think your eyes are fine. But there was some bleeding above them, and they found glass in one of the cuts. They just wanted to be sure your eyes are okay. And they're waiting until they get to the hospital for that."

She placed the voice. Some of the panic eased. "Thomas?"

"Yes."

"The... dragon got me."

"I told you not to talk. For once do what you're told, okay?" His voice sounded thick, as if he was speaking with difficulty. His hand tightened around hers. "I'll tell you everything I know."

She heard him speaking to someone else, although the words seemed far away. Then he was speaking to her again.

"The paramedic says you're bruised, and they'll want to watch for internal damage. But your vital signs are all stable, which is good news. You probably have a concussion, and they'll have to X-ray one arm and your ribs. Probably the arm you fell on after—"

"I...was beaten up."

"Yes."

The thickness was gone now. She heard steel in his voice. He was coldly furious. She knew him well enough already to detect that much. She could almost envision his face. No feelings would show. But they would be there, behind the remote expression that was such a part of him. She knew that about him. He cared too much. She hadn't thought about it before, but now she understood. He cared too much.

The thought comforted her.

"How... long?"

"I found you right afterward. I drove by the clinic and I..." The pause went on so long, she knew he was hiding something.

"What?" she demanded.

"I heard someone shouting. I stopped. The girl who lives upstairs was shouting for help. Apparently she heard you scream when... you were attacked. She had already called for help."

She could hear his voice near her ear. Everything was growing fuzzy. She concentrated on his words and the warmth of his hand. She didn't want to lose consciousness again.

"The ambulance got there before the police. Whoever did this was gone by the time I arrived."

"Your timing... stinks."

He squeezed harder. "Was it the Knights?"

"I... I don't know."

"You can't stay in the Corners, Garnet. We both know who it was and why. You're going to be all right this time, but what about next time?"

Intense. That was the word for Thomas. She had never met anyone so intense, so focused on what he believed in. She became aware of pain. It began to throb along her back, her abdomen, her arm. He had said she was going to be all right, and from what the paramedic had told Thomas, it seemed so. But what had Thomas said? What about next time?

"We won't talk about it now."

She heard his voice as if from far away. "I'm...not leaving home."

"We'll talk later."

"No."

"Save your strength."

"I'm staying. I know... I'll die there. I've always known."

"That's ridiculous. You're young. You don't have to die for a long, long time!"

"It's... inevitable."

"Nothing's inevitable. You can use your talents somewhere safer. But you've got to get out. These kids mean business! Who knows what they would have done tonight if someone hadn't heard you scream?"

"I'll... never leave. I couldn't desert..."

"Garnet." She felt his breath against her cheek. She knew his face was very near. "It wouldn't be desertion. It would just be good sense. There are people everywhere who need help."

"My people. I'm going home."

She felt him sigh, heard it, saw it inside her mind.

"Garnet," he said at last. "There is no home anymore. Whoever went after you lobbed a fire bomb inside your apartment."

Her hand clenched spasmodically in his.

He continued. "Your neighbor smelled the smoke. She and a friend broke down your door and managed to get it under control with the hallway fire extinguisher until the firemen arrived. She was in your apartment when she heard you yell."

"Was anyone else... ?"

"No one else was hurt. I don't know the extent of the damage, but the girl... Serena? Serena said there wasn't much left."

"The clinic?"

"I don't know. Damage, I'm sure, but hopefully nothing that can't be repaired."

"We'll be back in business by next week. I'll...make sure of it."

"What can I say to you?" he asked.

"Nothing."

"It's my fault."

"No, of course—"

"I put Andre on the defensive. I ruined your negotiations with him."

"Not your fault."

"You have to leave."

"I will never leave."

"Then you're going to need protection. You can't live alone

anymore. You won't be any good to anybody if you're attacked again."

"I wouldn't put friends in danger."

There was silence. She drifted on the waves of pain that seemed to toss higher and higher. What if she had broken an arm? What if her eyesight was damaged? How much help would she be to anyone? Long ago she had made a commitment to herself and to her community. She would stay in the Corners, although there were better, safer places to go. She would stay, and she would do what she could. She would never, never run. And in the end, if the Corners took her life, that was the way she would die. But she would not live or die on the run.

There were some things worse than dying.

"Garnet."

She felt Thomas's hand tighten around hers. Somehow it eased her pain. Tears formed under her eyelids.

"Isn't there a man in your life?" he asked.

"A man? I haven't met a man in years."

"Then you'll have to live with me," he said.

The words were so gentle, so compassionate, that for a moment she thought it wasn't Thomas voice. "Thomas?"

"You can live with me," he said.

This time she was certain who it was. "Live...with a preacher?" She wanted to force a laugh, but she knew what a bad idea that would be. Every inch of her diaphragm throbbed unceasingly. "What.. .would your congregation think?"

"We'll have to get married."

She was drifting again. She had to concentrate harder. Surely she hadn't heard him right.

"We want the same things," he said. "And I'm willing to go to hell and back to make sure we both get them. I made things worse for you, but I'm not going to let anyone hurt you again. You don't have to be a martyr. Live with me. We'll watch out for each other. It would be better if you just got out of here, but since you won't..."

"Marry you? Are you crazy?"

"Come live with me. The marriage part will be for show. It'll make it clear to everyone that you're not vulnerable anymore."

"Marriage... for show."

"It will buy you time. And you don't have to pay me back. Not in any way."

She was still drifting. There were colors swirling in her head. Colors and shapes. And words. Marriage. Buy you time. Pay me back. No. *Don't* have to pay me back.

If she stayed in the Corners, the MidKnights could very well come back to finish what they'd started. This beating had been a warning. If it hadn't been, they would have shot her and been done with it.

The dragon had breathed his fiery breath in warning.

But warnings came with consequences if they weren't obeyed. She wasn't going to obey. Thomas was willing to help her buy time.

Time. She had so little. She'd always known that. She had seen too many tragedies, too much sadness. The rest of her life wouldn't be any different.

Thomas wouldn't be in danger if he helped her—at least, no more danger than he was in already. The MidKnights had threatened him, too. Thomas had said that he and she could watch out for each other.

"Marriage," she said.

"Don't worry about it now," he said. His breath caressed her cheek. "Just think about getting well."

"I never.. .wanted to get married."

"Hush now."

She felt the ambulance slowing down. She drifted, then was jerked back to consciousness when she felt Thomas's hand slipping from hers. "Thomas?"

"It's all right. I'm still here."

"Not a real marriage?"

"Don't worry about it now, Garnet."

"I'll do it. I want... time."

She felt his hand tighten around hers. "That's all I can give you."

"It will be enough."

5

When was a marriage not a marriage?

Garnet gazed around the bedroom that Thomas had given her to use. His apartment had only one, and this room had been his until today. Now he had evenly divided the closet and dresser drawers and turned his bed over to her. There was a sofa bed in the living room where he would sleep.

She sat on the bed and gingerly leaned back on her elbows. Pain still came and went, striking at odd times and in a variety of places. The MidKnights had worked her over good, but pain was the most lasting effect. A cracked rib, a concussion and a multitude of cuts and bruises weren't much, considering the kind of ruthless beating she had undergone.

She stretched a little to relieve the pressure on her ribs. Sitting was still uncomfortable, but she tired easily if she stood too long. Serena and Thomas had helped her pack what remained of her belongings, but even that effort had been too much.

She could see Thomas moving back and forth in the living room. Pacing. Like a lion in a cage.

She was sure he regretted his hasty offer of marriage. She regretted accepting it. At her most vulnerable moment, marrying Thomas had seemed like the answer to a prayer she hadn't found time to pray. It would give her time to continue her work here.

Strangely, Thomas seemed to have an impenetrable shield that surrounded him. His accomplishments in the Corners were small, but they were accomplishments. No one had interfered with his plans. No one had interfered with *him,* not even after he had openly defied the MidKnights. If the shield extended to her, so much the better. If it didn't, then they were two poor souls fighting the dragon together. Surely that improved their odds to almost one in a million.

She had been at her most vulnerable when he made his proposal. By the time she'd started to heal and Thomas had appeared at her hospital bedside with a minister colleague, her regrets had been legion. She was marrying a stranger. What did she know about Thomas Stonehill? Certainly she could step out of the marriage at any time, and *would* when it was convenient for both of them, but what problems was she creating in the meantime? Thomas had assured her that this would be a marriage in name only. But what did that mean other than the fact that they obviously weren't going to share a bed? What damage could they inflict on each other before the "I dos" changed to "I don'ts?"

And not that it mattered, but why *didn't* he want to share a bed?

Garnet lay back and stared at the ceiling. The plaster was cracked, and the paint was a hundred years old. Apparently the church downstairs had received all of Thomas's attention. The whole apartment reeked of neglect. The living room had fresh white paint because the children used it on Sunday morning for their classes. But she guessed that nothing else had been done. The furniture was worn, but salvageable if someone cared enough. The apartment had interesting nooks and crannies, if someone just noticed them and spotlighted their charms. But there was nothing here that indicated anyone had noticed anything. There were no pictures on the walls, no vases, no curtains, no pillows.... The list went on and on.

There was only one adornment, if it could be called that. Across the room, on an old side table, there was a framed photograph of a woman. Thomas's wife.

Garnet reminded herself that *she* was Thomas's wife now. Somehow she hadn't been able to form her objections in time. Thomas had appeared with the minister, and half the hospital staff, some sentimentally teary-eyed, had come to witness the grand event. Garnet's room had looked like a train station at rush hour. And suddenly she was on board, speeding to a foreign destination as the stranger to whom she was being married slipped a thin gold band on her finger.

Now Thomas's footsteps grew louder, and she knew that this time he had paced his way to the doorway.

"Go ahead and say it," she said.

"What am I supposed to say?"

"We made a mistake. This was a terrible idea. Maybe being married is just for show, but I'm going to make you so miserable you'll end up begging the Knights to come in and finish what they started."

A deep, rich chuckle came from the doorway.

Slowly, with grave reservations, she sat up again. "Tell me you weren't thinking exactly that."

"I was thinking that your stuff will never fit in here."

"You'd be surprised. Besides, half of what I owned is in the garbage now."

His smile disappeared. "I wish I could have spared you the sight of your apartment."

"I'm just glad the clinic didn't burn, too."

"There is still a fair amount of water damage."

"Nothing we can't fix."

"*You* aren't going to fix anything for a while. You heard the doctor."

"I'm a nurse. I say I'm cured."

"You don't look cured. You look pale. Your eyes look tired."

She had seen herself in the mirror over his dresser. She looked worse than pale and tired. The bruise on one side of her face had turned a sickly gold. The other side of her face was still a little swollen. No telling what color it would turn before it healed. There was a bandage on her forehead. The cut it covered had taken three stitches to close. Luckily for her vanity, the scar would blend into her hairline.

"Well, at least I can see why you don't want to sleep with me," she said. She watched his face. Nothing changed. He was really very good at this.

"Did I ever say I didn't want to sleep with you?" he asked.

"You've made it clear."

"I said I wasn't going to sleep with you. Can you hear the difference?"

"Well, it seems like you should get some compensation for being my bodyguard."

"Your wit will be compensation enough."

She smiled enticingly but not so enticingly that he might take her seriously. "You don't know what you're missing."

"I have a pretty good idea."

She heard something behind his words. Nostalgia for the delights of sharing a marriage bed? No, she didn't think that was it. Nostalgia was much too tame a word. What she had heard was raw and unrefined. Her smile died. She had the sudden realization that she was playing with fire here. If she really offered herself to this man and he accepted, she didn't know what would be left of either of them.

She changed the subject. "Is that your wife's picture in the living room?"

He stared his ice-blue stare for a moment; then he shook his head. "I can't believe I didn't put it away."

"Don't worry. I'm not offended. Just curious."

"Her name was Patricia."

"She was lovely." Garnet had only sneaked one glance at the photograph, but she had seen the kind of pleasant, blond good looks that had enraptured the teachers in the private academy where she had spent her adolescence. The woman in the photograph wore an expensive white wedding gown with the requisite pounds of seed pearls and acres of lace. Her expression indicated that her thoughts were on the man she loved.

Man she *had* loved.

"When did she die?" Garnet asked.

"Almost three years ago."

"Illness? Accident?"

"She died in a struggle for her purse."

Garnet's gaze didn't falter. Thomas had barely managed to choke out the words. She knew so little about him, but now she knew that he hadn't yet accepted Patricia's death.

And she knew a little more. "A very senseless way to die," she said softly. "Almost as senseless as gang violence, right, Thomas?"

"What?"

"Did you marry me because of what happened to your wife?"

"You know why I married you."

"And I understand it a little better, I think."

He left the room. She watched him go and knew that she had scored a hit. But she didn't know how deep. Had he married her because he knew how easily she could end up like Patricia, and he wanted to help? Or had he married her because he felt an overwhelming responsibility for his wife's death, a responsibility that would not go away unless he saved someone else?

The two motives might look similar on the outside, but in her mind they were a million miles apart. One suggested a desire to stand beside her because his goals and hers were the same. The other suggested a desire to somehow atone for his sins.

What were his sins, and what was behind his offer to help her? She lay back and stared at the ceiling again. Patricia's image danced in her mind. She wished she could question the pleasant-looking young woman about Thomas's motives. But the only way to do that was a quick trip to heaven.

And Thomas himself was standing in the way of that.

Garnet's fragrance, a provocative, subtle scent, clung to everything she owned. And her possessions were so obviously hers that they might as well have been emblazoned with her name.

Thomas stood in the living room and surveyed the wreckage of what had once been a neutral, tranquil space. Now it was covered with Garnet's things, and Garnet was asleep in his... her bed.

So much of what she owned had been destroyed, but she had shrugged off most of the loss. As he had before, he sensed that she did not let herself become easily attached. She behaved as if she expected to have things taken from her. She had said as much the evening of her attack.

I'm staying in the Corners, she'd said. *I know I'll die there. I've always known.*

And she meant it. He supposed that her belief that she would die violently, and that her death would come sooner than later, affected her attitude about everything.

Yet she wrung life from every second with a zest he couldn't deny. Her possessions testified to that. There were no neutral colors here. Primary colors leaped at him from every surface. Colors and textures and scents so exotic he was transported to another continent where marketplaces filled the streets and the simplest food tasted of a thousand spices.

Out of nowhere anger filled him that someone who lived life so fully, who dared the devil and spent her time performing small miracles, had been threatened by death. Garnet Anthony.. .no, Garnet Stonehill was a woman of great audacity and cynicism. She was often sure she was right about things of which she knew nothing at all. She challenged everything, accepted almost nothing and had no regard for traditions or piety.

But she caught each second and drained it dry. She sucked up whatever beauty came her way and flaunted it for everyone else to enjoy.

And she cared. About everyone. About everything. More than she would ever admit. More than she would probably ever understand. She cared enough that she had entered into this sham of a marriage just so she could continue to stretch out her graceful, seductive arms to embrace a world that often didn't seem to notice.

Thomas walked to the window and peered into the bedroom. Evening had come, and still Garnet slept exactly where she had first stretched out. He knew she must be exhausted. She had insisted on being released from the hospital a day before the doctor had wanted to let her go. Then she had insisted that Thomas take her straight to her old apartment to see the damage and collect what she could.

She had walked the rooms with the baby from the apartment next door on her hip. Her eyes had been dry. But he knew what a toll the experience had taken on her.

She slept on. Her hair fanned out over the bedspread as if it had sought its own soft comfort. His heart clenched at the sight of the bruises, but bruises would heal. Her face was interesting in repose. There was a sharpness missing from it as she slept; she looked more vulnerable, more childlike. The unusual combination of features that was so striking when she was awake seemed merely beautiful now. He supposed it was the mobility of her expression, the smoking green of her eyes, that set her apart from other beautiful women he had known.

He wanted to touch her hair.

He didn't know where the thought had come from, or what had propelled him across the room to stand by her bedside. He watched his own hand reach out and stop just short of the tangled strands. She was too far away. He was too far away. A million desolate miles.

As he watched, the small room was lit with the warm glow of green fire. She stared at him.

"Come to claim your conjugal rights?"

He wanted to throttle her. He wanted to embrace her. He slipped his hands in his pockets. "I've come to wake you up for dinner. You're probably starved."

She sat up warily. He didn't know what she was afraid of, but he stepped back a little to give her all the room she needed. "Darn. Just food. No sex."

"I haven't made anything yet. I don't even know what you like to eat."

"I like to eat everything. You said dinner?"

"It's seven o'clock. At night."

"What have you got?"

"Frozen dinners. You can have your pick."

"Over my dead body. What else do you have?" She worked on a smile as he frowned at her. It came surprisingly easily. "Thomas, don't you cook?"

He didn't. Cooking took time from more important things. He shook his head.

Her smile widened. "Well, I do. You're a lucky guy. I'll run down to the store."

"No, you won't."

Her eyes narrowed. "Am I in prison?"

"Only if you think of it that way."

"I can't go to the store by myself?"

"You can do anything you want. You know that. But so can I."

"In other words, I've got a constant companion?"

"Either that or we can tie a target around your neck."

She pouted. "I don't like being caged."

"I'm sure you don't."

"You must have something we can eat."

"Let's go see." He watched her stand. She stretched like a cat, as naturally, as sinuously before she dropped her arms and winced. Her kelly green sweater tightened across her breasts. His mouth went dry.

He followed her to the tiny kitchen, around boxes spilling over with clothing and toiletries, books and DVDs. Her stereo had been ruined, but the CDs that had been inside the cabinet looked as if they had escaped harm. They had salvaged some furniture, too, a carved bedside table from India, a cupboard painted with designs—now blistered—that reminded him of Australian aboriginal art.

"Tomorrow I'll find places for everything," she said. "Unless you want me to find somewhere to store it."

"You live here now. The place is yours, too."

"Do you care what I do with it?"

He shrugged. "Just be sure there's room for the kids to gather here on Sunday morning."

Her response was barely audible. "When I'm done with the place, they'll be happier to gather here."

In the kitchen she took stock of what she had to work with. Thomas stood to one side and watched her. He wondered if he should leave her alone or offer to help. He compromised and just stood silently, taking up more than his share of the space.

"You've got hardly anything in here to cook with, Thomas. Didn't your wife cook, either?"

Patricia had cooked faithfully. Good, solid American cuisine with an emphasis on the food pyramid and parsley. He remembered that parsley had decorated every dinner she had served.

Her father, the bishop, had teased her once by bringing her half a dozen pots of parsley to set on her windowsill. She had taken the joke in quiet good stride, and the pots had flourished.

"I gave most of our things away after she died," he said.

Garnet looked up. There was a lock of black hair falling across his forehead. He was the picture of a strong man who refused to admit his vulnerabilities. "That bad, huh?"

"I didn't need them."

"Well, at least you kept a bowl. And a spoon. And one pot. One pot, Thomas? Do you mix everything together? Never mind, I know you said you don't cook. I'm just having trouble understanding how that's possible."

She bent and continued her inventory. Finally she stood. "Well, at least we won't have a problem finding room for my kitchen things."

"We could go out for dinner."

"Know a place that doesn't have a plate glass window? My ducking reflexes are a little slow."

"Carryout?"

"I'll manage." She opened the refrigerator. "Let's see. Eggs, milk, cheese, bread. Mustard..." She poked her head in deeper. "A can of tuna? Didn't your mother tell you that tuna goes in the cupboard?" She peeked around the door. "Did you have a mother?"

"I still do."

"Me, too. Two sisters, too, but Ema probably told you that."

"The other one's..." He tried to remember.

"Smart. Jade hitchhiked to California when she was sixteen and never found her way back."

"You should have done the same thing."

"What? And miss the chance to be married to the mysterious Thomas Stonehill?" She took everything out of the refrigerator and set the pathetically small array on the counter.

Thomas was right beside her. She was suddenly aware of his

presence in more than a cursory way. He hovered over her, sharing her oxygen, sending the warmth of his body to heat the air around her.

She looked up at him. He was watching her intently. Plankton under the microscope. “Does this seem as strange to you as it does to me?” she asked.

“Everything about it’s strange.”

“Was this a terrible mistake?”

“Not if I get a good meal out of it.”

She smiled. A smile seemed surprisingly intimate in the small space. “I can surely give you that.”

He knew he should move away. The air seemed heavy with something he didn’t want to identify. The fragrance he had noted earlier seemed to hang between them. Her hair crackled around her shoulders, and he could almost feel the electricity sting his skin.

He wondered what else she could give him. He had married her expecting nothing. And now, in this instant, he knew he had underestimated her.

Some long-denied part of him responded. She was woman. Every bit a woman. And he was nothing more than a man. Sensation crept along his nerve endings. Hormones charged through his system. Life stirred inside... and out.

“Do you want to help?” she asked. “If not, don’t stand there taking up all the space.”

“I’ll set the table.” He turned to leave, and the spell, the bewitching, pagan spell, of Garnet Anthony Stonehill was broken.

~

He made up the sofa bed at about ten o’clock. Garnet had been in the bedroom with the door shut for twenty minutes. He assumed she had already gone to sleep.

The bed looked less than inviting when he had finished. By rights he should have been tired after lifting and hauling boxes all day. And Garnet's tuna and cheese strata was still melting deliciously into every internal crevice of his body. Well fed and exercised, he should fall asleep with no difficulty.

He wouldn't sleep until the early hours, if he slept at all.

He was a married man. Automatically his eyes sought Patricia's wedding photograph, but he had shoved it in a drawer the first time Garnet's back was turned. His relationship with Garnet might be nothing more than that of church-sanctioned roommate, but it had still been inconsiderate to expose her to Patricia's photo. Her wedding photo.

His first wedding night had been nothing like this one. Patricia had been too shy to relax easily. It had taken too much of the evening to convince her to undress, and much more to convince her that wedding nights could be fun.

But theirs hadn't been. She had relaxed later on their honeymoon, possibly even into a certain degree of enjoyment. As the years had gone by she had relaxed still more, until by the last year of their marriage, she had come to him to initiate lovemaking.

Except that by then, he had been too tired or too busy much of the time to accommodate her.

Thomas slipped into bed. He was wearing new pajamas. He had never slept in pajamas, not even on his first wedding night. But he wasn't going to parade naked around this apartment with Garnet in the next room. That was an invitation he couldn't afford to issue.

He read the same four paragraphs of an article in *Christian Century* three times before he realized that reading was hopeless. His mind was on the woman in the next room. He told himself that having Garnet so close was a unique experience and one he would quickly grow accustomed to, but he wondered who he was trying to kid. She would not fade into the background of his life as Patricia quickly had. Garnet was not going to be his wife in any meaningful way, but before she left she would leave her mark on him and on everything she touched.

"Good. You're still up. I found something for us in one of my boxes."

He looked up to see the woman in question standing in the bedroom with a bottle in her hand. "It's not alcoholic, I don't drink. But it's my favorite fizzy stuff."

She was wearing a satin nightshirt that skimmed her legs at midthigh. It was royal purple, loose and comfortable and surely no shorter than the skirts she wore. But judging by the reaction deep in his gut, it might as well have been a transparent negligee.

"I don't usually drink," he said. "But not because it's against my religion."

"Jesus drank wine, didn't he? I'm betting you're no better than he was." She padded barefoot into the kitchen and came back with two juice glasses. "I'm glad you're not too stuffy, Thomas. Or living with me would give you palpitations."

His heart rate bordered on palpitations already. He was seeing nothing more of her body than he had seen already—except, possibly, for the swaying of her unrestrained breasts—but *his* body was reacting as if everything was new. He moved over as she approached the sofa bed so that she could sit on the end. She did, campfire style.

"Couldn't you sleep?" he asked.

"Sleep? Now? I'm a night creature. I prowl until the wee hours. I'll annoy the hell out of you before this is over—if I haven't already."

"What do you do this late at night?"

"Listen to music. Take long baths. Polish my nails. Dance."

"Dance?"

She smiled. "By myself."

He had a vision of her swaying provocatively to music, stretching and swaying and pirouetting.

"You weren't sleeping, either," she observed.

"No." He watched as she filled the two glasses nearly to the top.

"It's raspberry and lime. Is the bed uncomfortable?"

"It's fine. I was reading." He reached for his glass. "I wasn't succeeding."

"No? What were you trying to read?" She grimaced when he held up the journal. "Well, there's nothing like taking your work to bed with you. No wonder you couldn't concentrate." She slid off the bed and disappeared into the bedroom. She returned with a paperback. "Here's something you won't have any trouble with."

He took the book. The company was already relaxing him. *"A Morbid Taste for Bones?"*

"Think of it as a transition book. Something between *Christian Century* and Travis McGee. A mystery series about a Welsh Benedictine monk, Brother Cadfael. Different century and religion, but you can relate. Then, when you're done, we'll move you to lighter stuff. Hard-boiled detectives, men's adventures, lurid potboilers." She winked. "I'm going to be good for you, Thomas."

He watched her as he sipped. She was lounging comfortably now. Despite the bruises and bandage, her face looked contented.

"You don't ask for much from life," he said. "Your world has spun like a top in the last few days. You've got a gang of kids with guns after you, and you're married to a stranger. But instead of banging your head against the wall, you're lounging on my bed planning my midnight reading."

"What should I ask for?"

"What do you want?"

"Not the same issue at all."

"No? Why not?"

"Because people don't get what they want, do they?" It wasn't a real question. More of a challenge. She set her empty glass on the floor. "Tell me this is what you want, Thomas. Tell me that when you were a little kid you prayed or asked Santa Claus—or your wealthy parents or whoever—if, when you grew up, you could come and live in a ghetto and minister to a congregation that can't pay you ten cents. Tell me you hoped and prayed that the wife you obviously loved would die young and you would get stuck with a melting-pot hellion who has bruises all over her body and more bruises in store."

"I never would have put it to God or Santa Claus quite that way."

She saw the quick flash of humor in his eyes. She couldn't do anything but smile at him. "See? People rarely get what they want. So what good does it do to want anything?"

"A bishop friend of mine always said that God knows best what we need."

"Your bishop hasn't spend much time in the Corners."

He wasn't going to admit how true that was. "You haven't always been this jaded. What did you want when you weren't afraid to ask for it?"

"Does my memory go back that far?" She tapped her cheek with her index finger until she realized the cheek still hurt. "The things other people take for granted, I guess. A safe place to live, someone in my life to count on, children I could give everything to that I never had myself. Very basic, unadulterated dreams."

"Not impossible. Not if you get out of here."

Something, the late hour, the warmth in his voice, was having an unusual effect on her. Out of nowhere her throat seemed strangely thick. She couldn't smile, and she couldn't shrug. "I forgot to mention that part, didn't I? See, all those dreams were supposed to happen here. This is where I live and who I am."

"So you've said." Thomas set his glass down, too. She was only a foot away, but two very different lives separated them. He didn't want to be separated. In that moment, he knew that he didn't want to be apart from this woman.

He leaned over and surprised them both. He touched her hair. His hand slid to her shoulder, then to her arm. He saw her pupils widen, startled, then mystified. He urged her forward. In a moment she was in his arms, sprawling against his chest. He tightened his hold when she squirmed in protest. "Garnet," he said softly, "just stay here a moment."

"I don't need this."

"You do. We both do." He rubbed her back; his cheek rested on her hair. She fit in his arms and against his body as if she had been intended by some master planner for him. He was caught somewhere on the continuum between desire and compassion.

"I wanted so little, didn't I?" she asked. "There are so many people who want so little."

And so many who were afraid to reach for anything. His arms tightened around her. Her scent enveloped him; her warmth seeped into his soul—or what was left of it.

She lifted her face, and blue eyes stared into translucent green. He read centuries of sadness, of repression, of yearning. He saw the Corners in her eyes, and he saw more, so much more. He saw a magnificent, proud and brazen woman who would not be defeated, who would not be transformed, who would not let anything more be taken from her without a fight to the death.

He lowered his head to hers. He took, and she gave freely. His lips touched hers, searching for whatever she was willing to give. There was none of the minister, the shepherd, in his kiss. He forgot about leading, about gently bestowing gifts. He lost himself in her scent, her touch, the silken caress of her lips against his.

She pulled away at last, until they were no longer touching. Her eyes were dry, but her poor bruised face looked sadly vulnerable. "We'd better not plan to do this very often," she said. "You're a man, and I'm a woman, and neither of us is a virgin. If you want a wife, Thomas, say so and I'll give it some thought."

"Has comfort been such a rare experience in your life that you can't recognize it?"

"Was that just comfort? So be it, then. I recognize the intent.

But I also recognize the potential outcome." She slid off the bed and stood. "Enjoy the book."

He had enjoyed the woman. He no longer lied to himself; lying had once been his fatal flaw. No, he had enjoyed the woman. Enjoyed touching her, holding her, talking to her. Kissing her. And he had no right to any of those things.

"Good night," he said.

She didn't close the door between them. Even an hour later, immersed in the book she had given him, he was still aware that she hadn't closed the door.

6

"It's the most conservative thing I own." Garnet came into the living room and posed in the doorway. She was wearing a bright turquoise knit dress that nipped her waist and emphasized the swell of her breasts. It stopped only an inch above her knees. "Do I look like a minister's wife?"

Thomas had a vision of one of Pharaoh's daughters posing just this way for a beleaguered Moses. He wondered if the prophet had been sorely tempted not to lead his people out of Egypt.

"Doesn't make it, does it?" she asked with a grimace. "I didn't think so."

"You look lovely."

"Ah, but that's not the point. Do I look properly docile? Chaste? Virtuous?"

"We can't ask the impossible."

Her teeth flashed in a blinding smile. "I'll look more chaste if you zip it for me."

"You'll look more chaste if we button a full-length coat over it and add knee boots."

"But *I* don't have to go outside to go to church. I just walk downstairs, and presto!" She spun around, and the skirt of the dress flared around her legs. Her fingers gathered her mane of hair into one thick loop, and she lifted it off her neck.

He saw that she had managed most of the zipper. But the section she hadn't managed revealed a long swipe of skin. He crossed the room and grasped the tab. Her skin was a rose-tinted olive, smooth and glowing. There were no signs of bruises here. In the half-dozen days since she had come to live with him, most of the visible signs of her injuries had vanished.

The zipper glided slowly to the top. He wanted to blaze the trail with his hand, test for himself the resilience of her flesh, the silk of her skin. But he knew better than to initiate such intimacy. Their arrangement would only be successful if intimacy was a dream and friendship the reality.

"Really, Thomas. I don't want to embarrass you." She faced him. "I know you're trying to make a go of the church. And people are going to wonder why on earth you married *me*."

"Can you really believe that?"

She stared at him until a tiny smile tilted her lips. Her eyes steamed a tropical forest green. "Well, thank you very much."

"I'll announce our marriage from the pulpit."

"They'll wonder why it was so sudden...no matter what my charms."

"Everyone wants to believe in fairy tales and love at first sight."

"Do you?"

"Do I want to?" He shrugged.

"Do you *believe?* I don't. I don't even know if I believe in love, period." She thought for a moment. "Cancel that. I don't believe in it. But you were married before. Maybe yours was one in a million marriages. A love for all time."

"I've got a few things to do downstairs before people start to arrive." He started toward the door.

She watched him go, only too aware that she had breached

the unspoken agreement they had entered into along with their wedding vows. "You know, you did have another life once, and I had one, too. If we're going to live together, our pasts are going to come up once in a while. Aren't you even vaguely curious about who I am and where I've been?"

"You don't owe me any explanations."

"In other words, don't ask questions, because that could complicate this crazy arrangement of ours? Instead of marriage wouldn't it have been easier just to hire a bodyguard or buy me a suit of armor? It might have been a lighter load to carry around."

He turned to her. "Did you think this was going to be easy?"

"Obviously I didn't think at all. I didn't have time to, or even a brain that was working properly."

"I'm sorry you regret it. It seemed like the best answer at the time. It still does."

She sighed. "You might not answer questions, Rev, but I know a few answers already. You're not the windup preacher doll you pretend so hard to be. Can't you just show a little more of who you really are once in a while? I know this is hard on you, too. God knows, I'm not a piece of cake to live with. But wouldn't it be more fun if we got to know each other a little? Wouldn't this seem less like a waste of time?"

To Thomas, the last thing their marriage seemed was a waste of time. In the days since Garnet had come to live with him, time had passed swiftly. Seconds became minutes before he was aware of their passing. There was color, texture and music in his life again, where before there had been a gray progression of days. He didn't want to think about the changes the sham of a marriage had made, or his own surprising reaction to them. He was not a windup preacher doll, but what he was instead had to be worse. Much worse.

"Who am I?" he said. "I don't even know anymore. I wouldn't even know what to tell you."

"You could start with easy things. Why did you come here? Who were you before you came?"

"I came because there were people here who might need what I could give. And those people are going to be waiting downstairs for me to unlock the front door."

"Have it your way." She shook her hair. She'd had every intention of tying it at her neck in a stab at appearing civilized. Now she decided to let it slither over her shoulders. There was only so far she would carry this charade of a marriage, and apparently Thomas felt the same way.

He didn't sigh or shrug, but she thought she saw an apology in his eyes. "Thank you for coming with me this morning," he said.

"I guess it's the least I can do to thank you for trying to help me."

The preliminaries were finished. Greg had performed a rollicking prelude, the choir had sung, opening prayers and readings had been dispensed with, and Thomas had made his big announcement. There had been the requisite discreet turning of twenty-five or so heads to gaze at the new bride and the same number of welcoming smiles.

When the fuss had died down, Garnet sat alone in the back of the church and stared at the man standing in front.

She wondered if a woman could ever grow tired of staring at Thomas. He was an enigma, and that was part of his attraction. A woman could imagine him to be almost anything or anyone. Even his wife could indulge in fantasy about him—since she had no more idea than anyone who he really was.

But behind the aura of mystery was simply an overwhelmingly attractive man. Garnet could say that dispassionately. Her husband, possibly the only one she would ever have, was easy to stare at and hard to take lightly. There was nothing about him that was simple or forthright. He was hard-edged and hard-hitting. He was a brilliant, un-flickering flame, and his congregants were moths drawn to his majesty and power. He spoke, and the church immediately grew silent. Every eye in the room was focused exclusively on him.

His true appeal didn't come from his good looks. Perhaps that was the first thing that attracted others, but the sheer masculine beauty of his face and the width of his shoulders were quickly passed by. There was something elemental about Thomas, something that cut through all pretension, all polite meanderings, right to the heart of life.

She didn't understand what that something was. Magnetism, charisma. These were words she had thought she understood. But now she knew they didn't go far enough. They didn't grasp the essential fact that somehow this man had been honed in a fire, perhaps one of his own making, and the man who had emerged was someone different, better, finer than the man who had entered.

She might never understand exactly. What she knew about Thomas she knew only from clues. And the clues were rare but oh, so potent. The emotion-laden voice she had been forced to listen to so carefully on the rush to the hospital. The warm flash of Thomas's eyes and the ice-blue caution that always followed. The offer of marriage to a woman he hardly knew, simply to protect her.

He began to speak, and the words rolled off his tongue as if they had never been rehearsed, as if every one of them came directly, spontaneously from his heart. His voice was resonant, and he had a way of making love to a word until it became another, then another. She had never been a churchgoer, but she knew that she could listen to Thomas Sunday after Sunday. He loved language, its nuances, its cadences. He made his listeners love it, too. And somewhere in the loving, in the attraction to the minister, the congregation forgot him entirely and somehow focused on the higher meaning, the higher being toward whom Thomas was leading them.

"There is very little I can tell most of you about courage. Many of you had to brave great odds to come here this morning. Many of you are facing difficulties in your personal lives, and I can only imagine the courage it takes for you to get up each day and face the world. But this morning I want to tell you about others who showed great courage, men who heard a voice and saw a vision. Men and women who, by their beliefs and their integrity, changed our world."

The front door opened. For a moment Garnet ignored the interruption. She didn't want Thomas to stop speaking; she was sliding somewhere far away on the sound of his voice, somewhere where the brave stood up for their beliefs and risked their lives to make the world a better place.

Thomas fell silent, and Garnet turned to see why. Andre was standing in the doorway with Ferdinand beside him. In front of him, sitting proudly in her wheelchair, was Beulah Rollins, Andre's mother.

Garnet glanced at Thomas. He hadn't moved, but she knew he had tensed. His eyes searched for her, as if measuring the distance and how long it would take to reach her if there was trouble. Then his gaze flicked to Andre. Finally he spoke.

"Come in. You're welcome here."

Garnet watched Andre's face. Something passed over it. He was a match for Thomas; his feelings—or what was left of them after nineteen years on the Corners' streets—were just as impossible to read. He grunted something to Ferdinand; then, flanking the wheelchair, they moved to the opposite side of the church, past the middle aisle and the section where Garnet was sitting.

Ferdinand and Andre sat on the end of a row, and Beulah guided her wheelchair to the space beside them.

"Once there was a gang of twelve," Thomas began again. "More than two thousand years ago there was a gang. The twelve hadn't always been members. Some had been fishermen, some common laborers. They didn't even know they had the makings of a gang until one day a man came to them and said, 'Follow me.'

" 'Follow me.' Two words. Straightforward. Easy to understand. Follow me. But what do you say when a stranger, a man with no degrees, no prestige, no skills except those of a simple carpenter, comes to you and asks you to give up everything? What do you say when He tells you to leave behind the boat that has brought you your livelihood, the quiet, blue lake that has fed your family, the family itself who depend on you for support and sustenance?

"Follow me." Thomas left the pulpit. He stood in front of the first row. "What do you say when someone, anyone, asks you to follow them? What do you say when a stranger asks you to become part of a gang? When a stranger tells you to give up everything that is dear to you and promises you no reward on this earth. What *can* you do?"

His gaze traveled to settle on Andre. "Gangs have their pleasures, don't they? You leave behind the things you love, the family, the old friends who are frightened by your new ones, but you gain something in exchange. Suddenly you're part of a larger whole. The world expands. There are people who will stand up for you, who will avenge you if need be, who will protect your interests, so that life is no longer the lonely struggle it once was.

"Maybe you'll be called on to do some things you don't believe in. But what price do you pay if you don't? If you're on the outside, and there is no one to stand beside you, the world is a lonely, frightening place."

Pain flashed across his face. Garnet knew that no one in the room doubted that Thomas personally understood what a lonely, frightening place the world could be.

He continued. "The gang of twelve was different, though. There was no one to stand up for them. Even their leader was nailed to a cross, and there was no one who could stop it from happening. They died, one by one, and there was no one to interfere, no one to avenge their deaths, no one to drive by in the night when the streets are dark and dangerous and shower the houses of their persecutors with bullets. No one to wear colors for them, to spray-paint buildings with threats for them.

"But there were those who lived to carry on their message. They met in secret places and wrote their stories, their beliefs, for others to use. They had their 'bible,' the same way our gangs do today. They had juice—influence. And as the stories spread, as the beliefs were weighed and practiced, the gang of twelve became a gang of millions."

Thomas walked down the aisle until he was standing in front of Beulah. "And in the name of that gang of twelve and their leader, Jesus of Nazareth and his apostles, wonderful things have happened, but terrible things have happened, too. We have evoked their names as we've gone to war, led murderous crusades for purposes that Jesus would never have sanctioned, kept our brothers and sisters in poverty or looked down upon them because of their race or creed.

"That can happen, can't it? Even a gang with the best of intentions can get out of control. Even leaders—" he looked right at Andre, then at Ferdinand "—even the best leaders, the most intelligent and courageous, can make bad decisions."

Finally he turned away. "But wonderful things have come from the gang of twelve, too. Men and women have reached out to their brothers and sisters in more ways than I can tell you about today."

He walked up the aisle. Garnet listened as he extolled the beauty of Christianity, the purposes and principles of the gang of twelve, the way the world could be made a better place because of what one gang, two thousand years ago, had begun.

Then, as he had done the last time she had heard him speak, he focused on what *they* could do in the Corners to use those principles to make their community a better place. There was nothing radically new about what he asked for. Brotherly love. Reaching out to those in need. Standing up for what was right. Moving, one step at a time, toward goals that would enhance the quality of life for everyone.

He ended in the pulpit, his gaze fastened on Andre and Ferdinand. "The gang of twelve still has memberships available," he said. "The initiation rites differ from church to church, but at the heart the intent is the same. We must practice what the gang's leader preached. The commandments are simple. Love one another. Love God. The rest falls into place.

"But it is never easy. No matter what form your membership takes, no matter what your level of commitment, membership is never easy. If your life must be simple and uncluttered with decisions, if you don't want to question anything your friends or even your leaders tell you, then membership is not for you. But if you are willing to take risks, if you are strong enough to do what you know is right and sometimes to sacrifice, then there is always a place in the gang of twelve for you."

There was silence. Garnet forgot to breathe. Then Thomas brought his hands down on the pulpit and announced the final hymn.

She expected Andre and Ferdinand to flee at the first opportunity, and perhaps they would have if Beulah had been easily able to maneuver the aisles of the church. But by the time Beulah's chair was humming toward the doorway, Thomas was already shaking hands with departing parishioners.

Garnet stood back, accepting congratulations on her

marriage to Thomas from members of the congregation. Dorothy Brown, pillar of the Corners community, was the first to hug her and wish her well. Dorothy had been the first Corners resident to help Garnet solicit funds for Mother and Child, Dorothy with her white gloves, disarmingly gentle smile and razor-sharp tongue. Dorothy, now pushing eighty, still maneuvered and plotted and stirred the community to action. She was a voice for both stability and change, and Garnet wished there were a thousand more like her living on the Corners' troubled streets.

"So, I picked the right Sunday to come here to church," Dorothy said, after the hug had ended.

"You're not a member?"

"Not me. I make the rounds. That way I keep all the preachers in this neighborhood straight."

"Well, I'm sure Thomas is properly honored to have you today."

"That man of yours, he's not so bad at what he does," Dorothy said. "Maybe he'll be even better now that he's got you. More relaxed."

"Why?"

"You can't figure that out, this marriage is in trouble already," Dorothy said with a wink.

Garnet grinned and gave Dorothy another hug before the older woman moved away to speak to Thomas. Garnet continued to smile and shake hands, but she kept Andre and Ferdinand in her line of vision, just as she'd done when she spoke to Dorothy.

Thomas had told her about his conversation with Andre the night she had been beaten. Andre had been at home and could not have taken part. But Andre was a MidKnight, the closest thing to a leader the gang had, and she knew where his loyalties lay. Even if he had not ordered her abuse or taken part in it, he would support those who had. She was not fooled by his attendance in church. She imagined it was a scouting mission. He was finding out how the land lay, and it would be only a matter of time before he used the information in negative ways.

Thomas had wasted his sermon.

She watched as Beulah waited patiently in line to leave. Since they had once lived on the same street, Garnet had known Beulah most of her life. Garnet had admired the woman's courage when multiple sclerosis forced her into the wheelchair. As a teenager she had spent one memorable spring day planting flowers along Beulah's front walkway as Beulah supervised; then she had sat in Beulah's sparkling clean kitchen and eaten homemade cookies as reward.

Beulah had taught Ema to crochet. Jade had found her to be a good listener when their own mother was too busy earning a living cleaning offices day and night. Beulah had been a friend to neighborhood children, a kind, loving mother to her son. There was no reason she should be held responsible for Andre's failures.

Garnet squared her shoulders and moved forward, past a fidgeting, tattooed Ferdinand to Beulah's side. She squatted. "Beulah, do you remember me?"

Beulah turned. Her face, a chart of life's sadnesses and triumphs, lit up. "I thought that was you, Garnet honey."

"How are you?"

"Still getting around. Andre's always there to take me anyplace I need to go."

Garnet looked into Andre's face. He was watching her closely. "I'm glad to see he takes care of you," Garnet said, turning to Beulah. "Do you come here often?"

"Never before. But I heard this preacher was good. My preacher left, and the new one preaches hellfire till I go away each Sunday morning with a sunburn." She laughed. "Between you and me, this one's prettier to look at, too."

"Between you and me, I'm married to him."

Beulah slapped her thigh. "No... Well, congratulations!"

They chatted as the line shortened. Then it was only Andre and Ferdinand between Beulah and the door.

Thomas held out his hand. "Hello, Andre. I'm glad to see you again."

Garnet watched Andre's struggle. Then, as his mother looked on, his hand shot out for a quick squeeze. Afterward Thomas held his out again, this time to Ferdinand, but he didn't relinquish it quickly, as he had Andre's.

"You're the artist, aren't you?"

Ferdinand looked startled. "Me?"

"Dorothy Brown tells me that you're very talented. I believe some of your work was once on that wall." He tilted his head toward the wall where the graffiti had bled through.

"So?"

"So? I'd like to see some more of what you can do. There's a whole big space up there where something beautiful and creative should be. I don't have much money to give you, but maybe we could come to terms?"

Ferdinand sneered. Beulah slapped his wrist before he could say no. "You do what the preacher says," she ordered. "You're just dying to get your hands on some paint and a big space that people'll want to see. Don't be tellin' him no when you be dying to say yes."

Ferdinand mumbled something unintelligible.

Thomas moved to Beulah's side and took her hand. "I'm pleased to know you, Mrs. Rollins."

"You know my boy?"

Thomas nodded. "We've met several times." He looked at Andre and watched the young man's eyes narrow. "Your son's a born leader," he said, looking at Beulah.

"He's a good boy."

Garnet swallowed a laugh. Suddenly life was funny again, as it hadn't been since the attack in the darkness. They were kids, these phantoms who had moved through her life leaving pain in their wake. Dangerous and volatile, but kids nonetheless. She watched Thomas push Beulah through the door and down the sidewalk a little ways. She put one hand on Andre's arm and one on Ferdinand's to stop them from following.

"Did either of you gentleman beat up a defenseless woman in a parking lot a couple of weeks ago? I can tell you right now, I'm not going to make it into the gang of twelve if forgiveness for something like that is one of the initiation rites."

Andre shook off her arm. Ferdinand seemed to feel trapped.

"Well?" she asked.

"You were warned," Andre said.

"As a matter of fact, I know you weren't there," she admitted, "but I sure as hell expect better from you, Andre, than to condone it. Your mother deserves better."

She turned to Ferdinand. "And you, you big hulking heap of God-given talent, get a life, why don't you? Paint Thomas's mural. Stop hanging out with junkies and criminals. And don't ever lift a finger toward another woman or I'll make it my mission to be sure you serve time for it!"

"I wasn't there," he mumbled. "I didn't have nothing to do with it."

"Are you bragging or whining?"

His string of expletives was as colorful as his art.

"Well, apology accepted," she said. She dropped her hand and watched him sidle through the doorway.

Thomas came to stand beside her as Andre and Ferdinand followed Beulah down the sidewalk.

~

"Andre taught himself to read before first grade. I'd forgotten that until today." Garnet sprinkled a combination of herbs into fresh vegetables she had stir-fried while Thomas watched. Then she added tomatoes and chick-peas and set the mixture on a back burner to finish steaming.

In the days since she had come to live with Thomas, she had begun to cook more vegetarian meals. From the sparse furnishings in his apartment to the worn necks of his suits, the man advertised that he lived on a tight, tight budget. Between them, she suspected, they did not have enough money to eat meat as a mainstay.

"I've been to his house. Where did you live in relation?" he asked.

"Three... no, four houses down. The house was shabby then. Now the porch is gone and the roof is sagging. They'd condemn it if it had been built anywhere but the Corners."

"And you knew Andre and his mother pretty well?"

Garnet shrugged. She was chopping garlic and onions to add to bulgur wheat. The vegetables would be served over it. "Andre was a cute little boy, and I had all the requisite maternal hormones of a budding young woman. I used to play school with him. Mostly we did recess—I wasn't much of a teacher. But by the time I got interested in playing with big boys, Andre was reading by himself."

"Was he a success in school?"

"You're kidding." She looked up from the cutting board. "What planet did you grow up on? Smart kids don't do well in schools like the one in our neighborhood. The classes are huge, and the teachers are burned out. There's nothing for gifted kids to do while the other kids are struggling along, so they make trouble to get noticed. Pretty soon they've been noticed right out of the system and onto the streets."

"Are we talking about Andre or you?"

"Tricky, Thomas. Very, very tricky. Why don't you just ask me about myself and see if you get an answer?"

He was silent. She clamped her teeth together and remained

silent, too. She was at the stove again, and the tiny kitchen was filled with mouth-watering smells before he spoke.

"Start wherever you feel comfortable."

"In other words, I don't owe you any explanations I don't want to give."

"You don't."

She wielded the spatula like a professional chef. "What do you want to know?" she asked, placing the conversation squarely in his lap.

"Tell me about life on your street when you were growing up."

It was as impersonal a request as she had ever heard. Her answer was the same. "We had about twenty houses on our block. The garbage was collected on Mondays. The ice cream man came on Tuesdays and Saturdays in the summer." She tasted her concoction and added salt.

"We're playing games."

"Yes, we are."

Garnet made a pleasing silhouette at the stove. Her hair was tied back, and her feet were bare, despite the faulty heating system in the apartment. Thomas watched her bend and sway as she stirred, as if the popping and hissing of frying vegetables was music for dancing. He could not pretend he didn't want to know more about her. "Tell me about *you*."

"Much better question." She looked at him and realized she did want to share. It seemed important, somehow, to tell him who she really was.

"I was one of those kids like Andre," she said at last. "Not nearly as bright, but what I didn't have in brains, I made up for in spunk. By the time I was eleven, it was pretty clear I wasn't getting much out of school. I had a well-meaning teacher that year. She heard that Light Academy for Young Women was looking for scholarship students."

"I know about the academy."

"Well, you've got to understand, they had all these incredibly rich young ladies who needed ex-po-sure, thank you, dahling, to the real world. So they wanted a few students from the real world to give it to them. I was chosen. I wasn't quite riffraff, not quite civilized. A perfect choice."

He detected unhealed pain under the hard shimmer of her words. But he wasn't sure. Garnet was a master at suppressing her feelings. If he asked if she was hurting, she would tell him no, and probably believe it, too.

"How long did you attend?"

"Long enough to finish convincing myself I was worthless. The Corners started the process, the academy finished it up nicely. By the time I was fifteen, I was skipping school more often than I was going. The headmistress would call my mother to complain, but Mama was hardly ever home. She worked twelve-hour days, and when she wasn't working, she was trying to wring a little fun out of life with whatever man she'd taken under her wing that month. She was only sixteen when she had Ema, eighteen when she had me and an old woman of twenty when Jade was born."

"You weren't close to her?"

"Wrong. We adored her. Still do, in fact. She moved to Florida a few years ago, but I call her every week. She did everything she could for us. She never got angry. She hugged us and praised us and cooked big elaborate meals whenever she was home. She just wasn't home very often."

"Were you suspended from the academy?"

"Dropped out." She looked at him. "I got pregnant."

He stood very still, then he nodded, as if that was perfectly understandable.

"Damn it, Thomas, take off your minister hat. It's okay to react. I was sixteen and pregnant. I was also in terrible shape by then. I'd been drinking and smoking steadily for a year, and I'd been doing worse. The drawer beside my bed was a pharmacy. If a friend gave me something to try, I tried it. I wasn't hooked on anything except trying to blot out the reality of my life, but that was bad enough. I weighed half what I weigh now, and I'd forgotten what it felt like to be sober."

"The baby?"

"Died." She stopped stirring and put a top on the pan. She faced him, leaning against the stove with her arms folded. "When my mother found out I was pregnant, she marched me to the public health clinic in the city. A nurse sat me down and showed me pictures of babies whose mothers had lived the way I was living. My mother cried. I cried and sobered up fast. By then I knew I wanted to have the baby. No one could persuade me otherwise, though God knows they tried. I started taking care of myself from that minute on. But it was too late."

"You miscarried?"

"No. I delivered at seven months. My mother's car was in the shop, as usual. By the time she found a neighbor who would take me to the hospital, I was too far along to move. She called an ambulance, but it took an hour to arrive. Even for a preemie the baby was tiny, but she was breathing when she was born. We did what we could while we waited. But the ambulance arrived too late to save her."

For a moment he wanted to go to her. He wanted to take her in his arms and comfort her. But everything about the way she was standing told him that was not a good idea.

"You wanted to know about me," she said.

"Why that story? Why not the time you fell off your bike and scraped your knee, or the first time you went to a movie with a boy? Are you trying to shock me? You haven't."

"Because it tells you everything you'll ever need to know about me, Thomas. After I recovered, I took a good look at my life and saw I had two choices. I could go back to living the way I had before I discovered I was pregnant, or I could start telling other girls what it's like to lose a child and know you're directly responsible, along with the Corners, and its lack of health care services."

She shook her head when he started to interrupt. "So I chose option number two. I went back to high school and graduated near the top of my class. I won a scholarship to the state university and got my nursing degree. Then, when I'd had some experience, I came back here and pounded on doors until I had the money to fund Mother and Child. And I'm not leaving again. Not ever. Not as long as there's a pregnant woman or a little child left in this hellhole. Not until they drag me out of here in a pine box!"

"Which may happen sooner than later."

She took a deep breath and let it out slowly. Something inside her eased. She had told Thomas her story, and he hadn't flinched. She had needed his acceptance, and without so much as a smile, a tear, a touch, she knew—somehow she knew—that she had it.

"A long time ago," she said softly, "I realized there was a lot that could be taken away from me. But one thing that couldn't was my determination to stay here and beat my head against the wall. Maybe that's all I'm doing, and maybe it will never make a difference. But maybe if enough of us keep beating and banging and complaining and staying on here..."

He understood better why she had married him. There was no decision as important to her as the one she had made at her baby's death. Every other decision was weighed against that one. Even marriage to a man she hardly knew.

"My story," she said. She waited, hoping he would tell her his.

"You are an extraordinary woman."

She saw no answers in his eyes. But what she saw was nearly as riveting. Something was blazing there. Something warmer than compassion, stronger than understanding. He knew what she had gone through, knew it deep inside him, because he had been scorched by the same fire.

"The dragon got you, too, Thomas, didn't he?"

"One dragon at a time tonight," he said.

She thought it was a promise of sorts. Someday—if they were

married that long—he would tell her what had brought him here, what drove him.

He surprised her by reaching out to touch a lock of hair that had escaped to snake over her shoulder. "Extraordinary."

The word felt almost like a kiss. For a moment something shivered in the air between them. She felt herself lean toward him. She saw him lean toward her. But they didn't meet.

He turned away. She let out a deep breath.

They spoke about the news and weather over dinner.

7

Even though he'd lived with Garnet for two weeks, Thomas was still aware of the different fragrances subtly perfuming the air in their apartment, even when she was gone. Bath oil and pastel soaps, scented candles, hand lotion and more. Like the woman, the result could not be ignored. Together the scents were bold yet elusive, flamboyant but somehow starkly elemental. The flowers in the Garden of Eden had undoubtedly combined the same divergent notes. The woman in the Garden of Eden had undoubtedly combined them, too.

The apartment was silent now except for the noise of cars passing in the street below. When Garnet was home, the apartment was never silent. But Garnet was gone. Finn, Tex's cop husband, had arrived just minutes before to whisk her off to Mother and Child.

Finn was a gift. He had appeared the morning after Garnet moved into Thomas's apartment, just—he claimed—to pass the time with her. For the past two weeks he had continued to appear faithfully each morning the clinic was open. Finn drank a cup of coffee while Garnet finished dressing; then he walked her to work. Casually, as if nothing could please him more. Casually, eyes darting right and left, hand hovering close enough to his gun that anyone watching would have thought he just might be expecting trouble.

So far there had been none.

In the stillness, Thomas located his worn-out briefcase. He had a little time before he was scheduled to be in his office, but the apartment seemed unwelcoming, as if all the life had been sucked from it with Garnet's departure.

Two weeks had passed. Two weeks of a marriage that was, by anyone's standards, a fraud. Yet there were times when Thomas felt married to Garnet. They had already fallen into a routine. He arose in the morning before she did, and while he showered, she made breakfast. Invariably it was manna from heaven. She could take the simplest ingredients and cook food fit for the gods. Sometimes she made flour tortillas filled with beans spiced with garlic and herbs, ham, scrambled eggs, cheese. The list of fillings was as long as the woman's imagination.

Afterward he cleaned the kitchen while she showered and changed. She sang in the shower. Her voice was throaty and sensual, and she always chose love songs. Steam edged through the cracks in the doorway, scented steam that penetrated the pores of his skin—but never more than the songs did. When she emerged dressed in white, he didn't stare, but secretly he searched out the small details that made her unique. The colorful costume jewelry. The ribbon or scarf in her hair. The bright sheen of her cheeks and lips...

He caught himself staring at nothing. He didn't want to reflect on the ways that Garnet had changed his life in the weeks of their marriage. Reflection was a pastime for those unscathed by the dragon.

Downstairs he unlocked the front door of the church and left his study door wide open, even though doing so defeated the purpose of his small electric heater. He had no appointments to prepare for. He had made his office hours known to his congregation and to anyone else who might be interested. He was available to anyone who might need him during that time, easy to find, receptive and, more often than not, alone.

Once he had needed a secretary to monitor his time and schedule his appointments. She had been trained to knock discreetly and to apologize to whatever parishioner was in the office before she ushered in Thomas's next appointment. There had been no breaks, no time for meditation or prayer. He'd had a running argument with the church board. The board had hired another associate minister, and there had been funds available to hire an assistant to lighten his load, but Thomas had refused the help.

Now he didn't need help; he didn't even need a secretary. And he had all the time for prayer that any man of God could want.

More than *this* man of God had need of.

His desk was empty, no stacks of phone messages to answer, no carefully coded correspondence needing his attention. His desk was as clear of self-important hustle and bustle as his life. There were a telephone, a blotter and one sheet of scratched-up notes for Sunday's sermon that he had worked on the previous evening.

He stared at the notes. Evenings, after he and Garnet returned from work, were fraught with subtlety and innuendo. Dinner was as creative, as sensuous a treat, as breakfast. While Garnet chopped and sautéed they talked about their days as two strangers talk, but sometimes there were moments of surprising intimacy. The shared smile, the clink of glasses, the husky laugh, the insightful comment.

He had come to look forward to that time together as he hadn't looked forward to anything in years. Sometimes during the day he found himself thinking of things he would tell Garnet; sometimes he found himself thinking of things she had told him. Sometimes—as now—he thought of the curves of her body, the forbidden length of leg under a satin nightshirt, a glimpse of her neck when she lifted her hair.

At night, after dinner, when he knew she lay in the next room listening to music or reading, thoughts of her kept him awake.

He had married Garnet to protect her and for no reason other than protection. Now he wondered how he was going to protect himself.

By the time the front door slammed, there was a second sheet of paper, even more scratched up, to attest to his struggle to concentrate. But he still had no firm idea of what he was going to say on Sunday. He leaned back in his chair and waited for the visitor.

Ema came to the doorway and smiled her tentative smile. "I'm bothering you, aren't I?"

He stood in welcome. Something like relief filled him at the sight of another human face. "Of course not."

"I could come back."

"Sit down, Ema."

"I can only stay a minute."

"Make it two, at least."

She smiled, exactly the same frightened doe smile, and sat. "I shouldn't be here."

"No?"

"I told Ron I was going out for groceries."

"And he'd be angry if he found out you were here?"

"He...keeps track of me." She looked around the room, as if hoping there would be something there to comment on.

"Are the girls in school?"

"They're supposed to be. They're.. .they're at a neighbor's."

He sat a little straighter, alert now to barely perceptible signals that she was distraught. She was twisting the handle of her purse in her hands. He was so used to seeing her eyes red-rimmed and swollen that he hadn't noticed immediately that this time the tears were fresh.

"What's going on?" he asked.

"Did you know my real name is Emerald?" She laughed, and the sound wrapped around his heart. "Imagine that. Someone like me with a name like Emerald. But Mama didn't have anything else of value. Garnet's probably told you all about that."

"Not much."

She looked at him as if that was hard to believe.

"Your sister and I..." His voice trailed off. He couldn't find words to explain his marriage to Garnet.

"I know. She told me why you married her. But I thought..."

"Thought what?"

"Well, Garnet's pretty good at making the best of things." She looked away. "Anyway, Mama named us all for jewels. She said it was the only way she'd ever have any. You know? She called us her little treasures."

"And you were treated like treasures?"

She seemed to consider the question. "By Mama," she said at last. "But we were poor, and this is a hard place to grow up. Garnet and Jade, well, they turned out different from me. Jade ran away and started a new life. Garnet just fought everything that stood between her and the kind of world she thought the Corners should be. And I..." Her voice trailed off again, and so did her gaze.

"You got married to a man who beats you," Thomas said.

"Well, not all the time."

"Once is too often, Ema."

"Do I deserve better?" She forced her gaze to his. "I want to know, Reverend Stonehill. Do I?"

He marveled at how simple some answers were to give. "Yes."

"Ron says women started all the trouble in the world."

"Ron is a sick and violent man."

"I can't please him."

"No one could."

"I try. I cook foods he likes. I keep the apartment clean. I don't complain when he comes home drunk."

"It comes down to two choices, Ema. You can stay with him, knowing that things will stay the same or get even worse. Or you can leave him and start a new life for yourself and the girls. But there is no third choice. You can't stay and hope that he'll change."

"He doesn't mean to hit me."

"He does. And he means to hurt you. And someday he may mean to hurt your daughters."

"Oh, he's never--"

"Even if he never lifts a finger to Jody and Lisa, he's still teaching them it's all right for men to hit women. When your girls grow up, they may look for men like their father, and if they do, they'll probably act just like their mother when those men hit them."

The handle of her purse snapped in two. Ema looked down at her lap. "I don't want to teach them that."

"Do you want to stay with your husband?"

"Is it all right... does the Bible say... ?"

"Marriage is sacred, but only if both people treat it that way. Love, honor and cherish aren't answers to a multiple choice question. Until death do us part doesn't mean that one partner has the right to cause the death of another."

She flinched. "Sometimes—" She looked up. "I hate him."

"I'm sure you do."

"But that's wrong."

"Sometimes it takes anger to get a job done. You'll have plenty of time after you leave Ron to work on forgiveness."

"That's not what the others told me. You're not like any other pastor I've been to."

He doubted that, in the most important ways, he was like any pastor anywhere, but he wasn't going to explain that. "This is not the Middle Ages, and I'm not alone in this," he said. "I can promise you that there are pastors all over the world who would give you the same advice."

She nodded, as if absorbing that.

"Do you have a place to go?" he asked.

"Mama offered to let me come there. She lives in Florida, and she has friends who will help. I think it's too far for Ron to follow me. Jade offered, too—"

"Why aren't the girls in school today?"

She twisted what was left of her purse handle. She seemed to be debating. Finally she spoke. "I've got bus tickets."

"For when?-"

"Ron goes to work at one. Our bus leaves at two."

"Does Garnet know?"

"I thought maybe you could tell her?"

"Why don't you tell her yourself?"

"Because she'd make a speech about how I'm finally doing the right thing. And I know she'd be right, but I don't want to hear her say it."

"May I say it?"

She looked up again. "Please."

"You *are* doing the right thing."

"Am I really?"

He nodded.

His words seemed to strengthen her. "Will you tell Garnet I love her? Tell her I just wanted to do this because I know it's right, not because somebody pushed me."

"And will you call?"

"When I'm all settled, I'll call."

"Good."

"You won't tell Ron where I am if he comes asking around?"

"I don't know where you're going. I didn't let you tell me exactly."

She smiled a little, and for a moment the worry lines in her forehead smoothed. He saw Garnet in the momentary sparkle of her eyes. Ema's eyes *were* green, like her sister's. And someday they might sparkle often.

"You've helped me," she said. "I needed a place to come where I could think. I needed a place where somebody cared about me, not because they had to, like family, but just because I was a human being. You made me *remember* that's what I am. You and *your* God. Ron made me forget, but you helped me remember."

"Don't forget again," he said.

"I'm going to try not to." She stood. "I'll get a few groceries, then I'm going back to Ron. For the last time. I'll be okay," she added, before he could ask. "He waits till he's done with work to start his heavy drinking. He'll really have something to be mad about when he comes home tonight, won't he?"

Thomas stood and walked her to the door. "He'll always find something to be mad about."

She paused in the doorway, then shyly rose on her tiptoes and kissed his cheek. "Goodbye. Take care of my sister. And thank you again. You gave me something to hold on to. It's the first good thing that's happened to me in a long, long time."

She had been gone for minutes before he turned back to his desk. He was glad he had given Ema something to hold on to. He gazed upward, although he had never really believed in a bearded, complacent God on a cloud-borne throne.

"Does that make me a hypocrite?" he asked out loud. "She's holding on, and I let go."

There was only silence, a greater silence than he had ever heard. But perhaps years ago he had never taken the time to listen for answers, anyway.

~

"I don't know where she is, Ron. I just hope it's somewhere thousands of miles away." Garnet held the telephone receiver six inches from her ear. When the torrent of abuse receded she responded. "Try *any* of those things, Celabraze, and I'll have you in jail so fast your head will be spinning for a week! I'm not my sister. I'd like nothing better than to see you turned into fish bait and fed to the sharks."

"Sharks?" Thomas asked, after she had hung up.

Garnet tried to control the anger that had boiled over at Ron's accusations. "Big ones. Ema's left Ron. He went home early, probably got the itch to beat her up before midnight for a change, so he sacrificed drinks number ten through fifteen. Anyway, he found a note. Do you happen to know where she went?"

"Somewhere she and the girls will be safe." Thomas poured Garnet a glass of mineral water. The clinic had been open late that evening and, as always, Finn had escorted her right to the church's front door. Ron's phone call had come only minutes after her arrival.

His face was inscrutable, and for once she couldn't pass it off as vintage Thomas. "So you know? And you're not going to tell me where?"

"I don't know. I didn't *want* to know. You don't, either, in case Ron goes to the police and accuses her of kidnapping the children."

She told herself he was right. She told herself to be calm. "I don't think he will. There are too many people who could testify about the way he beat Ema. And he has a whole file drawer to himself at the cop shop. The law would move very slowly to assist Ron Celabraze."

"Then a toast might be in order." He lifted his glass.

"Ema told you, but not me."

He drank alone.

"Why?" she asked. "I wouldn't have said 'I told you so.' She knows me better than that."

He heard the hurt under the anger. Garnet was struggling for control, but the wound was apparent. "She wanted to be sure that you and everybody else knew she was doing it on her own. It was her decision completely."

"Then why did she tell you?"

"I think she needed an objective stamp of approval."

"God's?"

"Maybe so. I couldn't give her that, but she got mine."

"She thinks you speak for God, Thomas. They all do. I watch their faces on Sunday morning. Those people drift in from the street to hear you preach, and they all think you speak for God." She stood up and strode to the refrigerator to see what she could make for dinner.

"I don't. And you're angry."

"She's my sister, and you're nothing to her!"

He rose and went to stand behind her. He hadn't expected this. He'd thought she would be happy that Ema had found the courage to leave her husband. When Garnet straightened, he put his hands on her shoulders. "I'm nothing," he agreed. "But what she found at the church is something real and vital, Garnet. Maybe you don't understand it. Maybe I don't—"

She turned. "What? You're going to say you don't understand it, either? Come off it. God's what you do for a living."

They were married, yet she didn't know him at all. That fact had never been more apparent to him. Nor had it ever been more apparent that he could never share his heart with her.

He grasped her shoulders again. "I'm trying to say that your sister found the strength to do what she's needed to do for a long time. She found it in her own way. I'm sure if you hadn't stood by her for so long, supported her, spoken your heart to her, she never would have found it at all. But now she's made the break. Be happy."

She couldn't pull her gaze from his. Little by little the anger drained away, until finally she spoke. "Damn it, Thomas. I'm sorry. What's wrong with me? Of course I'm happy for her. I was just thinking about myself. I'm selfish and vain and envious. Now that Ema's gone, you'll have to work on changing *me.*"

"I don't want to change anything about you."

As she often did, she found a refuge in audacity. "No? I don't have any of the qualities a man like you needs in a wife. I'd need to be docile." She lifted her arms and pulled her hair from her face in the semblance of a bun. "Self-sacrificing." She lowered her eyes. "Reverent." She began to hum something that sounded like "The Old Rugged Cross" with a reggae beat.

He felt a stab of irritation. "Since you can't be any of those things, then just be yourself."

"Well, at least there won't be any danger that someone might take this marriage seriously."

He was beginning to take it seriously. He realized it before her words had stopped echoing through the kitchen. He had offered her the charade of a marriage for complex reasons, but he had never expected it to profoundly change his life. Now he saw that nothing could be further from the truth.

His hands dropped to his sides. He had kept himself from her in all the important ways. She was, for all purposes, married to a stranger. And most of the time she had kept herself from him, as if by open agreement. Yet somehow she had crept into his life, into his thoughts, into...

"Don't tell *me you're* taking it seriously," she said, when he didn't answer. "Thomas, I'm closer to the boy who delivers clean linen for the clinic than I am to you."

He turned away. "Don't let me keep you from making dinner."

"Answer me!"

"You didn't ask a question." He felt her hand on his arm.

She was still riding the wave of emotion that had crested with the news of Ema's flight. Humor, irreverence, repression. None had brought her to firm emotional ground. Now she couldn't control her words. "Here's the question. Are you taking this marriage seriously? Or are we just playing house like a couple of preschoolers?"

"You cared about Ema, and now she's gone. You're feeling a lot of things. Don't take them out on me."

"Cool, Thomas. Collected, rational. Thank you for the objective analysis, but I'm still waiting for an answer to my question."

He turned. She was only inches away. The mocking light was gone from her eyes. She was awash in emotion. He understood why. The last weeks had brought so many changes in her life. Even Garnet could only shrug off her feelings for so long.

He understood so much, but he felt so much more. She moved closer to him.

"You don't tell me anything about yourself," she said, eyes narrowed. "You don't share your feelings. You don't touch me. You don't even smile very often. Maybe we agreed to all this. Maybe it's best this way. But don't go looking at me like the rules changed and you forgot to mention it. Don't go looking like I've wounded you because I said out loud what we both know. This marriage is not serious. I'm nothing to you, and even if you get just the teeniest twinge of desire for me sometimes, the Reverend Thomas Stonehill is too much of a god himself to be tempted by someone as lowly as Garnet Anthony."

"We were both wrong to think we could pull this off without it affecting us."

"*I'm* not affected. I sleep in that bedroom and I cook in this kitchen. Sometimes I talk to the God-fearing robot who passes through these rooms." She stopped. Slowly her hand dropped from his arm. "Damn!" She faced the refrigerator.

He understood turning points. There had been some so crucial in his life that, after them, nothing had been the same. He recognized this one. Every part of him screamed that he should back away and give her time to compose herself.

Instead he put his arms around her. She was as tense as he had expected; he could feel the tension everywhere he touched.

She was also warm and enticingly female, and immediately his body cried out for what hers had to offer. She didn't yield easily, but he pulled her against him. "Maybe you're not affected," he said. "But I am."

She was very quiet. For a moment he wasn't even sure she was breathing. "What's wrong with me?" she asked at last.

"A very difficult situation."

"What's so difficult? You've given me a place to stay, protection, your name—just in case it helps to scare off the little boys with the guns! How can that be difficult?"

"Because we've taken a sacred institution and made a mockery out of it."

"Sacred? Maybe in the world you come from. Here marriage is just an institution, like prison or the closest psychiatric hospital. My mother was married to Ema's father. It lasted six months before he left her pregnant and alone. She thought she was married to my father until she discovered he was already married to somebody else. She didn't bother fooling herself about Jade's father."

"It's a sacred institution."

"Was your marriage sacred, Thomas?" She turned in his arms. "Your real marriage, not this one. Did God bless it? Did He honor it? When Patricia died, did you have that to comfort you?"

"I had nothing to comfort me."

She saw pain in his eyes, a pain so deep, so powerful, it threatened to suck her into its vortex. She had been prepared to taunt him again, but she found she couldn't. Somehow she knew there was nothing she could tell him that he didn't tell himself every hour before dawn.

"I could give you comfort," she said softly. The words came from nowhere, yet she didn't want to call them back. "Maybe it wouldn't be enough, but it would be something."

Her breasts pressed against his chest; her scent enveloped him. As he stood with his arms around her, powerless to release her, she smoothed her hands up them. He felt the cool slide of her palms on his neck, against his heated cheeks. Her fingers burrowed into his hair, and she pressed his mouth to hers.

The taste, the feel of her lips against his, was as pleasurable as he remembered. His arms tightened around her. She was soft and giving; her warm flesh was as pliant as her spirit was not. She was his wife before man and God.

His hands traveled to splay against the curve of her hips. With a helpless groan he delved into the secrets of her mouth. She was everything womanly and desirable. Their tongues moved together giving and taking pleasure; their bodies moved together, too. They were married strangers, yet her touch, her curves, her taste were familiar, as if he had always partaken of them with this heady rush of desire.

He had partaken in his dreams. Thomas knew it as surely as he knew he had never touched her in these ways before. He had dreamed of her in the hours when dreams aren't remembered, when sleep is so deep it buries all thoughts and feelings, all desires.

All desires.

Garnet drank in the heady pleasure of his body against hers. She had not indulged in fantasies about him. She had admired his body, saucily assessed the potential of his hands and lips, but she had not allowed herself to imagine being in his arms. Now she knew why. There were realities so potent that fantasy was too poor an imitation. She had known, before she had been conscious of knowing, that passion with Thomas would be light-years beyond imagination.

"Come to bed, Thomas," she whispered against his lips. "If the rules have changed, then come to bed and make this marriage real. Even your God couldn't object."

She had said nothing of love and commitment, but he knew if he took her to bed everything would change. And still, he was helpless to say no.

Garnet unfastened the top button of his shirt as she kissed him. The second was as easy, and the others followed in quick succession as her trembling fingers would allow. She smoothed her hands over his chest, murmuring provocatively. She did not give herself easily or casually. She had always been wary of relationships that bound her too tightly. She was too enamored of freedom to give control of her life to anyone.

But Thomas hadn't asked for control. He had given her freedom when he married her, given her the chance to continue doing what she had to do, to continue walking the streets of the only neighborhood she would ever call home. He wanted nothing, asked for nothing. And in return, because he made no demands, she could give him what little she had to give.

There was more, though, and as desire swept her away, she was compelled to face it. Her gift wasn't unselfish. At that moment she wanted him with an urgency no other man had ever provoked. She wanted him inside her, where intimacy would destroy all mystery. She wanted all barriers lowered, all defenses exploded. In every way, she wanted to know the man she had married.

He kissed her forehead, her cheeks, and clasped her closer. She pressed her knee between his legs and felt his response. He wanted her, too. There was no mystery there. He was a man desiring a woman. He was not the minister, the husband of Patricia, the slayer of the Corners' dragons. He was simply a man, like every other, a man aroused enough to enter a woman and make her his.

"Come to bed," she repeated huskily as she started to slip his shirt over his shoulders. "It's time, Thomas. It's right."

He felt her knee stroking the sensitive flesh between his thighs. Thought, doubt, creeds and rules melted away. He was nothing but a man, a man alive and hungry and aching for a woman. He felt himself growing to meet her, growing with need, bursting with desire, throbbing and aching to bury himself inside her.

And then, as strong as his response had been, as potent as his need, he was no longer ready.

If the world had depended on their joining, if all the stars in the heaven had decreed it, he could not have made her his.

Garnet felt the new tension in Thomas's arms, in the muscles of his back. It was no longer the tension of a man bursting with passion. It was no longer the tension of a man denying himself what he most needed.

It was the tension of a man who no longer wants nor needs the woman in his arms.

She felt his response to her disappear. She shifted her weight so that she was no longer against him; then she stepped back and stared at him.

"What is it?" she whispered. "What's wrong?"

He shook his head.

"I..." She didn't know what to say. Humiliation washed over her. She had forced this, read signals that weren't there. She had believed he wanted her, and she had admitted how much she wanted him. But somewhere she had gone desperately wrong.

He saw her confusion and shame. He touched her hair; it seemed to singe his skin. "Don't," he said. "Don't think any of the things you're thinking."

"I'm sorry," she said.

"For what? For acting like a married woman? Sorry because I can't act like a married man?" He turned away and straightened his shirt. "Can we go on like before?"

"Like before." Something new boiled up inside her. She wanted to laugh or cry, but she choked down both. She wanted to reach out to him, but she had already learned what a mistake that would be.

"*Can* we go on like before?" he repeated.

"Yes. I guess... No! Are you saying we'll pretend this didn't happen? That one minute you wanted me and the next you thought better of it?"

"Thought?" He faced her. "Thought had nothing to do with it! Were you thinking? Was either of us thinking?"

"I was thinking that I wanted you. And somewhere along the way you were thinking you didn't want me."

"No!"

"Then what happened?"

"You ran up against the truth. This marriage is a charade. It can't be real."

"For a few minutes it felt real. It felt real to you, too. You can't deny it."

"It was a few minutes of dreaming."

"Then let's dream a little longer. Maybe we'll wake up and find out we weren't dreaming at all."

"Maybe we'll wake up and find out that we're in the middle of a nightmare." He put his hands on her shoulders. His eyes were bleak. "I can't make love to you, because I can't. Not because I don't want to. Because I can't."

She stared at him, then she shook her head. "What are you saying? I don't believe you."

"You're wasting your vote of confidence. I haven't made love to a woman since Patricia died. And this isn't the first time I've tried."

"But you wanted me. I know it. It's not something you can hide."

"Wanting has nothing to do with it." He dropped his hands.

"Thomas, I-"

"This wasn't supposed to happen. I just didn't factor in-"

"What?"

"How desirable you are."

"If there's something wrong there are doctors, medication, clinics—"

"I've been to doctors. There's nothing physically wrong with me. It's all in my head and even little blue pills can't solve that." He turned away again. "You didn't sign on for this. I married you to keep you safe, not to make you my sex therapist, Garnet. I'm not going to try to keep you here. If you have a better alternative than this farce of a marriage, go. I'll understand. I'll wish you well."

There were better alternatives. She knew that now. She could have found a more acceptable plan for her life than marriage to a man she hardly knew. But she had let Thomas rescue her, not because she had no other alternatives, but because...

"I married you because I needed your strength," she said after moments had dragged into more. "And because I felt something for you. I don't know, maybe just curiosity, but something."

"Now you don't have to be curious anymore."

"I've never met anyone who was more of a man."

His laugh was short and bitter.

There were no words in any language to reassure him. She knew that instinctively. And she knew that there were no words to reassure her. All that was left were words that should have come naturally, words like "goodbye." And those words wouldn't form.

"I'll choose this over the other alternatives for now," she said at last. "If you'll still have me."

"You're welcome here."

She wondered what it had cost him to say that. She knew she wasn't really welcome. She would be a constant reminder of failure at the deepest level.

"I'll make dinner," she said.

"Don't make anything for me."

"Are you going out?"

"For a while."

She watched him button his shirt and find his coat, watched as the door shut quietly behind him.

She was still awake long after midnight when she heard the door close again.

8

In his heart, Thomas was still married to Patricia. She had been gone from his life for three years, but obviously she was not gone from his heart. In every way that mattered to him, she was still his wife. If he made love to Garnet, he was being unfaithful to Patricia.

It had to be as simple as that.

Garnet set the table for supper, even though Thomas wasn't home. It was unusual for her to arrive at the apartment before he did, but tonight she'd had to let herself in with her key. There had been no note or phone call explaining his absence. He simply wasn't there.

In the week since they'd nearly made love, nothing had followed the pattern set in the early weeks of their marriage. Thomas had taken pains to avoid her, and when he hadn't been able to find an excuse to disappear from the apartment, he had drawn into a shell she couldn't penetrate.

After a week of silent questions, of suffering alternately from anger and tortuous self-doubts, Garnet had come to a conclusion. The reason for Thomas's impotence had to be a commitment, even after death, to Patricia. He was a married man, sorely tempted by an adulteress—never mind that the adulteress was now his wife in the sight of man and God. He must have loved Patricia beyond death, beyond his own ability to adjust to her passing. Even with the advantage of breath in her body and a beating heart, Garnet could never hope to prevail over Patricia's memory.

Bested by a dead woman.

Garnet had failed repeatedly in her life, but the last few years had taught her the joys of being a winner. She had grown to like herself, to feel pride in what she had accomplished. She had learned to believe that she had much to offer. Now, a memory offered Thomas more than she could.

She bent and turned up the portable radio on the floor another notch to discourage more analysis. The station was Spanish-speaking, the music sensuously Latin. She hummed along, forcing herself to concentrate on the words. Her Spanish was as mongrelized as her heritage, but she eventually caught the gist of the musical story. A man had lost his lover, and all he could do was dream of her. He would dream of her until the day he died.

She snapped off the radio and kicked it with her bare toe. Pain shot up her leg.

"Sony might design next year's model to kick back."

She looked up and saw Thomas leaning against the doorjamb, his arms folded. She wondered how long he had been watching her. "Well, I'll be ready for it."

"I thought I'd probably missed dinner."

"Your cell phone wasn't working? A call would have been appreciated."

"I'm sorry."

She was in no mood for an apology. "Is that all you're going to say? You're sorry? That's not enough, even for someone as unimportant as a roommate, Thomas. *Why* were you late? Embroider a little. Give me a sentence or two about your day. Pretend I matter."

He stared at her; then he turned and left the kitchen.

She followed him, tired of backing down. If no other kind of interaction was available, she would take a fight. "What's wrong? Is pretending against your moral code? Too much like lying? What is it, the eleventh commandment or something? Thou shalt not pretend your wife matters if she doesn't?"

"I guess I don't have to ask what kind of day you had."

"Yes, you do have to ask. If we're going to live together, you have to ask!" She listened to the reverberations of her voice. She was coldly furious, or at least, that was the impression she was giving. Furious, and she hadn't even realized it.

She hadn't known he mattered so much.

"I am sorry I'm late, Garnet." He faced her. For the first time she noticed how bleak his eyes were. "And I should have called. I just didn't realize how late it had gotten."

"Where were you?" She tried to temper her tone. She didn't quite succeed.

"At the hospital... and the funeral home."

And obviously he had been doing his job, a job sometimes as grim as her own. Her desire for answers faded. Silently she cursed her bad temper.

Thomas saw the anger fade from her eyes. He saw her glance away and noticed the beginnings of regret.

He recognized the last with ease. He knew all about regret. He had wallowed in it for the past week. Regret that he couldn't make her his wife. Regret that he had tried. Regret that he had ever believed this phony marriage would benefit her. He had married Garnet on a wave of sentiment so intense it had wiped away whatever logic he possessed. He had wanted so desperately to protect her, the way he hadn't protected Patricia. Nothing else had mattered.

Now everything did.

"I'm sorry," she said. "I don't know what came over me. You didn't sign an agreement saying you'd call if you were going to be late. I've never even asked you to call."

"You've never had to."

She met his gaze. Still bleak. Still looking as if something inside him had died. She asked the question she really didn't want answered. "Did someone in your congregation...?"

"Dorothy Brown died this evening."

"No." She looked away again and swallowed. She had seen death a hundred times. Dorothy was an old woman who had lived a good life. Hers was not a death to mourn. The death of children, the death of young mothers, the death of warring teenagers, those were deaths to weep for. But not the death of an old woman whose time had come, who had probably met death with her arms wide open.

"No." She blinked back tears, but they would not disappear.

Thomas stepped forward and enfolded her in his arms. It was as natural, as perfect an answer to their mutual sorrow as existed. "I was with her. She'd had a heart attack. She had the hospital call me."

"Why you, Thomas? There were a hundred people she could have called."

He held her tighter. "She wants.. .wanted me to do her funeral service. She was organizing right up to the end. She wanted me to go to the Knights and the Coroners and demand that they come to honor her. She thought it would help unite the community if they would both come peacefully to her service."

Garnet moved far enough away to see his eyes. She could feel the tears gliding down her cheeks at the same time she felt something different bubbling in her chest. "She was planning her funeral service?"

"She was."

"While she was dying?"

"No, she was just polishing the details. She's had it planned for years. She just hadn't decided on a preacher until today. She said I'd find instructions at the funeral home. She already has a casket. Everything's paid for."

Garnet tried not to smile.

He saw the glint of humor behind her tears, and something eased inside him. He framed her face with his hands. Her smile broke through.

"Garnet." He shook his head.

"I'm sorry, Thomas," she whispered. "But don't you see how 'Dorothy' she was right up until the end? I can just see her with St. Peter right now, demanding a house on the one heavenly street that's not paved with gold. Before you know it she'll be organizing angel committees, circulating petitions..."

He kissed her. It was the only thing he could do, although he could feel the shock register in her body. The sorrow that had plagued him at Dorothy's death began to drain away. He held life in his arms. Dorothy's essential spirit was still alive in others, most notably the woman he had married. Since he'd been called to the hospital, he had forgotten that the world still contained hope and joy.

And love.

He tasted hope against his lips, tasted the potential for joy. Garnet was so warm, so quintessentially female. But she was more than just a pleasing feminine form, a pliant, willing lover. She was strength and courage. Her commitment to what was right resonated in every movement, every decision she made. She was the real slayer of dragons, not he. And the dragon she was slaying right now was his despair.

He gave himself up to her ministry. For that moment he forgot that he couldn't take what she offered, that his capacity to take solace and joy from a woman had vanished. He let himself drink in her comfort, bathe in her life-giving femininity.

"Thomas." She broke away, bewildered.

He pulled her to his chest. His shirt was already wet from her tears, but he didn't care. "She made me pray with her," he said. "She didn't care that—" He broke off abruptly.

"Care about what?"

He shook his head.

"That your religions were different?"

He was silent for a long time.

"But she wouldn't care, Thomas. I doubt she even belonged to a particular church. The last time I saw her, she said that she visited all the churches in the Corners to keep them on the straight and narrow." She slipped her arms around his waist. Standing against him felt better than her most forbidden dreams. Seeking comfort, giving comfort, were experiences too new to test. She just stood there, her body melting against his, and let warmth flow over her.

"She left money in her will to the church. I'm supposed to use some of it to pay Ferdinand to paint a mural."

"He'll do it. If you approach him again and tell him it was Dorothy's request, I think he'll do it."

"He'll be at the funeral, along with the other Knights. I'll ask him then."

She stood in his arms, absorbing the heat from his body, the satisfaction of his comfort. Then his words penetrated. "The Knights?"

"And the Coroners."

"No." She put her hands on his chest and stepped back. "Wait a minute...."

"That was Dorothy's request. I told you. That's why she wanted me to do the service. She wants them both to come. She wants her funeral to be a step toward uniting the community."

"Thomas..." She realized that he had already told her as much. But she had been so shocked by the fact of Dorothy's death, she had somehow blocked out the rest. "My God, what could she have been thinking?"

"She was thinking of this community. She gave her life to it. Now she wants to give her death."

"Look, no cute little twist of words can change reality. You ask both of those gangs to show up, they'll tear this place down, and you with it. You know what they're capable of. Look what they did to me!"

"I know. And that's why you won't be at the funeral."

"What do you mean, I won't be there?" She put her hands on her hips.

"My head's not in the sand, Garnet. I know this is a potentially volatile—"

"Potentially volatile? Try explosive, why don't you? Try cataclysmic, for God's sake!"

"A potentially volatile situation. Dorothy knew it, too. She asked me whether I could handle it. I told her I could. And one of the ways I'll handle it is to ask you not to be there."

She stared at him.

"I couldn't function at all if I thought you were in any danger," he said. "I would only be worrying about you. I wouldn't be able to do what needs to be done."

"You've really lost it, Thomas." She shook her head. "First you tell a dying woman you'll let a mob of bloodthirsty kids gang bang at the church in place of a dignified funeral service. Then you tell me that I'm not free to attend and keep score? Where do you get off playing God? You think you can really control the situation so that everything comes off with a happy ending? You think the Coroners and the MidKnights are going to walk out of that church saying prayers and making plans for a picnic in the park?"

"I'm not a fool." He grasped her shoulders. "Listen to me for once, okay?"

"For once? What's that supposed to mean? When do you ever talk to me?"

"Now!" His fingers dug into her shoulders. "Tomorrow I'm

going to Andre, and I'm going to Francis's brothers. I'm going to tell them when and where the funeral is being held, and I'm going to request their presence. I'm going to remind them of every good thing Dorothy Brown ever did for them. I'm going to remind them that they're human beings and that as such they have duties. And one of those duties is to hold their violence in check during that funeral service. Then, when they arrive, I'm going to have people stationed at the doors to take their weapons."

"People? Don't you mean cops?"

"No. Members of this congregation. No cops. Because everyone at the funeral is going to show respect and dignity."

"You're out of your mind."

"Well, be thankful you aren't going to be there to witness the worst of it."

His jaw was clenched, and his eyes were bleak again. Silently she mourned the comfort they had given each other. It had been so short-lived.

"I will be there," she said. "If you think I'm going to let you stand up there alone, you don't know anything about me."

"If you come, I'll be--"

"Shut up." She put her fingers over his lips. "Just shut up, Thomas. This marriage may be a joke, but as long as it's still legal, I'm your wife. A wife doesn't let her husband face hungry lions by himself. Even if we did it for the wrong reasons, you and I vowed before God that this marriage was for better or worse. Well, I can't imagine anything worse than this funeral, can you?"

He turned away, his shoulders hunched forward defiantly. She shut her eyes, knowing she hadn't reached him.

"Then you'll sit in the front," he said at last. "Where I can get to you quickly."

"I'll sit in the front to honor Dorothy and support you."

"You're making this harder for me."

"That's not possible. It couldn't be harder." She hesitated;

then she put her hand on his arm. Tentatively. When he didn't jerk his arm away, she moved closer. "You've been married before, Thomas. You should understand that I have to do what I think is right, just like you do."

"Patricia would have done exactly what I asked."

She supposed it had never been clearer to him that she wasn't Patricia. She dropped her hand.

She was sorry those were the last words he spoke, because they seemed to resound through the silent apartment for the remainder of the evening.

Thomas stood in one side of the doorway. Kimmy and Frankie's father, Jack, stood in the other. Thomas had turned down Finn's offer of assistance, because even in plain clothes, Finn looked like a cop. He was in attendance, but only as a guest—a guest who would keep one eye on Garnet at all times.

When Jack had heard about the circumstances surrounding Dorothy's funeral he had volunteered to help with security. Jack had just found a new job, the breath of hope for his small family, but he had taken off the afternoon without pay to stand beside Thomas.

There were uncanonized saints walking every city street, angels without halos, prophets and priests who would never be asked to preach a sermon. Thomas gazed across the space separating him from the thin-framed, stoop-shouldered father of two and felt humbled.

"Here they come," Jack said. "The first to arrive."

Thomas looked outside. The day was relentlessly gray. A drizzle one step removed from sleet darkened the sidewalks and made the November chill more bitter. He had awakened that morning sure that Dorothy's funeral would not be well attended.

For better or worse, he had been wrong.

The three young men approaching the door were dressed in Army surplus jackets. One wore a red baseball cap turned backwards. One wore a pound of gold chains around his neck.

Thomas blocked the entry way. "Welcome," he said.

"If we're welcome," the spokesman for this small group of Coroners said, "why are you standing in our way?"

"Because we're taking weapons at the door. This is God's house. There will be no violence here, out of respect for Dorothy Brown."

"You think we're going in there without being strapped, like itty-bitty lambs to the slaughter?"

"I'm asking you to respect a woman who had nothing but respect and concern for you. Everyone else who walks through this door will be asked the same. Those who can't comply will not walk through."

"Yeah? You and him gonna keep 'em out? You got that much heart?"

"We have all the heart we'll need." Thomas held out his hand, as if he expected the young man to cooperate. "You're the ones who can make or break this," he said. "You're the first here. If others see that you had enough courage to leave your weapons at the door, they'll do the same."

The spokesman's expression was insolent. He was a handsome teenager with a teardrop tattooed under each of his heavily lashed green eyes, symbolizing the loss of two fellow gang members to violence and flames tattooed down the side of his neck. With the right haircut and without the tattoos, he could have passed for an Ivy League fullback.

"You couldn't stop me from coming in if I wanted," he said with a sneer.

"Knowing won't stop me from trying. But I don't want to try. I just want you to do what's right for this occasion."

Thomas waited, hand still extended. Then, just as he was sure he'd lost this first encounter, the young man shrugged. He reached inside his trench coat and pulled out a handgun. As if on cue, the others divested themselves of knives. Thomas nodded. "Thank you," he said. "You'll get them back on your way out."

"Yeah?" The young man snorted. "You'd better mean what you say."

Thomas nodded solemnly. "I always do."

The next half hour passed swiftly. There were more confrontations, more near losses. The church filled up with the Coroners, along with a growing number of members of the Corners community. There were also people who were obviously from outside the neighborhood, people who looked distinctly uncomfortable with the almost primitive simplicity of their surroundings and the caliber of the others attending.

During a lull between arrivals, Thomas felt a hand on his shoulder. He knew without looking who stood behind him.

"It's after four," Garnet said.

He didn't turn. He was afraid he couldn't afford even that weakness. "There are more coming."

"How do you know?"

He didn't. He had gone to Andre, just as he had gone to Francis's brothers, and pleaded his case. Andre had stared at him, his dark eyes suspicious, but he had not made any promises. Nothing had passed between them to give Thomas hope. But still he waited.

"Is it fair to make the people who did come sit there and stare at the coffin?" she asked. She dropped her hand, wondering if her touch had made him more stubborn. There was no evidence it had any positive effect on him. In the days since he had told her about his plans for Dorothy's service, there had been no evidence that anything she did or said had any effect on him at all.

"We'll wait five minutes," he said, still not turning. "Then we'll begin."

She knew better than to argue. "Shall I go up and ask Greg to start the prelude?"

He was forced to face her. She was dressed somberly in black. It only served to make her more exotic, more alluring. "Go sit with Finn and Tex. It's bad enough you came," he said in a low voice. "Don't put yourself on display."

She searched his face. There was no rebuke there, only something akin to concern. "I'm fine," she reassured him. "I'll stay fine."

"Please. Go sit down."

She looked past him, and suddenly the doorway was filled with young men in dark hoodies, do-rags and watch caps pulled low. Andre stood at the head of the line. "Jesus," she said softly. It was as much a prayer as any words she had ever uttered.

Thomas turned, stepping in front of her for protection. "I'm glad you came," he said.

"You think we be coming 'cause you asked?" Andre said. "We're here for Dorothy. That's all."

"She would be pleased."

Andre stepped forward, but Thomas blocked his way. "No guns," he said. "No weapons of any kind. This is God's house."

"And you think you be speaking for God?"

"No. That's one thing I don't claim."

Andre folded his arms. He was the picture of insolence. "So who makes the rules, Padre? If it's not your God?"

"I made them, at Dorothy's request. Nothing good can come if you walk through this doorway with weapons."

"And you're going to stop me?"

Garnet heard laughter in the ranks on the sidewalk. From her limited vantage point she looked for Demon, but couldn't find him. She hoped he'd been left behind.

"I can't stop you," Thomas said. "You know that. There are two dozen of you, and only two of us here. I'm putting my faith in you, Andre, you and your goodwill. You came to honor Dorothy Brown, not to dishonor her. Cross this threshold with a gun or a knife, and she will be dishonored."

"We got no weapons." Andre pulled his hoodie up to display a black shirt. The others took his cue and did the same. There were no weapons of any kind in sight. "You gonna search us, Padre?"

"That would dishonor *you.*" Thomas stepped aside. "I believe you. You're welcome here."

"Thomas." Garnet stepped forward. She couldn't believe that he had taken Andre at his word.

He turned, and the anger in his eyes told her how far she had overstepped her bounds. She couldn't tell him that it was fear for his safety and his safety alone that had made her speak out. She couldn't tell him of the vision of impending disaster that knotted her stomach and clutched at her throat.

But there was nothing she could do about that vision. Now she could only show Thomas her support. "Thomas, make sure you show them where the memorial book is so everyone can sign." She turned to Andre. "It will be sent to Dorothy's sister in California. She couldn't attend."

Andre's eyes narrowed; then he shrugged. She turned away, but not before she saw Thomas staring at her, his eyes still angry.

Somehow she walked slowly to her seat, while every second she expected a shot to ring out behind her. There was an audible rustling as heads turned and those already seated watched the MidKnights find chairs.

Greg began the prelude. There was nothing somber about the music Dorothy had chosen. The medley of hymns was as cheerful as Dorothy's smile had been, but the room was still tense when the hymns had ended. Garnet could shut her eyes and still feel suspicion and anger choking off her oxygen. The little church was a conflagration waiting to ignite.

"Let us pray." Thomas bowed his head. Garnet bowed hers with effort, but she doubted that many other heads in the room twitched in response.

"We come together to honor a woman's life, a life that has touched each of us because of the contributions she made to this community. As we both mourn Dorothy Brown's passing and celebrate her life, help us to remember that we have been called here to listen to her last words to us, words we may not desire to hear. Give us courage, O Lord, to listen with open minds and willing hearts. Amen."

She was surprised at the abruptness of Thomas's prayer. She tried to compare it to other prayers she had heard him give, but surprisingly she could not. Upon reflection, she could not remember the substance of one, much less its length. Thomas seemed to spend as little time as possible invoking the Lord's assistance.

There were opening words. Several close friends of Dorothy's did readings. Several others spoke of her role in their lives, of the important differences she had made in the lives of others. Community leaders who had worked with her stood to pay her tribute. Two songs, both favorites of Dorothy's, were sung.

Then it was time for Thomas's eulogy.

As he always did, he abandoned the pulpit at the first opportunity. He came down the aisle and stood in the middle. The Coroners and the MidKnights had aligned themselves perfectly along each side. Had they stood, faced each other and bowed, the scene would have looked like the opening strains of a deadly minuet. Now, with Thomas standing between them, they looked only like volatile young men bent on destroying their lives and the lives of anyone who loved them.

"Dorothy asked me to dispense with praising her life," he said. "It was a life worthy of praise, an exceptional life, but I, like most of you here, would never dare disagree with Dorothy Brown. So I am not going to do a eulogy. Instead, I am going to do exactly what Dorothy asked of me."

Thomas hooked his thumbs in his pockets. He was wearing a suit, but he didn't look like a preacher. His hands were clenched. His mouth was grim. His eyes blazed with almost unearthly light.

"This service will be concluded when Dorothy's body is

respectfully carried out to the hearse waiting in front. Then there will be a short ceremony at the graveside. In her last moments Dorothy named her pallbearers. I can't tell you how glad I am that they're all here today. I can't tell you how much I hope that each of them will stand when I call his name and come forward to carry Dorothy's casket out that door."

Garnet felt her heart beat faster. She knew what was coming next. Dorothy, damn her saintly soul, was about to make her final statement.

Thomas looked around the church as he spoke. "Dorothy named six young men whom she was especially fond of. She was color-blind, and blind to all other immaterial differences that keep us from respecting and loving each other. She chose young men who she believed would someday take her place in this community as leaders. She believed that each of them can help change the Corners from a place of despair to a place of hope. She believed that each one of them would stand proudly today and take his place beside her casket."

He paused to let that sink in. "May her belief in the goodness of others, may her good instincts and supreme faith be rewarded with this final act."

He turned and pinioned Andre with his gaze. "Andre Rollins, Dorothy believed in you." He found Francis's older brother Xavier with his eyes. "Xavier Ramon, Dorothy believed in you."

There was an audible gasp, as if the two hundred or so people crowded into the room had all realized, at the same moment, what Dorothy had intended.

Thomas continued calling out names until three MidKnights and three Coroners had been singled out. Thomas straightened, and his arms fell to his side. "It's time to take your places beside Dorothy Brown's casket."

Garnet shut her eyes. She had no hope that any of the six young men would comply. Thomas had asked too much, too publicly. They would not stand, and when the import of what had been asked of them was understood, they would react with anger.

And their anger would be enough to ignite the church.

She heard a rustle. She could not block out the inevitable. She opened her eyes in time to watch Andre slowly get to his feet. He started toward Thomas. She lifted her hand as if somehow, even from yards away, she could protect her husband. Then, as she watched, Andre brushed past Thomas and started toward the casket. The other two MidKnights stood and moved to join him.

"God," she said softly. It was another prayer.

Xavier Ramon got to his feet. "For Dorothy," he said clearly. He snapped his fingers. The other two Coroners who had been chosen rose and joined him.

Garnet took a deep breath as the Coroners reached the casket and took their places on the opposite side from the MidKnights. Then she forgot to breathe again as they lifted and shouldered the heavy casket as if they had practiced together for hours.

The procession, with Thomas at the head, was slow and silent. Those gathered to witness it rose, as if they were one body, and stood respectfully until the casket was gone. Then they filed quietly and tearfully from their seats.

Garnet, following Tex and Finn, was the last to leave. At the door she turned and stared at the picture of the multi-faceted Jesus that Dorothy had given to the church. Then she closed and locked the door behind her.

9

There had been no violence. Maybe Dorothy Brown, wearing angel wings, had been just out of sight directing her own funeral, or maybe God himself had rained blessings on the Church of the Samaritan.

Or maybe, even more miraculously, a man named Thomas Stonehill had displayed enough courage, enough commitment and charisma, to convince the teenage fiends from hell to act like human beings for one afternoon.

Garnet peered out the window for the fifteenth time, hoping to see Thomas's car pull into the parking space just below. She had gone to the graveside to assure herself that the truce in the war between the Coroners and the MidKnights was going to last. Then, when the service had ended and the only remaining mourners were a few community leaders and family members, she had gotten a ride home with Tex and Finn.

Now she waited impatiently for Thomas to return. She didn't know how to tell him she was sorry. She had showed an abysmal lack of faith. Granted, all her reasoning had been sound. She had lived here forever. She knew these boys and what they were capable of, both good and bad. They did not respond well to coercion or public tests, and even the respect they felt for Dorothy Brown would not outweigh devotion to their chosen gangs.

She had been sure she understood so much more than Thomas, but in the end, he had been the one who understood. He had understood about miracles. Dorothy, even on her deathbed, had understood about miracles, too.

While Garnet waited for Thomas to return, she put the finishing touches on the table. She had worked swiftly to turn the apartment into a place to celebrate. The table was covered with her favorite blue tablecloth, and she had unearthed her most festive pottery to set it. There were candles in the center and an arrangement of dried flowers. She had even defrosted a steak she'd intended to divide for three nights of stir fry and set it to marinate in cooking wine and herbs in preparation for broiling. There were potatoes roasting and a salad in progress.

And no Thomas.

She changed her clothes. Black had hardly seemed appropriate for an event as uplifting as Dorothy's last stand. She put on cropped pants and an oversize dark red T-shirt and let her hair hang loose around her face. Her necklace was a double strand of papier-mâché watermelon slices and her earrings matching hoops of watermelon seeds.

And still there was no Thomas.

She had just finished making dessert, her mother's favorite Key lime pie, when Thomas walked through the door.

"If you were a drinking man, I'd say you needed a drink," she said.

Thomas felt completely drained; there was nothing left of him. He had watched Dorothy's coffin being lowered into the ground, a simple pine coffin that held the remains of one of the finest women he had ever known, and he had felt such despair that he had wanted to throw himself in after her.

He hadn't wanted to come home. In the past few days the

tension in his apartment had been nearly as thick as the tension in the church today. Garnet was impossible to ignore. He was sure she had no idea how aware he was of every move she made, every sensuous, provocative move. She couldn't know how his eyes followed her, how his traitorous body reacted to her presence, how desperately he wanted to talk with her, touch her, replenish himself with her warmth and wisdom.

But he owed her more than that. He owed her a life free of his inadequacies. He could not bind her to him in any way; she had to be able to leave when the time was right. In the meantime, he had to keep his distance.

But how could he keep his distance at this moment, with Garnet gazing at him and her earthy Garden of Eden smile flooding the room with light? How could he keep his distance when she was not about to keep hers?

"Since you're not a drinking man," she said, "how about hot cider? It's all made."

He wanted to turn and run. After the funeral he had found a hundred excuses to avoid coming home. He should. have found a thousand.

"Thomas?" She walked toward him, frowning. "Are you all right?"

"I'm fine."

She stopped just an arm's length away. "You're burned-out," she said. "I know the signs, preacher man. You've given your last for today. Sit down." She pointed at the closest armchair. "Sit and let me take care of you, starting with some cider."

"You don't need to wait on me."

She tossed her head, and her smile widened. "Sure I do. This is my party. We're having a wake for Dorothy. Just you and me, and probably Dorothy, looking on from above."

He wanted to protest again, but she had already gone into the kitchen. He sank into the chair. He did not have the strength to leave. God help him, he had never had the strength to do what was right.

His eyes were closed when she returned. His hair fell across his forehead, and he had managed to loosen his tie.

But he looked like a warrior who had returned from a battle so terrible he would never be the same man again. She set his cider on the table beside him. When he didn't move to take it, she squatted to look at him, resting her hand on his arm.

"Thomas, that funeral was the most wonderful thing that's happened in the Corners in years. Those boys stood together without a fight or even an angry word. I know you must be exhausted, but I hope you realize how important that was. There's still hope here. Maybe all hell will break loose tomorrow, but today there was hope. And that was something."

He opened his eyes. For once her face was devoid of all defenses. Her expression was earnest, her lovely mobile mouth rounded in entreaty.

"It wasn't enough," he said.

"No? Well, you didn't save the world, that's true. But this little corner of it looked brighter for a while."

He wanted to deny even that much, but he couldn't. He reached for the cider and swallowed some as she watched. It was hot and spicy, and it spread warmth in its wake, chasing away some of the chill that had felt almost natural.

"Your problem, Reverend Stonehill, is that nobody ever taught you how to celebrate. How can you possibly slog through life without celebrating the good things that come along? Even the church has more pizzazz than that. For every Good Friday, there's an Easter."

He searched her eyes.

"I'm sorry I doubted you," she said softly. "No, that's not quite true. I never doubted you. I just doubted that even you could pull off something this impossible. But you did, and I'm sorry."

"I don't want an apology."

"Too bad." She smiled. "Seems to me there's a lot of things you say you don't want, but I think you're lying to yourself."

"Garnet-"

"For instance, I think you want to rest right now and let some of your sadness drain away. Then I think you want a good dinner with good company." She began to untie his shoes.

"Garnet-"

"I think you really want to be quiet and relax. You want me to wait on you a little, maybe turn on some soft music and dim the lights before I go and broil the steak. You want to sit here and remind yourself that something good happened today until you feel it inside you a little more." She slipped off his shoes.

"No one ever taught you the meaning of the word no."

"And you won't be the one who does, so relax."

He didn't want to feel better. Feeling better was dangerous. It made him believe that life could be good, that he had something to offer in return for what he got. But she was gone before he could protest again. Gone just far enough that he could still hear the husky music of her voice murmuring love songs with the radio.

His body responded to the sound of her voice as it had responded to her presence. His desires were still imprisoned deep inside him; only his ability to relieve them had disappeared. The torments of hell existed inside him, and there was no escape. The connection between desire and fulfillment had somehow been lost, and he was doomed to suffer until death.

He shut his eyes again and willed himself to relax. He could get through this evening as he had gotten through others. Garnet would back away if he remained uncommunicative. He didn't want to hurt her, but there was more hurt just around the corner if he let himself respond. He had nothing to give her, just as, in a different way, he'd had nothing to give Patricia. But the biggest difference between the man he was and the man he once had been was that now he knew the truth about himself.

He was a fraud and a liar.

In the kitchen Garnet sang along with the radio. Under the broiler the steak spat and crackled. She put the finishing touches on the salad and tossed it as she kept her eye on the oven. But beneath all the bustle and good spirits was a certain anxiety that, despite all her plans and intentions, Thomas was not going to respond.

He had come to her fresh from Dorothy's hospital bed, and he had shared himself in a way he never had before. She had rewarded him by doubting his abilities. She hadn't trusted him. She had let fear for his safety stand between them. Now it was too late to go back to those moments of sharing.

She turned off the broiler and finished setting the table. Then, when everything was done, she went into the living room to tell Thomas.

He was half reclining on the sofa, asleep. In repose his face looked younger, less the Roman soldier, more the man. But sleep, which should have been rejuvenating, seemed to suck something essential from him. As she watched, his head turned restlessly, as if he was following movement with his closed eyes.

She knelt beside him, studying his face. He looked younger, but even more troubled. She wondered what he was living or reliving, what fear or memory had him in its grip-

"Thomas?" She touched his arm. "Thomas?"

He jerked upright. His hand grasped her wrist, and she gasped from shock.

"Patricia?"

She shook her head. "You were dreaming. Thomas, you're hurting me!"

He seemed disoriented. "No... I can't—"

She wrenched her arm from his grip. "I'm not Patricia. I'm Garnet. You were dreaming."

His eyes focused slowly. He saw Garnet, nothing like Patricia, alive and vibrant and... hurt. He reached for her hand. "I'm sorry. I'm so sorry. I saw..."

"What?" She cradled her throbbing wrist with her other hand. "What on earth did you see?"

"The man who killed her."

She forgot her own pain. "Oh, Thomas." She leaned toward him. "I'm sorry. But I'm glad I woke you."

He shut his eyes.

"You said she died in a fight for her purse," Garnet said. She touched his cheek in sympathy. "Did they find the man?" She didn't know what else to ask. She didn't know how Patricia had died, or even why, exactly. Except for that one fact, she knew nothing at all about his past.

"No." He turned away, as if to escape her touch.

She refused to allow it. She followed him, her stroking hand offering the comfort he didn't seem to want. "You said you saw the man who killed her. Then the police know who it was?"

"They don't know anything. I don't know anything!" He pushed her hand away. He could not tolerate her touch. His throat was blocked with emotion; his head was threatening to explode. And her touch, the soft warmth of her hands, was threatening to send him over the edge.

"Then it was just a figure in the shadows?"

"I don't want to talk about it." He sat up straight and opened his eyes.

"Well, I do," she said softly. "Because it's eating you alive. And I'm not going to let that happen. You don't deserve it."

"You don't know what I deserve." He rose on unsteady legs and found his way to the window. The room, which had seemed pleasantly warm when he'd first come in, now seemed unbearably hot. He opened the window and stared out at the gray streets below.

"You don't deserve to suffer," she said. "I've tried leaving you alone. I thought you'd tell me about your past in your own good time. But you won't. I know that now. You'll keep it locked inside you to fester. I'm tired of being shut out."

"Are you?" He turned. "Believe me, it's for the best. You don't want to be where I am, Garnet. It's not a fit place for any human being, especially not one like you."

"Like me?"

"That's right. You're so full of life, and I'm so full of regrets."

She folded her arms. She was standing beside him, but not close enough to touch. She knew what a mistake that would be. "Tell me about them."

"Leave it alone."

"No. I don't think so. I think it's time we faced each other the way we really are. You see shadows in your dreams? I see them every waking day. I see them every time I look at you. I want to see the real Thomas Stonehill. I deserve that much."

"You don't know what you're asking."

"I do know. Exactly."

He turned away again and slammed the window shut. Then he leaned against it, his cheek against the cool glass, and shut his eyes.

He had no right to keep his past from her. Not anymore. Their marriage had never been real, yet in more ways than he could have guessed, it bordered on reality. If he'd learned anything from his years with Patricia, it was the mistake of not sharing. Patricia had died because he had kept the most essential parts of himself from her.

"You look at me, and what do you see?" he asked.

She felt for words, discarded them. "A voice crying in the wilderness," she said at last.

"You've been to Deering Hills to see Candy and Francis. Have you passed the Deering Hills Community Church?"

"It's not possible to go through Deering and not pass the church. The town's practically built around it."

"I was pastor there for six years."

She whistled softly. The mega church was a phenomenon. It sat on a hill like an ancient temple. The parking lot took up a square block. A fleet of buses and vans was parked along the roadside to gather in the faithful on Sunday mornings.

"We had six thousand people on our local mailing list," he said, "and another six thousand nationwide who subscribed to my sermon series. The attendance on Sundays doubled the first year after I was called. We went to three services the second year, two in the morning, one in the evening. The third year I began my own radio show to reach the people we couldn't fit in the pews. My fourth we added two wings and knocked out a wall to double the capacity of the sanctuary. During my final year we were looking into a television ministry."

"And then something happened," she said.

He faced her. "I always wanted to go into the ministry. My family is influential. One brother is a vice president in the family bank. The other is an attorney in an old, old Philadelphia firm. I was the youngest, the one who didn't fit in. Eventually my parents saw that I wasn't going to change my mind. I wanted a pulpit, and I wanted to be heard. So I went to seminary, but my father told me that if I was going to pursue this nonsense, I'd better be the best damn minister in the business."

"And were you?"

"I went to seminary at Harvard. I did postgraduate work at Yale. I interned in one of the largest churches in New York, and while I was there, I married the bishop's daughter. Patricia's mother died when Patricia was a teenager, and she took over her mother's duties without a blink of an eye. She was perfectly suited to become the wife of an upcoming star in the denomination. She knew exactly what to say, what to do, in any situation. She could listen and lead-unobtrusively, of course—and she could entertain. She looked wonderful in the front pew every Sunday, refined, feminine, prayerful. The only thing she couldn't do was get my attention."

He turned to the window. "She wanted children. I was in agreement, just as long as she assumed full responsibility. Children are an asset to a minister's image, but congregations don't, as a rule, understand that they also need some of a father's time. As it turned out, it didn't matter. Patricia couldn't get pregnant. We were never sure exactly why. She had several problems that were corrected, and I had none. We followed all the rules. But she never conceived."

"That must have been difficult for you both."

"I didn't have time to be concerned. In a way, I guess, I was relieved. I was climbing the ladder so quickly I didn't want anything to slow me down. And Patricia was such an asset, I didn't really want her to be sidelined by children. But she wasn't relieved. She was devastated. I realize now that she saw motherhood as a role that had nothing to do with her image as a minister's wife. She knew by then that she would never really have my attention. I was focused totally on my career. She expected children to give her the love I didn't have time for. When she couldn't have them, her life no longer had meaning."

"But there were other things she could have done."

"She knew that." He watched Garnet's image in the glass. She was standing just behind him now. He turned so the real woman was visible.

"She tried to talk to me," he said. "She really tried. I made promises and didn't keep them. There was always a meeting I had to attend, a hospital to visit, a sermon to prepare. There was never time to get away with her to plan our lives. My life was fine the way it was. I refused to understand that hers was not."

He was still facing her, but he shut his eyes again. "Then one evening she came to the church to see me. She never made it to my study, but I found out later that she had come to tell me she was leaving me. She had confided that much to a friend. Afterward, the friend made sure to let me know. The police put together what must have happened after Patricia got out of her car. She started toward the front door. When she got there, she was accosted by someone. There was a struggle. That much we know. She wasn't the kind to struggle, but I think by then she was distraught. She was tired of standing by and letting others rob her of everything that mattered. So when the man went after her purse, she fought him. The police think he shoved her. Hard. What we know for sure is that she fell backward and hit her head on the corner of the entryway. She probably died instantly."

"Thomas." She didn't know what else to say.

"I stayed at church until almost midnight. I wanted my sermon the next morning to be perfect. There was to be a meeting of the board of deacons after the service. The television ministry was to be discussed. I wanted everyone going into that meeting to know that I was worth whatever funds we had to raise, that my ministry would be a credit to the church. When I came out the front door, I stumbled. At first I didn't know what had caught my foot. Then I saw her...."

"I'm so, so sorry, Thomas." She put her hand on his arm.

He jerked away. "Why? It's fine to be sorry for Patricia. She died without having a chance to live. I made sure of that. But don't be sorry for me. I brought it all on myself with my greed and vanity. I stole her life and used it for my own purposes!"

"She had choices, too."

"And when she decided to exercise them, she died."

"But how could that be your fault? You didn't know she was coming to see you that night. Maybe if she'd stood up to you sooner, she'd be alive today."

"It was not her fault. I rode over her. I molded her into the image I thought I needed in my ministry, just like her father did before me. She never stood a chance. I never once thought about her needs. Don't you see what that says about the man I was? I wasn't thinking about her, I wasn't thinking about the people I was ministering to, I was thinking about myself. And Patricia died because of my sins!"

"You have this all out of kilter."

He didn't meet her eyes. Some part of him wanted to believe her. A larger part knew he was guilty and would remain so until the day he died. "I've had years to put it in perspective. I resigned my pastorate the day of Patricia's funeral, and then I left the state. I spent two years wandering. As far as my family and friends knew, I was dead. I took any job that came my way, slept in doorways if nothing did. I drank my way through a hundred gallons of rotgut liquor, but I sobered up after six months. I wasn't even a successful drunk. Alcohol just made my nightmares worse."

"What happened then? What brought you here?"

"I found out that you can't run away from who you are."

"And who you are is a man of God, with God's message to proclaim."

He met her eyes this time. "No."

"But isn't that where your story is leading? Isn't that why you came back? Because you knew you had something to offer? That your own experiences had taught you about the pain, and you wanted to start a church in a place where you were really needed?"

"That part's true."

"Then I don't understand."

"I'm not a man of God, Garnet. There hasn't been any God inside me since Patricia died."

She still didn't understand. But she did understand that now his eyes were not empty of emotion. They brimmed with it. They burned with it.

"I'll make it simple," he said. "I stand up on Sundays and preach. And I say what's in my heart. I talk about ways people can change their lives. I talk about the community coming together to make things better for everyone. I tell stories about men and women who have done that throughout the ages. But I don't pretend those messages come from God. Because I gave up on

God the day He gave up on Patricia. I can no longer speak with assurance about something I don't really believe in."

"You don't believe in God?"

"That's as close to the truth as anything, I guess."

He was struggling to hide his feelings, but nothing could hide his torture. "I don't believe you," she said, and she didn't.

"Sometimes I don't believe myself. I don't believe I have the gall to speak of things I no longer understand. But when I stopped speaking of those things, I was in hell. When I came here and began to speak of them again, I put hell on hold. I can make a difference in the Corners. Maybe I can even keep someone else from suffering the way I suffered, the way Patricia must have suffered."

"But how did you... ? How could you... ?"

"I woke up one morning and realized that even if I have nothing else left of all those years in the ministry, I could still do some good in the world. I've been trained to counsel, trained to preach and organize. I could use that training or I could sleep in doorways. And put that way, the choice seemed simple."

She still didn't believe him. She knew he was telling the truth as he saw it, but there was more behind his words. She could sense as much, even if she didn't know what, exactly.

"So I resumed a life of sorts, here in the Corners. I send cards to my family from time to time, and they do the same. They'd prefer not to acknowledge my existence, but they're too upstanding to give in to that impulse. Most of my friends and colleagues still don't know where I am, and I've preferred to keep it that way."

"You've been so alone."

"Now you know what an impostor I am," he said, as if she hadn't spoken. "You wanted the truth, and you've got it. Our marriage isn't the only thing I've faked. My entire life is as counterfeit as a three-dollar bill."

She looked at him for a long time. She saw the same man she

had known. A man of integrity. A man of courage. A man of compassion. The blue eyes that could snap with life when he preached were desolate now, as if by admitting the truth he had doomed himself. But they were the same eyes.

"We have a celebration dinner waiting for us," she said at last.

He shook his head. "What do we have to celebrate?"

"The first day of our marriage."

He shook his head again.

"I was married to a stranger," she said. "Now I'm married to someone made of flesh and blood. And I like this man better."

"Garnet..."

"Thomas." She smoothed his hair off his forehead. He brushed her hand away, but she wasn't intimidated. She touched his cheek. "Something wonderful happened at the church today, even if you can't see it right now. You made a difference. Dorothy made a difference. Come with me. We'll toast Dorothy with mineral water and eat our meal in her honor. And we'll do it as two human beings with a thousand flaws between them who are still, despite everything, trying to do what's right."

He stared at her. He had told her his darkest secrets, secrets he had never admitted to anyone. And still she touched him. She strove to heal his pain.

He took her wrist, but he couldn't push it away. "I could hurt you, the way I hurt Patricia," he said. "Even in the short time we'll be together."

"I'll take my chances."

"Why?"

She shrugged. "Why not? Because you've admitted you're human? That you made mistakes? That you have doubts? Those are just more reasons to care about you."

"Don't care about me!"

"I'm afraid you're too late." She withdrew her hand, but she felt as if she was still touching him. She wanted to ease his pain, to wipe away all his terrible memories and his guilt.

But she had done all she could tonight. She knew better than to say any more. And she knew better than to touch him again, even though she ached to give him solace.

"Now will you come and have dinner with me?" she asked.

He watched her start toward the kitchen. She had disappeared before he realized that he was going to follow. He waited for the all too familiar feeling of defeat. He had failed again, failed to warn her away, failed to make her understand his sins.

But the feeling didn't come.

"Thomas?"

Even as he tried to steel himself against her, he was drawn toward the sound of her voice.

10

Outside the window a truck gunned its engine in sync with the out-of-tune morning chimes from St. Michael's blocks away. In fifteen minutes Garnet would be late for work. She had awakened late after a restless night, and judging from a peek at the living room couch, Thomas hadn't awakened at all.

She imagined his night had been restless, too. Their celebration dinner had lasted into the wee hours. She had borne the greater part of the conversation, but he had relaxed as the evening wore on. She knew how painful his revelations had been, but she believed—or hoped—that it had helped him a little to tell her about Patricia.

It had helped her. She paused in the middle of twisting her hair on top of her head and examined the face staring back at her. She had been so wrong about his first marriage. Thomas did not look at her and wish she was Patricia; he did not even want her to be like Patricia. He had loved his wife—his sorrow would not be as profound if he hadn't— but she didn't think he wished for marriage to someone like Patricia again. He needed a woman who would stand up to him, who would insist that she be included in his life. Ironically, when Patricia had finally rebelled, she had died.

The face of a brash, worldly-wise woman stared at Garnet, but this morning she could see more than the obvious. The woman in the mirror had blamed Thomas's rejection on herself. She had believed herself to be the cause of Thomas's impotence. He had not wanted to make love to her because she had failed, just as she often had, to be good enough, bright enough, attractive enough.

The worthless teenager who had turned to drugs and alcohol, to absences from school and unprotected sex, stared at her. Garnet knew she had come a long way in the intervening years, but apparently she had not come far enough. She could still let her own perceived inadequacies drag her down. She could still blame herself for things that were not her fault.

"So grow up already," she said, turning away from the mirror.

In the living room she noted that Thomas slept on. Finn had called almost half an hour earlier to tell her that he wouldn't be able to walk her to work. He was ill and furious at his body for forcing him to take the day off. She had promised him she would let Thomas accompany her. But Thomas had never gotten up, and she wasn't about to wake him. Not when he seemed to be sleeping so peacefully.

His arm was thrown over one stubbly cheek. The covers were twisted around his hips, and his pajama shirt was unbuttoned. She studied him, but not dispassionately. Naming what she felt when she looked at Thomas wasn't easy. Desire wasn't broad enough. Love was too frightening. Yearning? Well, perhaps that was closest.

She yearned to be held in his arms. They were strong arms, arms that could hold back the world as well as embrace it. She yearned for the intimacy of passionate nights and lazy, sensuous mornings.

Thomas was all man, yet he claimed not to be able to

consummate their marriage. What secrets were still locked away inside him?

They were married. Husband and wife. But she had never seen him without his clothes. She let her gaze rest on him for another moment; she knew if he awoke, he would see longing in her eyes.

Thomas slept on as she finally closed the door quietly behind her. She left the building through the church, although there was another exit. She supposed it was silly, but she wanted to see if the room had changed somehow after yesterday's triumph. The impact of Dorothy's funeral would be felt in the Corners for weeks to come. She wondered if success lingered in the very rows where the two gangs had sat.

The church didn't look any different, but Garnet walked through it and felt different. She felt hopeful, a luxury she had carefully schooled herself against in days past. She worked hard to change things, but she rarely let herself believe that things could change on the most basic level. Believing was too painful. Now she was close to believing anyway.

She locked the front door behind her, instinctively scanning the street before she turned the lock one last notch. She planned to take precautions, but this morning she wasn't really worried about her safety. There had been no trouble on her walks with Finn. And she hoped, after yesterday, the MidKnights and the Coroners had better things to think about than harassing her.

There were cars passing, it was nearing rush hour. But there was no one on the street who looked as if he didn't belong there.

She started down the steps. It was a rare, crisp November morning. Yesterday's drizzle had stopped, and the sun was peeking between the units of Wilford Heights. No one was sleeping in Kensington Park. She could almost pretend that all the city's homeless had been taken care of for the night at the Kensington Hotel and places like it.

She said good morning to a grandmother with a stroller and

"They're cleansing the wound now, but she'll be able to go in an hour or so, just as soon as the police are finished taking her statement. Do you want to come and get her, or do you want me to drop her off?"

Thomas hung up after assuring Tex that he would be by to pick up Garnet himself.

He had one hour. He could go and make a fool of himself at Garnet's bedside, or he could find Andre. The choice seemed simple. Perhaps Garnet had seen a red bandanna, but it wasn't the Coroners who were angry at her. She had helped Francis, one of their own, when she had delivered Candy's baby. Unless they were trying to confuse this issue for purposes he didn't understand, there was only one explanation for what she had seen. The MidKnights wanted to throw suspicion on the Coroners. And they had done it by false flagging, by showing Coroners red when they shot at Garnet.

She could have been killed. He found himself in the chair beside the telephone table. Shock washed over him. She could have been killed. Yesterday's truce in the war between the Coroners and the MidKnights had lasted only a few hours. Now it was in full swing again, and Garnet was still a target.

She could have been killed, and he could have been left with nothing. Until that moment he hadn't realized how much she filled his life. She was light and warmth. He had married her to protect her, but she had never needed him the way he needed her. His contribution to her life was debatable. Despite their marriage, she had almost died today. But her contribution to *his* life was so far-reaching that he couldn't even see an end to it.

Except the ending that would come when she left him.

He found Andre in a boarded-up house the city had promised to tear down ten months before. When they needed a private place to gather, kids in Deering Hills got keys to their parents' summer cottages. MidKnights had no keys or cottages, nor did they need them. They had made this house theirs, despite numerous complaints to the authorities. The outside walls were sprayed with graffiti to warn away strangers. When the city finally got around to tearing down the house, the block would become a battlefield.

Thomas took the steps to the porch two at a time. The door rattled under the assault of his fist. There were two shorties lounging on the porch throwing signs at each other. They were the youngest of gang members, no older than thirteen, and the elaborate hand signs that proclaimed their membership in the MidKnights looked like the slapping, clapping games of another more innocent generation.

"Hey, you can't go in there," one of the boys said when Thomas shoved the door open.

"You're supposed to be in school," Thomas said. "Get going."

"Yeah?" One of the kids stood. He didn't stretch to Thomas's shoulder. Thomas stared at him. The kid rested his hands on his hips, but he didn't meet Thomas's eyes.

"Why aren't you at school?" Thomas asked.

"'Cause I don't like them teachers at the middle school."

"Why not?"

"They be saying the Knights are bad."

"If you don't show up, they'll think the Knights made you stay away."

The kid cursed like a pro. "I don't gotta listen to you."

Thomas stared at him. "I think I know your grandmother," he said at last.

The kid squirmed.

"In fact, I know I do," Thomas said. "Letitia Whitney. Right?"

"So?"

"So, when I leave here, I'm going to give Letitia a call and tell her we had this talk."

"So?" The kid cursed and squirmed some more, scuffing his toe against the porch.

"So maybe if you leave right now you won't be more than an hour late for classes. Letitia doesn't have to know about our chat."

The other kid stood. "Don't let him—"

"And you're Annie Wade's kid, aren't you?" Thomas asked.

The two boys scurried off the porch. There was no guarantee they were going to school, but at least they started in the right direction.

"I'm going to call the attendance office this afternoon," Thomas shouted after them. They walked faster.

"What you doing here?"

Thomas turned to find Andre in the doorway. His hair was in neat cornrows that hung halfway to his shoulders. Thomas was struck with the young man's proud male beauty. With his fierce dark eyes and mahogany skin, he looked like an African deity. He never should have had to fight the battles of urban America. His fitness for other things, for anything he chose, had never seemed more apparent.

"Garnet was nearly killed today. By a bullet from a Knight's gun. Or am I boring you with old news?"

Andre lounged in the doorway, smoking a cigarette. Behind him, Thomas could see movement. Andre was not alone. Thomas didn't care.

"I heard," Andre said.

"You heard right."

"What makes you think it was us who done it?"

"There was no reason for anyone else to do it and pretend it was one of the Coroners."

"Maybe it *was* them."

Thomas fought to read Andre's expression. He knew that the most important communication would not happen with words. There was only so much that Andre could say. But his eyes spoke volumes.

"I don't think so," Thomas said. "And you don't, either."

Andre shrugged.

"You didn't plan it, did you?" Thomas asked.

Andre shrugged again.

"So who did? And don't shrug again, damn it. You're upset about it, too."

"I don't know."

Thomas was silent, assessing Andre's answer. Then he nodded. "Okay."

"She's not supposed to get hurt."

Thomas was surprised Andre had admitted that much. "No?"

Andre tossed the butt of his cigarette into the bushes beyond the porch. "That's what I said."

"Well, she was."

"Yeah. And I don't like somebody busting a cap like that without my say so."

"Can you find out who it was?"

Andre's head barely moved, but Thomas took it as a sign. "The police should be told," Thomas said.

"Cops?" Andre snorted. "We take care of our own business, Padre."

"It's not your business to take care of. There are courts and higher justice."

Andre folded his arms. "Higher justice? Like your God, maybe?"

Thomas didn't answer.

"You don't say much about God," Andre said. "I hear you talk a lot, but I don't hear you talking about God. You believe in God, Padre? Or just in trying to pretty up the Corners?"

It didn't surprise Thomas that Andre had picked up on his greatest failing. The young gang leader was highly intelligent, and years of life in the Corners had taught him to pick out anyone's weakness and twist it to his advantage. He had survived, even risen to be a leader, by his abilities.

"I believed with all my heart until a few years ago," Thomas said. "Then my wife was murdered, and I didn't believe anything anymore."

"What kind of preacher can you be?"

"The honest kind. The kind who doesn't pretend the world's filled with easy answers."

"You walking and talking a lie."

Thomas looked past the young man's ridicule. "You understand what I'm talking about," he said. "You're a lot like me. You'd like to believe, too. You've seen things in your life that make it hard. You've done things you're ashamed of."

"I'm not ashamed of nothing."

"You're a better person than you believe you are."

"You don't know nothing about it."

"I think I do."

"You can leave now."

Thomas nodded. "Whoever shot at Garnet should go before a court of law. Will you think about that?"

Andre didn't answer. Thomas wondered how much of what he had said had fallen on deaf ears. He hoped none of it. He felt a strong kinship with the young man. He and this product of the Corners streets had a lot in common.

~

"Tell me you're done," Garnet said. The policeman who had come to the emergency room to get her statement was Finn's partner, Jake.

Jake, who had the dark good looks of a television cop, grinned. "Just about."

"I lost blood today, pal. I've got to go eat a hamburger or something."

"Yeah, right. I've lost more blood shaving."

"Well, go nick yourself again and leave me in peace."

"Just one more question about the gun you say you saw."

"Say I saw? If you don't believe there was a gun, go pry a dozen bullets out of the wall of the discount store!"

"Garnet, Garnet." Jake shook his head. They were old friends. Tex and Finn had tried repeatedly to match them up, but Garnet had never had the urge to be hooked to a cop. Nor, of course, had she ever had the urge to marry a minister.

She looked up, and the minister himself was standing in the doorway. He looked surprisingly the worse for wear. "Don't come in," she said. "Not if you're going to read me the riot act, Thomas. I've been through enough."

"Are you really all right?"

She could have drowned in the emotion in his eyes. She stood on unsteady legs. "Fine. Really."

He crossed the room and enfolded her in his arms. He didn't care that a cop was looking on. He needed to hold her to be sure she was really all right. She seemed to melt against him. The sensation was delicious. She was pliable, boneless.

She was unconscious.

"Damn." Thomas lifted a sagging Garnet in his arms and carried her to a gurney in the corner. "Get a nurse," he told Jake. "What are you doing questioning her when she's in this shape?"

Jake got up. "She seemed fine. She insisted."

"She would have." Thomas rubbed Garnet's hands as Jake left. After a minute her eyes opened.

She looked at him for a long time, as if she was piecing together this final chapter of her morning drama. "I can't believe I did that," she said at last.

"Garnet, you're going to stay here overnight so they can keep an eye on you. I'm going to insist!"

"Not a chance. It's a reaction. That's all."

Thomas looked up to see Tex in the doorway, with Jake right behind her. "She fainted," he said.

"She's been through a tough time. It's probably just starting to hit her."

"She needs to stay here overnight."

"They've got people sleeping in hallways here. I think she'd be better off somewhere else, someplace where she could get some rest."

Thomas realized there was wisdom in Tex's words. He looked at Garnet. Her eyes were closed, and she looked very pale. He thought of their war zone apartment and discarded that possibility immediately. "I know a place," he said finally.

"Hawaii?" Garnet asked. "Bermuda?"

"Close. Are you up to a short trip?"

She opened her eyes, and surprisingly, they filled with tears. "I would like to get out of here for a while," she said softly.

He pushed her hair off her forehead. Until that moment he hadn't even realized his hand was trembling.

Thomas's marriage to Patricia Collins had been celebrated before five hundred family members and friends. Their wedding gift from her father the bishop had been a small cottage on a lake just three hours from Deering Hills. Before the wedding he had warned them of the need for a minister's family to get away from time to time. Owning the cottage gave them few excuses not to.

Thomas had used every one of those few excuses over and over again.

Now, as he pulled onto the gravel road that led to the lake he tried not to remember the times he had refused to come here. The cottage had been too far away. He had been too busy, too invaluable, too obsessed with his own importance. Finally they had found a renter, with the intention of using the rental income for occasional nights out together. Those nights had been few and far between, too.

"Are you going to tell me where we're going?" Garnet asked.

He debated not telling the truth, but even to be tactful, he couldn't lie. "There's a lake up ahead. The house we'll stay in belongs to Patricia's father now, but it used to be Patricia's and mine when we were married. I gave it back to the bishop after Patricia died. He only took it on the condition that I would come here whenever I wanted."

"Did you come here often with her?"

"Almost never."

"And since?"

"Not at all."

He slowed to a standstill. The brush beside the road ahead, rustled visibly. As they watched, two deer, a stag and a doe crossed in front of them.

Garnet put her hand on Thomas's arm and held her breath. The deer took their time crossing, as if no one had ever mentioned hunting in their presence. "Do you think there are others?" she asked.

"I've never been here when I didn't see deer. Everyone on the lake posts their property. I think the animals sense it."

"Hey, maybe we should post the Corners." She smiled, to let him know she was teasing. "This is wonderful."

She still looked pale, but the stress had seemed to disappear from her face with each mile they traveled. Thomas covered her hand with his. The deer passed from view, but the oaks and poplars lining the road swayed in the breeze against a brilliant blue sky. "Winter comes earlier here than it does in the Corners. We might see snow."

"Snow that hasn't already turned to slush." Suddenly she yearned for it. "There was a park across from the hospital where I took my training. I used to get up early on mornings when there'd been snow just to go over and look at it before everyone trampled it." She looked at him, embarrassed to have revealed something so sentimental. "That probably sounds silly."

"It sounds like you."

"No, too sappy."

"You're gifted at extracting beauty from little things."

She tossed her head. "Well, if you don't extract it from little things, you might not find any at all. There aren't too many Taj Mahals in the city."

He started the car again, and her hand fell to her side. He didn't want the moment of intimacy to end. He smiled at her. "There aren't any Taj Mahals here, either, but the sunsets are spectacular."

She felt as if he had filled all the bitterly cold places inside her with sunlight. "I wish you'd smile more often," she said. "It does funny things to me."

"I'll smile nonstop for the next few days."

"Few days? We can't stay a few days. You've got a church, and I've got a clinic."

"Tex is taking care of Mother and Child. Greg is organizing Sunday's service without me."

"What?" She turned, ignoring the rasp of the seat belt against her bandaged shoulder. "Thomas, that's crazy. Tex can't function without me. And Greg hasn't had any experience—"

His smile disappeared. "You are not indispensable, Garnet. And neither am I. The clinic and the church aren't monuments to us. If they don't survive while we're gone then they weren't meant to."

She sat back and let his words sink in. "If I'm not indispensable," she said as they entered a clearing, "then what in the hell am I?"

"A woman who needs a few days away from gangs and bullets and death threats."

"And who are you?"

"Her husband," he said.

"Tell me you need a few days away, too."

He needed a few days with her. He needed to be sure she was all right. He needed to be sure she would continue to be. But he couldn't tell her that, because it was too revealing. "I do," he said.

"The last time you said those words, they got you into more trouble than you'd bargained for."

"They might again." He stopped the car. The cottage was just ahead of them. He turned and touched her hair. "For the next few days we take care of ourselves and each other. We don't worry about anyone or anything else."

"Like two married people on vacation?"

"Yes."

She didn't ask how married they would be. Suddenly everything seemed possible. "Will you feel strange being here with me?"

"I've hardly ever been here," he assured her. "I'll only feel as strange as you do."

"Then you won't feel strange at all, because I think we were meant to come here."

"Meant to come here sounds surprisingly religious coming from you."

"I might surprise you in a number of ways." She smiled at him again and thought of days alone together in a lakeside cottage. Suddenly the world was a brighter place than she had believed it to be that morning.

11

The cottage was rustic, haphazardly built of logs and stone throughout a generation. Rooms had been added without thought of easy access or privacy. The living room, with a wall of windows looking over the lake, stretched the length of the house. The kitchen had to be entered through a bedroom. The second bedroom was perched on top of the first and reached by a steep stairway in a corner of the kitchen. A third bedroom was set away from the main part of the house with only a covered walkway to link it.

Garnet completed her tour while Thomas carried groceries and suitcases from the car.

"This is a great house," she said, when he brought in the last load.

"I always liked it. It has character. It's been painted recently, and the furniture's been changed around. It hardly looks the same."

"Does Patricia's... the bishop know we're here?"

"I called him."

"I'm glad he wasn't using it."

Thomas thought about that brief phone call. Patricia's father had sounded surprised that Thomas had asked permission. The cottage still belonged to Thomas, he'd said, and the bishop had just seen to its maintenance.

"Do you talk to him often?" Garnet asked.

"I didn't talk to anyone for almost two years. When I decided to rejoin the living, I got back in touch. That's how I got my denomination to finance starting the Church of the Samaritan. They agreed to fund a small salary for me and expenses for the building for three years. By then the church should be able to survive on its own. And after that the bishop expects me to take another big church and go back to the life I led before Patricia died."

"And will you?"

He turned. Garnet's question had been asked in a deceptively casual voice, but he sensed emotion behind her words, "What do you think?"

She shrugged.

"You still don't think I have a commitment to the Corners, do you?"

"This could just be a very colorful chapter in your life, Thomas. Minister loses wife, loses faith, and wrestles with demons on the hellish streets of the inner city. Then, when his faith in himself and his God returns, he goes back to preaching to the multitudes. With lots of new and dramatic anecdotes to spice up his sermons."

"I could do that." He dumped fruit into a wooden bowl on the kitchen table.

She reached for an apple. "Who could blame you? You could reach a hundred people in the suburbs for every one you reach in the Corners. Of course, they would be a hundred people with only a problem or two between them."

"Money solves a lot of problems, but it doesn't make life run smoothly. People get sick, have breakdowns, lose jobs or loved ones. Even in the suburbs." He took the apple from her hand. "You haven't washed this yet."

She forced a jaunty smile. "I like to live dangerously."

"So I've noticed." He strode to the sink and let the water run for a few moments before he plunged the apple under it.

"You never really answered my question."

"It was couched in preconceived notions and conceit."

"Conceit?"

He tossed her the apple. She caught it without flinching and dried it on the tail of her shirt.

"Conceit," he repeated. "You think you're the only person in the world who cares what happens in the Corners and places just like it? Guess again. You're just one."

"And you're one of the other half dozen or so?" She held up her hand. "Okay, okay. An exaggeration. I'll admit it."

"I care," he said. "And I'll be staying. If I ever have a large church again, it'll be the one I build on Wilford and Twelfth, one pebble at a time."

"On this pebble I build my church." She considered, then took a large bite of her apple. "That lacks something."

He leaned against the sink and dried his hands. "You're enough to drive a saint to sin."

"Exactly what I had in mind." She met his eyes. "There's a long line of women just like me in the Bible, Thomas. Eve, Delilah, Mary Magdalene..."

"Mary Magdalene didn't succeed."

"So men have proclaimed for centuries because it suited their purposes. But if she didn't, I'll just bet she livened up a saintly life or two along the way."

"You've certainly enlivened mine."

She took another bite of apple, but her heart nudged her rib cage. His expression was tender, as if the words that accompanied it had been a tribute. Her response lost most of its impact because she couldn't look at him anymore. "Well, our life together has been anything but boring."

"I could use a little boredom. No more phone calls telling me you've been shot at, for a start."

"Shot, not shot at." She struggled to be offhand. "Want to see my bandage?"

"Why didn't you wake me up this morning and tell me Finn couldn't go with you to work? Didn't you think I'd care?"

She turned to him. "Has that been bothering you? Of course that wasn't the reason. You just looked so peaceful, and I guess I was fooled by yesterday."

Suddenly all the shattered hopes of the past twenty-four hours were real again. She didn't have the strength to pretend anymore. "I believed... something good had come from that funeral. I felt safe."

"I *was* sleeping peacefully." He didn't add that his sleep had been undisturbed for the first time in a long time. He had confessed all his faults, all his sins, to Garnet, and she had taken them in stride. She didn't expect perfection from, him. She seemed to prefer honesty.

"And what good could you or Finn have done, anyway?" she asked. "I was paying attention to everything. The first time he passed me I even suspected the driver of that car might be up to no good. And I picked out a safe place on every block, so by the time that car turned the corner—" She swallowed. Her throat felt as if it had swollen shut. "By the time..."

"Garnet." He went over and knelt beside her, taking the forgotten apple from her hand.

"I'm sorry." Tears filled her eyes. "I don't know what's wrong with me."

"Don't you?" He pulled her against him. "You could have died this morning."

"I would have." She had no desire to resist. She put her arms around his neck and rested her cheek against his shirt. "Except that I saw the car coming out of the corner of my eye, so by the time he got a second round of shots off, I was lying at the bottom of some convenient cellar steps."

"Then he wasn't just a lousy shot?"

"He was trying hard, but the car was moving fast, and I was moving faster."

He stroked her hair. "You're so brave."

"No, just scared to death. I kept thinking I'd never told you that I care about you. I expect to die young. I've never believed in leaving any loose ends in my life. But there they were, the loosest ends of all."

"I know you care." He searched for more reassuring words. "You've been a good friend."

"I'm not a friend, Thomas." She pulled away a little so she could see his face. "I have friends. I play pinochle with them or go to the movies on Friday nights."

"And I don't play pinochle."

"You know what I'm saying."

He felt trapped, but hadn't he known that bringing her here would bolt the door behind him? And still he had brought her anyway. Not because she was a friend. Because he cared about her as he hadn't cared about anyone since Patricia.

Because he loved her.

He shut his eyes so she wouldn't see the truth. He felt as if someone had punched him in the stomach. He loved her. He, who was so unworthy.

"Thomas." She cradled his face in her hands. "Is it so bad that I care about you? I know we didn't plan it that way. You married me out of some misguided notion of keeping me safe, because you hadn't saved Patricia. Don't you think I see that? And I married you because I've always been alone, and just that once, it was too tempting not to let someone else shoulder some of the burdens of my life. But we've grown beyond that."

He opened his eyes. "Garnet—"

She couldn't let him speak. She had to push on, because she might never have the courage for this conversation again. "We've grown beyond those reasons. You matter to me now. I think about you when I'm not with you. I try to imagine what it would be like to be really married to you, heart and soul. And when I'm with you, I find excuses for being near you, for touching you or talking to you."

"Even if we wanted to try a real marriage..."

He let his words trail away. He couldn't choke out the words that should follow.

"You don't *try* a real marriage," she said softly. "You commit yourself for better or worse."

"I'm sure that's not what you told Ema."

"You're wrong. It is. And she did. Ema committed herself, but Ron didn't. She has nothing to be ashamed of. You and I do. We've been playing at something sacred. You've said as much yourself. But I don't want to play anymore, and I don't want to try a real marriage. I want to have one."

"And I can't give you that."

"Are you attracted to me? This isn't because you don't find me... appealing?"

He stood. "I find you appealing, damn it. It doesn't make any difference."

"You had a terrible thing happen to you, Thomas. It was bound to affect you. But you're on a different road now. Your life is different. That could be different, too."

He ran his fingers through his hair. "Let's not talk around it anymore. I'm *impotent*. We're talking about a man who can't make love to his wife, Garnet. Whether he's playing at marriage or wallowing in it. I can't make love to you, no matter how appealing you are. Something happens inside me. Some switch gets turned off, some defense goes up. I went for a thorough physical, and every cell of my body was poked and prodded. I'm in perfect health. I'll live to be a hundred, but I'll live those years celibate. It's just too bad I'm not a priest or a monk, isn't it?"

"You're afraid to try," she said. "You're afraid you'll prove your theory. Well, listen, you're talking to a nurse. I know a little about this. If you tell yourself enough times that you're impotent, you will be. You—"

"I don't need any two-bit psychology. I know it's in my head! It's just too bad it's not manifested there, isn't it? Because then I could claim you as my wife. And I'd like nothing better. If we're going to be honest, let's really be honest. I want you. I go to bed at night hard from wanting you. And I know as well as I know anything else in the world that if I try to make love to you, I won't be hard anymore!"

He wanted her. She was filled with triumph. "So what if that happens nine times out of ten? And what if the tenth time you succeed? What then?"

"What if it's ninety-nine times out of one hundred? What then? Could you stand the frustration? Would you feel anything for me by then except pity?"

"I don't feel anything like pity for you! And I never would. You're not a man to feel sorry for. You lost your wife in a terrible way, and you lost your faith. But you've climbed out of the hole you dug, and you're fighting back. Now it's time to fight back on this, too."

He shook his head as if one or both of them was crazy. "Can't you see? It shouldn't be a fight."

"But we can't have everything just the way we want it, can we? So we take what we've got, and we make it suit us." She stood and walked slowly toward him. "I suit you. I won't ever let you be pompous or self-important. I'll keep the gloom away when you come home feeling tired and defeated. I'll shake hands with your congregation on Sundays, but even better, I'll fight for them if they need me. I won't be Patricia. I can't be. But I'll be Garnet, and that'll be good enough."

"This has nothing to do with you suiting me!"

"But do I?" She put her hands on his shoulders. "You suit me. I love it when you touch me. And I love it when you bare your heart. I love watching you preach, because I know that under the sincerity, the passion and compassion, is the man who smiles at me over the dinner table, who sneaks my mystery novels and hums my favorite songs under his breath when he thinks I'm not listening."

She leaned against him. "You suit me, Thomas."

He covered her hands, as if to tear them from around his neck. But he loved the feel of her body against his. Her breasts pressed softly against his chest; her hips melted into his. The fragrance of her hair wrapped around him.

"And I suit you," she said. She pushed her hips more firmly against his. "You can't tell me I don't."

He wanted to tell her, but once again, he couldn't lie. She suited him too well. He hadn't married her just because he had failed to keep Patricia safe. He had married her because she was all the things he was not, and he had feared those things might die. He hadn't given his name to protect *a* woman. He had done it for *this* woman, a woman who had stirred him from the first moment he'd seen her.

"I don't care if we fail at making love," she said. "I don't care if we have to try a hundred times, or even a thousand. Will you give us a chance? Will you give this marriage a try?"

He could feel himself teetering on a threshold. And the voices in his head that screamed for him to run away were not loud enough. She pressed against him and rose on tiptoe. He shut his eyes as she kissed him; then, powerless to do otherwise, he groaned—in defeat, in victory—and kissed her back.

She was jubilant as his arms came around her. She had been so afraid he would reject her. She had never risked herself this way, because the stakes had never been this high. Now she let herself bask in the heat of his body, the strength of his arms. She had won this much.

"Garnet." There was nothing else for Thomas to say. His hands moved down her back. Even through a cotton T-shirt, her skin was warm and smooth. As he kissed her he traced the curve of her waist, the flare of her hips, the rounded perfection of her bottom. Her breasts tantalized his chest; her arms, velvet soft and utterly beguiling, brushed his cheeks as they tightened around his neck.

"I've never seen you without a shirt." She murmured the words against his lips. "And I want to now." She slid a hand between them and fingered his top button. "Will you look as sexy out of one as you do in it?"

He felt her fingers stroke the pulse point at the base of his neck, then feather over his throat to rest lightly at his collarbone before they played with the button again. "Your heart is racing," she whispered.

He couldn't answer. Conscious thought dissolved. He felt the first button give way. She trailed a finger along the skin she had exposed. The second button followed the first's example. So did the third and fourth. She kissed the base of his throat and murmured against it.

He felt her hands brush his chest, parting his shirt. He could feel each separate finger splayed across his rib cage. Her lips were warm and soft against his skin. His eyes closed, and without thinking he arched to give her better access.

She unfastened the remainder of the buttons with impatient swipes of her hand. Then she eased the shirt off his shoulders until it fell to the floor. "Thomas," she said, moving back to see him better, "you're beautiful."

"Aren't I supposed to tell you that?" His voice sounded strange. Hoarse and muffled.

"Not in the twenty-first century. Not unless the spirit moves you."

The spirit moved him. He lifted the hem of her shirt, a bright fuchsia, and slipped it over her breasts, over her upraised arms, over her head. Her skin was a warm rose, and her breasts, after he removed the bra, were the same provocative hue.

"You *are* beautiful," he said.

"Touch me." She moved closer, and her eyelids fluttered shut. "Tell me I'm beautiful with your hands."

He told himself he knew how she would feel against his palm, but reality was so much sweeter. He hadn't remembered that a woman could feel this way, that the differences he took for granted were so enticing, so overwhelmingly seductive.

She threw her head back and moaned as his thumb traced slow circles around one nipple. "Sweet and slow and perfect," she said. "This is perfect, Thomas."

The part of his mind that could still form words wondered how perfect their lovemaking would remain. He was aching for her already, a man who'd been celibate too long, face-to-face with the most enchanting temptress he had ever known. But what would happen when she was in his arms, pleading for release?

As if she knew his thoughts, she opened her eyes. "I want you, too," she whispered. "But maybe I'll be the one who doesn't please. That's always a possibility, isn't it? This takes so much trust."

He pulled her to him and felt her naked torso melt against his. Her hair danced over the backs of his hands; her lips caressed each place they touched. He slipped his hands inside the waistband of her panties, and the elastic stretched to accommodate him. His hands were filled with her flesh; his senses reeled at the onslaught. He was aware of fear, but more aware of desire. He wondered if he had ever wanted anything else as he wanted this.

"There's a bed in the next room," she said. "Our room."

He had never slept there with Patricia. She had always chosen the room upstairs, so he could prowl the downstairs at night without waking her. The bed downstairs was narrower and old-fashioned, made for lovers who wanted to spend the night entwined in each other's arms.

She led him by the hand. At the bedside she slipped off the rest of her clothes as naturally as if he had always intimately known her body. When she was naked except for a white patch of gauze and adhesive on her shoulder, she straightened and faced him.

He could have told her she was beautiful again, but the words seemed trite. She was all women, and still, somehow, only herself. She was everything female and enduring, a symphony of fluid, changing lines and curves. He understood why ancient man had revered and honored woman's fertility. He understood how men had been brought to their knees throughout history by the feminine form.

She held out her arms, but he didn't want to go to her clothed. He undressed as quickly, as easily as she had. Her smile was all-knowing. "I won't repeat myself," she said.

She sat on the edge of the bed; then, as sinuously as a cat, she rolled to her side, leaving room for him to join her. He stretched out beside her, riveted by her expression. She believed the battle was won. She knew her powers, and she could see his response.

She stroked his shoulder, but her eyes never left his. Her hand glided down his arm, then rested at his waist. She leaned forward, their gazes were still locked until the last moment before she kissed him.

Her hand trailed fire, moving slowly over the part of him whose ultimate destiny was to give her pleasure. His response was immediate. He moved against her hand as she wrapped her fingers around him. He felt one long leg drape over his hip as she inched closer. And all the while her hand worked potent magic.

He couldn't touch her enough. His palms, his fingers were limited receptors. He wanted to know her with all his senses, to immerse himself in her purest essence. He touched her breast with his lips, savoring the salt-tinged warmth of her skin. He filled his lungs with the erotic fragrance of her flesh. His eyes feasted on the hills and valleys of her body.

She was everywoman, that marvelous, enduring creature who from the beginning of time had peopled the earth with her hard-won bounty. But she was more; she was Garnet, the woman who could be his for all time—if he allowed her to be. The woman who wanted to make him whole again.

He moved away from her touch and leaned over her to better explore this prize. Her smile was as old as woman's first triumph. Her eyelids fluttered shut as he touched her again with his lips. Then, as he moved over her with the slow stealth of shadows at nightfall, she gasped and murmured endearments.

She was so alive in his arms. He wondered how any man could resist her. Every cell of his body seemed to swell with longing, but especially that intimate part that had betrayed him since Patricia's death. But never in the years since had he tried to make love to a woman he loved. Sex had been intended as a momentary release. Now it was more. So much more. Garnet was not just a woman; he was not using her in a way that was against all his principles. She was his woman. He loved her, despite not wanting to. He loved her, and she was his wife.

"Thomas, come to me," she said.

He had almost convinced himself that this time would be different, but as she pulled him over her, the fears returned, faint, nagging voices inside his head that fought to be amplified. He could feel her lips drinking the passion of his, feel the lush curves of her body press against him. For a moment, for one brief, victorious moment, he knew that she would win against the voices—that *he* would win—and they would become one.

And then he knew there would be no victory.

The longing didn't disappear. He had never wanted anything so much. His body screamed for release at the same time that it denied him the possibility. In seconds he went from man to eunuch. Half a man.

He sank against her, unable to complete what she had begun. Her fingers dug into his back, then soothed him with gentle caresses. She kissed his cheeks, his forehead, his lips. "Rest a moment, and we'll try again," she whispered.

He would have, if there had been any point to it, but there wasn't. That much he knew. "No."

She was silent for a moment. "I told you it doesn't matter, and it doesn't," she said at last. "What matters is that you want me, and that you trusted me."

He wanted to believe her; he also wanted to scream that she was lying, that this mattered more than anything. He moved away from her and lay beside her, his hand over his eyes.

She lifted his hand. Her hair snaked provocatively along his chest. Her eyes gazed into his. "You're a wonderful lover, Thomas Stonehill," she said huskily. "We've just got to work on the ending a little."

He pulled her closer so that her head lay against his chest and held her so that he didn't have to see her expression. He heard her small, surprised gasp as his hand moved over her. He parted her legs and sought the most intimate part of her. She gasped again, explosively this time, but she didn't move away. She twisted, then moved against him, giving him freer access.

He was quickly caught up in giving her satisfaction. Even as desperation filled him, some remnant of pride asserted itself, too. He could give her release and bring her pleasure, even if it was denied to him. He could fight back in this way. He was not quite worthless.

She moved with him, and when he bent to kiss her breasts, she gasped again. He could experience her pleasure building by the mounting tension in her body. She was more beautiful in this last moment of passion then she had ever been before. Restless and completely sensual, and somehow pure. There could be no artifice, no pretense. She was a woman, his woman, letting desire claim her.

And when it had, she lay in his arms, boneless with exhaustion. He cradled her head against his shoulder. He wanted to weep, although everything that made him a man told him he couldn't.

"I don't know if I could have been that generous," she said.

"Generous?" He stroked her hair. "I wanted to give you pleasure. As much for myself as for you."

"You did."

He knew he should move away. He had only proved how impossible their marriage was. But he was as powerless to leave her now as he was to make love to her.

The day to leave her would come soon enough.

"I've imagined sleeping with you," she said. "You wouldn't sprawl. You probably don't sleep that deeply. And even though some people might think you're aloof, I know better. You wouldn't move away to find your own space. You would sleep with your arms around me. Not too tightly, because you'd still want me to feel free. The perfect man to sleep with."

Perfect except in the most important way. But he didn't remind her of that; he was sure she needed no reminder.

"I think I'm falling asleep now," she said, laying her hand on his cheek.

"Go ahead," he said. "You need to rest."

"Will you stay with me?"

"I'll stay."

But he didn't say how long he would stay. There would be time for that discussion later. For now he held her and felt her body relax into sleep. And as she slept, he lay awake and contemplated his own failures.

12

The mural was in progress when they returned to the Corners. There had been no opportunity to negotiate with Ferdinand at Dorothy's funeral, and the following day had been too eventful. But when Garnet and Thomas walked into the church after their too brief holiday at the lake, there were whole figures blocked out on the wall that had once been tainted with graffiti. Ferdinand hadn't needed a key. No MidKnight needed a key to walk through a door.

The mural grew and changed over the next weeks, but no one ever saw Ferdinand inside the church. Several times at night Thomas heard noises downstairs when he was trying to sleep with Garnet breathing peacefully beside him. But he never left her to confront Ferdinand. Ferdinand would come to him when he was ready. It was enough that the young man had decided to cover the wall with the stirring New Testament images that spoke of his own struggles and pain.

The Thanksgiving holidays passed. Thanksgiving itself was a quiet day spent at the lake. Garnet cooked a traditional feast with his assistance. After dinner they walked through the surrounding woods together, scuffing autumn leaves and gathering fallen butternuts. And that night he tried and failed once more to make love to her.

Since their first time together in the cottage, she had never once indicated distress at his failure. She was supportive to a fault. He wanted her to rage at him, as he raged at himself. He wanted her to tell him that she doubted his masculinity. But he could detect no anger or doubts. She truly seemed to find pleasure in his arms. She truly seemed to believe that his impotence was temporary, and that together they would overcome it.

He couldn't discuss his failures with her again. He couldn't find words to tell her that he had given up hope that he would ever make love to her. There was no woman more seductive, more entrancing than Garnet. He couldn't imagine desiring anyone more. The fault lay somewhere inside him, in some dark, terrifying part of his mind. And nothing, not passionate nights in her arms, not years of therapy or prescriptions for miracle drugs, not meaningless hours of prayer to a God he no longer was sure of, would uncover the reason for his impotence.

With the end of the Thanksgiving weekend came the beginning of the Christmas season. The despair that gripped the Corners seemed to lessen with each store display and Christmas tree shining bravely through a living room window. A city crew appeared one morning and strung lights in Kensington Park, and surprisingly, they weren't vandalized. Thomas could see them from his apartment window at night, a secular symbol of an approaching holy event.

Once Christmas and Easter had been his favorite times of the year. They had been busy times, busier than any other for a Christian minister, but they had been days filled with wonder. He had felt humbler, more in tune with the son of God at those times than at any other. His days had never seemed fuller or more miraculous. His life had been touched by the Holy Spirit.

That feeling was gone now, even though he desperately wanted to bring it back. The approaching holiday season was something to get through, one day at a time. A committee was formed by enthusiastic, devoted members of the congregation to plan a celebration. He faithfully attended all meetings, but for once he couldn't provide leadership. He had no idea how the small church could make Christmas special for its members.

He was staring at a blank study wall one afternoon, taunting himself for his lack of inspiration, when Garnet appeared in the doorway.

"What are you doing off so early?" he asked.

"Have you noticed Christmas is coming?"

He knew *she* had noticed. Her white knit dress was festooned in ropes of green and red glass beads. Miniature Christmas tree bulbs swung merrily from her ears.

"Did Finn walk you home?" he asked.

"Yes, yes and more yes. I've got more protection than an armored truck. I'm here in one piece. No bullet holes, no psychological traumas. Just an overwhelming urge to buy a Christmas tree."

"A tree?"

"Yeah, you know. Green. Bushy. Symbolic. Something to drop needles on the rug?"

"Did the clinic close early?"

"It's your fault I'm home. You told me I wasn't indispensable. So I'm taking the afternoon off." She grinned. "But don't get cocky. We've got three nurses in training from the hospital giving shots today, and Tex is watching them like a hawk. They needed my office. I was in the way."

She walked to his desk, perched on the edge and brushed her shapely legs seductively against his. "So, how about it?"

He didn't want a Christmas tree. He didn't want a Christmas celebration. At that moment he didn't want to be the minister of a church that needed faith and wisdom he no longer possessed.

He looked at Garnet's shining eyes and knew he couldn't disappoint her. "Fine. I'm just drawing a blank here, anyway."

"No sick to visit? No lame to heal?"

"Your job, not mine." He stood.

She slid against him as she stood, too, and clasped her arms around his neck. "Are you all right?"

"Yes."

"Are you sure you're up to this? We could do something else."

He was afraid the something else she was going to suggest would be even more torturous. Even now his body betrayed him, as it always seemed to when she was in his arms. Yet he knew that if he took her upstairs and tried to make love to her, he would fail.

"Where did you want to look for a tree?" He unwound her arms, but he pressed a kiss against her palm so she wouldn't feel rejected.

"Somewhere I can stroll around the lot without having to duck bullets."

"Let's just drive out of the Corners and look."

"Do you have any decorations?"

"No."

"Mine were destroyed in the fire."

"Then we'll buy some."

"Good. I like the idea of starting over together, anyway. Let's get a smallish tree and just pick out a few things that we really like. We can add to our collection every year."

He looked away. She was planning for a future together that he couldn't envision. The time was as good as any to tell her not to hope for the impossible, but he couldn't find the words. Not now. Not when her eyes were sparkling with Christmas spirit.

"I'll meet you upstairs in a minute," he said. "You'll probably want to change your clothes first."

"Why, are you going to make me haul the tree to the car?"

"It was your idea, wasn't it?"

"Which simply means I'm the creative end of this project, and you're the muscle." The door closed behind her with a cheerful bang.

He was left to count the days until January.

Garnet made hot chocolate while Thomas struggled with fitting the tree—not a small one at all—into the tree stand.

The stand was new, the lights were new and the ornaments, two boxes of them, were new, too. Somehow, they had been of one accord on everything they had chosen. At heart she guessed they were both traditionalists when it came to Christmas. The lights were replicas of old-fashioned bubble lights, and the ornaments were colored glass copies of antiques. She had splurged on a dozen hand-crocheted snowflakes to fill in the emptiest spaces.

It would be a tree the children in the Sunday school would love. She planned to ask their help next week, when they came upstairs for their class. She would buy colored foil to cut into strips. The children could make chains to wrap around the tree, and they would feel that it belonged to them, too.

The thought of busy little fingers and innocent faces glowing with Christmas excitement gave her a funny pang. She missed her nieces, although she was fervently thankful that Ema had escaped Ron's abuse and was making a new life for herself. Ema was in Florida, Garnet knew that much now, and she had managed, with their mother's help, to find a job as a receptionist in a doctor's office. She and the girls had rented a tiny house just miles from the beach, and each time Garnet spoke to them they seemed happier than the last.

Until they left she had never realized the hole the girls had filled in her life. She had never expected to have children of her own. Her own child lay buried in a tiny grave miles away, and with her, Garnet had buried all hopes of another. She had committed herself to helping all the children of the Corners, and when she had done so, she had sealed away her own desire for a child.

But now that desire seemed to have forced its way to the surface. Perhaps it was her nieces' departure. Perhaps it was facing a waiting room of babies and toddlers nearly every day. Perhaps it was the small, well-scrubbed survivors of the Corners who arrived each Sunday morning for Sunday school.

Perhaps it was loving Thomas.

The last thought left more than a funny pang. It left such longing in its wake that she stopped her preparations and stared unseeingly at the refrigerator.

She loved Thomas. Love hadn't blazed into her life. It had crept slowly, insidiously, through all the cracks in her defenses, until one morning she could no longer pretend that what she felt was anything else. Desire was a part of it. Identification with his struggles, his hopes and dreams was another. Respect was an ingredient; compassion for what he had survived was another. But love was more than the sum of all those parts.

Love was waiting for Thomas to discover the reason for his impotence and overcome it.

"Are you trying to make the milk come to you?"

Startled, she turned to find Thomas standing in the doorway.

"The cocoa's all done," she said. "I was just... daydreaming."

"Your tree is in the stand. Your small, insignificant, inexpensive tree is scraping the paint off the ceiling."

"Goody." She went to the counter and got the mugs for the cocoa. Then, as he watched, she poured it and topped each cup with a plump marshmallow. She turned and offered him one. "Let's go sit by the fireplace and drink it," she said.

He reached for his. "We don't have a fireplace."

"We're going to pretend."

"Is that a habit of yours?"

"It's gotten me through some tough times. My mother taught me. There was one Christmas..." She stopped, wondering if he wanted to hear her childhood stories.

"Go on." He started into the living room.

She followed, setting her cocoa on the coffee table. Then, as he watched, she threw cushions against an empty wall. "Whoops, I almost threw that one on the fire," she apologized. "Get another log, would you? Then come settle over here with me."

"Where are the logs?"

She shrugged. "Wherever you stacked them."

He shook his head, but he stooped and pretended to lift something. Then, as she supervised, he leaned over and dropped his imaginary bundle against the wall. "Did I hit it?" he asked.

"Perfectly." She patted a pillow.

"Sorry, but the fire needs stirring. Hand me the poker and the bellows."

She leaned back, smiling smugly. "They're right beside you."

"You moved them again." He made an elaborate pretense of stirring the fire, then fed it gusts of air with the invisible bellows. Finally, satisfied, he settled himself against the cushions. "Warm enough?"

"Much better, thank you. Nobody makes a fire like you do, Thomas."

"No one enjoys one like you do. So, tell me about that Christmas."

"My mother's choice in men was abysmal. You've probably figured that out. I'm afraid Ema learned from her. Mother's lovers weren't all abusive, like Ron, but they all had major flaws. Anyway, the December I was eleven, the boyfriend of the moment stole everything that wasn't nailed down in our house, emptied mother's tiny checking account and drove off in her car. The car wasn't paid for or insured, and the boyfriend was never caught."

She sipped her cocoa. "Do you have stories like this one to tell?"

He thought of the Christmas he had received both a baseball autographed by Nolan Ryan and a pony. "Not exactly."

"My childhood was colorful."

He lifted his cup. "I'll drink to that."

She smiled. "You can guess there was no money left for Christmas that year. In fact, the landlord was threatening to evict us because the boyfriend had also gobbled up the rent money. Christmas was always more show than substance with us, anyway. Mother always wrapped up anything she could find. She'd buy us socks and wrap them separately. One year I got three plastic hair bands in three different boxes. But at least it was a celebration. The year I was eleven, there wasn't even money for hair bands."

"If you tell me it was the best Christmas of your life, I'll know this story isn't true."

"It sure as heck wasn't. But it was the most educational. On Christmas Eve Mother came home from cleaning up after other people's office parties, and we were all moping because we knew the next morning was going to be dismal. Mother got down our Christmas tree ornaments, which the boyfriend hadn't wanted, I guess, and told us to decorate the tree. Of course, there was no tree, but she kept insisting. So finally Jade hung a bulb on the coat tree in the corner, just to shut her up. It looked pretty silly, so I hung another. In half an hour, we'd strung it with lights and hung ornaments on every arm, even from the light strings."

She wriggled closer to him. "Then Mother told us to get out our presents and put them under the tree."

"That almost seems cruel."

"It wasn't. She told us all she could give us that Christmas was dreams, but that dreams were important. So one by one, we put our dreams under the Christmas tree. I wanted a new bike, so I wheeled it in. It was bright red, and the chrome was so shiny it reflected the lights from the tree. Ema wanted new clothes, and she modeled them for us, one outfit at a time. She looked beautiful. Jade wanted a piano. We stood around it, and she played Christmas carols for us."

She stopped. "It wasn't our best Christmas, but we survived it.

And sometimes I remember that Christmas Eve, and the next day when we ate canned hash and pretended it was turkey and dressing, and I use that memory to make my life better."

He wanted to ask her what she pretended now. Did she pretend that they were a normal married couple, reminiscing and strengthening their bonds? Did she pretend that this Christmas season together would be followed by others? Did she pretend that someday their own children would be standing beside them, gazing at another Christmas tree and bringing the Christmas miracle into their lives in a special way?

"Do you think I'm silly?" she asked.

"I think you're incredible," he said.

It was a compliment, but it was said with such sadness that she felt hollowed by it. "Your turn," she said.

"Mine?"

"For a Christmas memory."

He stared at the fire. It was almost real to him now. He wasn't sure why, but the memory that popped into his head was of a Christmas spent with Patricia. And he certainly wasn't going to relate a story about his first wife.

"How did you and Patricia celebrate?" she asked, when he remained silent.

He turned his gaze to her, surprised. "Why do you want to know?"

"Well, she was part of your life. An important part."

"Most of the time I was too busy for much celebration. But there was one year..."

She rolled to her stomach, propping her chin on her hands. "Tell me about it."

"She kidnapped me." He smiled at the memory. "After our midnight candlelight service. Everyone had gone home, and I was still at the church, making notes on what I'd do differently the next year. She came into my study and told me there was an emergency. She said she'd tell me about it as she drove me there.

I followed her out, already a little suspicious. When we got in the car, she got right on the interstate going out of town. She told me to go to sleep, that she'd wake me up when we got to the emergency. The emergency was a little country inn on a snow-covered lane. She'd reserved their best suite for a week. There were no phones, and a blizzard hit the next morning. I couldn't have left if I'd wanted to. There were half a dozen other couples there, escaping jobs and in-laws and stress. It was the best Christmas we spent together."

"Were you angry at her?"

"No. I think I was relieved."

"And you had a wonderful time."

"Yes."

"You were a better husband than you think."

He closed his eyes and lay back on the pillows. "It was one week, Garnet."

She crawled closer and rested her head on the pillow next to his. He had no choice but to put his arm around her. "And if you put your mind to it, you'd come up with other weeks and days and hours."

For a moment he wondered; then he shook his head. "She was going to leave me. There weren't enough hours."

"Maybe she was just trying to scare you into taking a look at yourself. Did she love you?"

"I don't want to talk about this."

"Fine. But give it a thought or two sometime. Because if she still loved you, threatening to leave might have been just a different version of kidnapping you that Christmas."

He wondered. He had assumed for so long that Patricia had stopped loving him. Now Garnet had planted the seeds of doubt.

She put her hand on his cheek and forced him to look at her. "People never change completely. You can tell me you're a different man now than you were, but I won't believe you. The man I know is the same man who was married to Patricia. Maybe at the time you were driven by your desire to succeed as a pastor, but underneath you were the man you are now. She married you because of who you are. I'm lying here with you because of who you are. I can't speak for Patricia, but I know I would have fought to keep you. I *will* fight to keep you if our relationship is threatened."

He wondered how she could imagine that it wasn't.

Loud knocking at the door saved him from making a response.

"I'll get it," Garnet said, getting reluctantly to her feet. "But I don't care who it is, we've got to decorate this tree before you go anywhere."

"Find out who it is before you open the door."

She obliged him by looking through the peephole he had installed. "It's Andre. Your choice. Do we open it?"

"Is he alone?"

"Looks that way."

Thomas joined her at the door. "I'll let him in."

"And I'll stay."

He didn't protest. He trusted Andre, although he wasn't completely sure he should. He opened the door and gestured him inside. "You look cold. The temperature's dropping out there, isn't it?"

"I didn't come to talk about the weather."

"I didn't think so."

Garnet took one look at the two men and made her decision. "Andre, we were just having cocoa. I'll make you some."

"I don't drink cocoa."

"Then I'll heat up some antifreeze or drain cleaner. Something for a tough guy." She flashed him a cocky smile and left for the kitchen.

"I know. She's got a mouth," Thomas said. "Come on in and sit down. She'll make you drink the cocoa, so you might as well get comfortable."

"Looks like I'm interrupting."

Thomas followed Andre's gaze to the pillows scattered haphazardly against the wall. "We were about to decorate the Christmas tree."

"I got my mama one yesterday."

Thomas was surprised he had admitted to something so absolutely normal. So harmless and sentimental. "And she'll probably make you decorate it, right?"

"I do that stuff for her. I take care of her plants and the yard. She can't be doing it herself."

"She's still a strong woman. Garnet says she was always there for the neighborhood kids. All of them."

"Yeah. I guess." Andre sat, then rose again immediately and walked restlessly around the room, finally coming to rest beside the tree. "I'm not staying for no cocoa. I just came to tell you I know who shot Garnet."

Thomas sat absolutely still. He was afraid to move, afraid Andre would stop talking.

"It's nothing you got to worry about. I took care of it."

"Did you?" Thomas stood. "Precisely how?"

"You don't got to worry about that, either."

"I am worried." Thomas joined him by the tree. "Very worried."

"He won't hurt you or her. I put him in check."

"Check?"

"It was a violation. He won't be coming back to the Corners. He knows if he do, he be looking at the Knights to take care of him once and for all."

"Who are we talking about?"

Andre was silent.

Thomas made his best guess. "It was Demon, wasn't it?"

Andre didn't deny it. "It was him who shot Wolfman, too."

Thomas remembered that Wolfman was the Knight who had

been killed in the drive-by shooting that had been blamed on the Coroners. "Demon did that? Why?"

"A mistake. He was out driving around, looking for Francis. He'd smoked a lotta weed, and it was dark. He saw Wolfman over by Wilford Heights and thought he was Francis, so he took him out. Then, next day when he found out what he'd done, he told everybody that he'd been talking to Wolfman just before the shooting, and he'd seen a car with Francis and his brothers cruising the streets as he was leaving."

"All to get even with Francis because Candy left him?"

"When he heard what happened at Dorothy's funeral, he started getting scared we was going to talk to the Coroners, maybe find out the truth. So he shot Garnet and made it look like it was the Coroners."

"But you knew better."

Andre didn't answer.

"A man who uses a gun to settle scores when he's unhappy isn't someone we need out on the streets."

"You think he's the only one?"

"No. But I think he's a lot more erratic than the rest of you kids with your guns and your swaggers and your signs. You've got some sense left, Andre. Ferdinand does, too. And those kids I saw on the porch a couple of weeks ago, they've got some sense left. Demon would just as soon shoot somebody as pass them on the street. And banishing him from the Corners isn't going to make a bit of difference to him. He'll just keep on shooting."

"He won't be able to shoot nobody for a long, long time."

Thomas didn't ask what Andre meant. The young man had already made it clear he had administered his own brand of justice. Thomas knew that in a lot of places and in a lot of gangs Demon wouldn't have survived to walk away.

"Tell me where he is now," Thomas said.

"What for?"

"So I can tell the police."

Garnet walked into the room with Andre's cocoa in her hand. "The police?"

"Demon was the one who shot you," Thomas said. "I imagine he was also responsible for beating you up. The big surprise is that he also shot Wolfman."

Garnet set the cocoa on the coffee table. Her hand was shaking. "Do you know how Wolfman got his name, Thomas?" she asked, looking straight at Andre. She didn't wait for an answer. "He and Andre were best friends when they were little. Wolfman had a dog, a big husky-shepherd mix. He called him Wolf, because that's what he looked like. He and Andre used to train Wolf to do tricks in Andre's backyard. That dog was still alive when Wolfman was killed. I don't know what happened to him afterward. What did happen, Andre?"

Andre stared at her.

"I would guess he died," she said, her voice shaking, too. "I'd guess that Wolf couldn't take Wolfman dying. What about you, Andre? Could you take it?"

Thomas let Garnet's question hang in the air for a moment before he spoke. "Demon will kill again. He will. There's only one way to stop him. If you can't go to the police, tell me where he is. I'll go to them. He has to be locked away."

"You'd like to lock us all away!"

"No. I wouldn't. I'd like you to live on safe streets. I'd like your mother living on safe streets and the kids you'll have someday living on them. *I'd* like to live on them. I don't want my wife shot at anymore!"

"If you knew the things I've done, you'd want me in jail, too."

"You are not Demon Harris."

Andre turned away, but he didn't leave. "You don't know nothing about nothing."

"I know about this."

The silence seemed to stretch into forever. Then Andre

walked to the door. He spoke without turning. "Demon's at his aunt's. She lives on Chester. Sally Harris."

"Who can testify to what you've told me?" Thomas asked.

"Raygun's the one who told me. Demon told him all about it. The car he was driving when he shot at Garnet is parked at his aunt's."

"The police kept shards of glass from the car window," Garnet said. "Maybe they can match them."

"With luck they'll get his gun first," Thomas said. He watched Andre turn the doorknob to leave. "Thank you, Andre."

"He shouldn't have killed Wolfman." He walked through the doorway, then he turned. He looked straight at Garnet. "Wolf's mine now," he said. "Wolfman's mama gave him to me."

She imagined Andre taking care of the old dog. She looked away, afraid he would see how moved she was that he had admitted it.

She heard the door close behind him and felt Thomas's arms come around her. She leaned against him. "I'm pretending I believe in miracles," she whispered against his shoulder.

He held her tighter. Because suddenly he was pretending, too.

13

Thomas stared at the finished mural. Emotion filled him. Ferdinand had used muted colors and vivid images. One scene blended into another. Jesus on a donkey riding into Jerusalem; Jesus walking on water; Jesus praying in the Garden of Gethsemane and at the Last Supper; Jesus on the cross; Jesus risen from the dead.

None of the multiple images of Jesus were the same. Like the picture Dorothy Brown had donated for the front of the church, these saviors had different faces, different colored skin. The Jesus presiding over the Last Supper was Asian, and his disciples were a mixture of races and nationalities. The Jesus praying in the Garden was Hispanic, dressed much as Ferdinand himself liked to dress, down to the tattoo on his left arm. There was a white Jesus on the cross and a black one risen from the dead.

The Jesus walking on water was female, and *she* looked something like Garnet.

Thomas could not look at the mural without something clutching at his throat. There would be people who would see it who would not understand, people who would think it was blasphemous. He felt sorry for them, because the images were the essence of Christianity. He believed that the man Jesus would have approved.

For a moment he felt that approval. Something moved over him. He felt as if someone had touched his shoulder, as if someone was in the room with him. He stood in a hollowed-out storefront, in a neighborhood that God seemed to have abandoned, yet he felt a presence he remembered from other, better times. A presence stronger, surer, brighter than he had ever felt before.

He turned instinctively, but the room was empty except for the mural and the picture looking down at him from the front of the church. He was as alone as he would ever be, yet he felt comforted and strengthened.

He bowed his head, but no words would come. Frustration warred with faith. He wanted to cry out, to command the tranquility that had ebbed away to return and fill him again. But the harder he struggled to hold on to that brief moment of inner peace, the less comfort he felt.

He stood with his head bowed until the pain was too great. He straightened, then started toward his study when the front door swung open.

Ferdinand walked in, thumbs hooked in the belt loops of his khakis. His trench coat was wide open, despite a heavy snow falling outside.

"So, what do you think, Padre?" he asked.

For the first time Thomas gazed at the young man through the lens of his own pain and saw a fellow traveler. Ferdinand had struggled for simple survival for most of his life, yet this masterpiece had sprung directly from the tortures of his childhood.

The young man understood pain, and Thomas felt a kinship with him that he could never have experienced in his days at Deering Hills Community. He beckoned for Ferdinand to join him in front of the mural.

He found he had to clear his throat to speak. "Thank you seems pretty lukewarm. I don't know what to say."

"Then you like?"

"I like." He waited for Ferdinand, and they stood together staring at the mural. "I can't even find words to tell you how much I like it."

"My mama went to church. She took me. I had to look some of this up, but I remembered some."

"You'll always be welcome here if you want to give church another try. You know that, don't you?"

"I'm going away." Ferdinand folded his arms. "My mama's been trying to get me to go live with her. She left when I was little because my old man beat her bad. She tried to take me, but he said he'd kill me first. He's crazy. He would have found us, and she didn't have no way to stop him. But she sent me letters all the time at my aunt's house, so I'd know she still wanted me. Now I'm bigger than my old man, and he's afraid of me. I guess I coulda left a while ago, but I didn't want to desert the Knights. You know?"

"I know. But now you're ready?"

"Yeah. I guess. She wants me to go to art school."

"Judging from this, you can probably show your teachers a thing or two."

"You think I'll make it?"

Thomas heard the young man's self-doubt. Ferdinand had never been anywhere except the Corners. He had never lived any other kind of life. And since adolescence he hadn't had to face life without the backing of his gang.

"I know you'll make it," Thomas said. "Dorothy Brown left money in her will for you to paint this mural. Did you know that?"

"I didn't do it for money."

"Dorothy would have wanted you to go to art school. We'll call it a scholarship."

"I'll be leaving soon."

"The Corners will miss you."

Ferdinand looked at him. "Now that Demon's gone, things are different."

Thomas knew what he meant. It wasn't only Demon's arrest that had changed the atmosphere in the community, but also the discovery that the Coroners had not been responsible for Wolfman's death. Suddenly there was no tangible reason for the two gangs to be at war. They didn't have the long history of hatred other big-city gangs had. They had sat next to each other in school classrooms, played together as children at city playgrounds. They had tenuous bonds as well as trumped-up excuses for anger.

There was hope here. Just a fragment, but more than there had been a week ago.

"Jails are crowded, and judges can't do much about kids like Demon. It won't be long before he's back out on the streets again," Thomas said. "What kind of neighborhood is he going to come back to, do you think?"

"Who knows?"

"If we make the right kind of changes here, he won't be comfortable. He'll move on."

"Buena suerte, Padre." Ferdinand gave Thomas a playful sock on the arm. "Me, I'm going to a place where I won't be comfortable. You know?"

"You can be comfortable anywhere. Just remember there are people here who believe in you. Believe in yourself."

"I think He believes in me." Ferdinand inclined his head toward the mural.

"I think so, too." Thomas waited for the rush of shame to come, as it always did when he mouthed platitudes he no longer felt. But there was no shame, only an emptiness waiting to be filled.

"Maybe I'll come back and see you."

Thomas turned to him and smiled his warmest smile. "I'll be waiting for that day."

~

"I've got the diapers. Six packs, but the way Candy says she changes that baby, they'll be gone in a week." Garnet rummaged through a series of shopping bags. "I've got her present, and one for Francis. I've got the sweater Tex crocheted for Matty—" She looked up. "Do you believe Tex crochets? Can you see me with a crochet hook in my hand?"

"Right now I just want to see *me* with a steering wheel in mine."

"All right. Let's go." Garnet picked up two of the bags and watched Thomas get the others.

She followed him out to his car. She still thought of it as his. When she had to drive somewhere she always took her own car. Their possessions were still separate, the possessions of roommates.

She settled into the passenger seat and relaxed as he pulled onto Wilford and wove through the streets that would take them out of the Corners. She had been looking forward to this jaunt all week. They were taking Christmas presents to Candy and Francis. She had talked to Candy often by telephone, but she hadn't seen Matty since his birth. She was eager to see for herself that he was doing well.

Thomas seemed less excited about the trip. He had seemed pleased that morning when he shared Ferdinand's visit with her. But as the afternoon drew closer, he had grown quiet. She knew returning to Deering Hills was hard for him. How could it not be? The symbol of his former success sprawled across a hill in the center of town, visible from almost everywhere in a five-mile radius. How could he help but compare himself and what he had achieved in the Corners with what he'd once had?

Did he compare her with Patricia? Garnet didn't have to take a long look at herself to see how different she was from the stereotypical minister's wife. She was no shepherdess, no beaming helpmate. Her skirts were too short and her vocabulary too colorful. She said what she thought and did what she wanted. She wondered if he was reluctant to take her to his old home.

"Why don't you show me around town a little while we're there?" she asked. She supposed the question was a test.

"What would you like to see?"

"Your church."

He was silent.

She considered the possible reasons he hadn't said yes. The visit might be too painful for him. The church, after all, had been the scene of Patricia's death. It was a symbol in Thomas's mind of all his failures.

Or perhaps he didn't want her there because it would be too blatantly apparent how drastically his life had changed.

"All right."

At first she wasn't sure she'd heard him correctly. "All right?"

"All right. As in yes."

"Really?"

"I've stayed away too long." He glanced at her. "I'm glad you'll be with me. I don't think I'd want to go back alone."

She stared straight ahead for the rest of the trip.

~

Matty was adorable, with a ready smile and dark curly hair. Candy looked well, and Francis looked as if his hours outdoors on a work crew had honed his body from a boy's into a man's.

They seemed happy in their new life. Candy helped Marcia around the house and no longer had to pretend. Marcia was frankly grateful for the help. Francis had already been promoted and given a raise. The reports were that he was an enthusiastic worker with real aptitude for construction. His boss, Stu Wilson, who had never been blessed with a son of his own, seemed to think Francis had the potential to learn all the building trades.

There was only one part of Candy and Francis's life that brought them sadness. They had grown up in the Corners. Their friends were there, and so were their memories. But they could not go home for visits. They were happy to live in Deering Hills, but they still wanted the Corners to be a part of their life, too. And even with Demon's arrest, they did not feel safe enough to go home with Matty.

"I feel sorry for them," Garnet said after the visit, as she and Thomas drove toward the Deering Hills Community Church. "They've been uprooted, with no chance to go back and renew their old ties. Candy has friends in the Corners with babies. She could sit and have a soda and talk to them about Matty. She likes Deering, but it's not home, and she doesn't feel like she fits in with the other young mothers in the neighborhood, with their private-school educations and their imported English prams."

Thomas was silent. The problem had been nagging at him, too. It was Christmas, the season of goodwill. Yet Candy and Francis were still afraid to return to the Corners. A young couple with their first child, afraid to come home at Christmas.

There had been another young couple...

"Thomas?" Garnet said, wondering if he heard her.

"Maybe we can do something," he said.

"What?"

"Let me give it some thought." His mind was whirling with possibilities. For a moment he forgot they were headed to the scene of his greatest failures. He forgot that the church he ministered to had only one member for every two hundred or more of the faithful at Deering Hills Community. He could think only about the celebration of Christmas that had eluded him all week.

He turned into the church parking lot, and suddenly all his

memories came crashing down on him. He parked, but for a moment he could not get out of the car.

"You were never supposed to be perfect," Garnet said, reaching for his hand. "There was one perfect man, or so the Bible tells us, and his name was not Thomas Stonehill."

"I was glorious in my imperfection," he said bitterly. "A man trying to play God."

"On anybody's sin list, trying to do too much good is way at the bottom."

"I did it for myself."

"I doubt it. Not at first, anyway. Later, well, maybe you got carried away. Power does that to people."

"I haven't been inside that door since I turned in my keys."

"Then it's time." She opened her door and got out. The parking lot was icy, and reluctantly he got out and went around the car to give her his arm.

"I'll bet the parking lot wasn't icy when you were the minister," she said, hoping he would smile. "I'll bet you were out here with your giant bag of rock salt and your snow shovel before the snow even hit."

"It didn't dare fall when I was the minister."

She laughed and rubbed his arm. The church loomed just ahead of them, one tall copper spire pointing straight to heaven, surrounded by a sprawling two-story building of tan brick that went on and on. From the outside Thomas pointed out the additions that had been constructed during his tenure. Then he opened the front door. She tried not to think about what had taken place on this spot.

He looked perfectly calm. His blue eyes didn't show any of the turmoil she knew he must be feeling. "We'd better let the office know we're here, then we can wander around," he said.

"Shall I come with you?"

"Of course. I want to introduce you."

She walked beside him, but she dropped his arm. The church

halls were cool, institutional beige lined with pale, tasteful watercolor landscapes of the Holy Land. She thought about Ferdinand's mural and tried to imagine it anywhere inside this building.

The office was a series of rooms. The main one faced the hall near the sanctuary, with glass windows, much like a doctor's reception area. An older woman with tightly permed gray hair looked up from her desk as they approached. "May I—" She stared at them, then pushed herself to her feet. "Thomas? Is that you?"

Before Thomas could respond, the woman was shouting behind her. "Thomas is here! Thomas Stonehill! He's come back to see us."

She disappeared for a moment, then reappeared followed by a small stream of women. In seconds she was hugging him ferociously while the others waited their turn. Garnet stood to one side, watching. She wondered if this answered the questions he must have asked himself about what kind of reception he would get here.

He hugged each woman in turn before he motioned for Garnet to join him. "I'd like to introduce my wife," he said. "Garnet Stonehill." He named each woman in turn.

Garnet shook hands, murmuring polite greetings.

Afterward the first woman, whose name was Barbara, put her hands on her hips. "Well, we heard you were back in town, but I had to see you to believe it. Why haven't you come back to visit us before?"

Garnet wondered if he would be honest.

He was. "There were too many painful memories connected with this place."

They all nodded and clucked sympathetically. Garnet had a vision of the women, as a unit, serving Thomas chicken noodle soup every day at lunchtime and tucking his napkin on his lap. They were all comfortably past middle age, beautifully groomed and—she bet—absolutely efficient at their jobs. She could see that they adored her husband.

Her husband. She wondered how the women felt about Thomas's new marriage. One of them, a woman named Marie, smiled at her, a very down-to-earth, genuine smile. "I'll bet Thomas has told you stories."

Garnet doubted Marie was talking about the stories Thomas *had* told her. "Not enough," she said with a smile.

"Well, *I* will fill you in." Marie took her by the arm. "Let me show you the office." Garnet looked over her shoulder as Marie pulled her along. Thomas smiled and shrugged.

She was regaled by Thomas stories for the next fifteen minutes. It was another side of Thomas's days in this church, a side he had never told her about. She heard about a man Thomas had befriended because, on a hospital visit to one of his own parishioners, Thomas discovered that no one ever visited the lonely old man in the next room. So he had added the old man to his visitation list, and months later, upon his death, the man—though atheist to the end—left a small fortune in stocks and bonds to the church.

She heard about the couples Thomas had married and others he had refused to marry, about the families he had comforted and the dying he had sat with. She heard about sermons that had filled the huge sanctuary and sermons so controversial that half a dozen deacons had resigned over them. She listened to the love seeping through the stories, the love of an older woman for a young man who, in a unique capacity, had shared some of the important moments of her life. Her husband's death, her grandchild's christening, the troubled antics of a teenage son.

Garnet came out of the office wondering if she had ever known Thomas at all.

She found him talking to a man near his own age. He gestured for her to join him. "Garnet," he said, "this is Chris Shallcross, the senior pastor at Community."

They shook hands. Chris Shallcross was tall and dignified, but his smile was warm and—she realized with appreciation —admiring.

"I was just telling your husband that I have big shoes to fill here," Chris said.

"And I was telling him to be careful not to fall into the trap I did and try to fill them," Thomas said.

"He was also telling me about your church in the Corners. I don't know if I could do what Thomas has done there, but it sounds like important work. I think our board would like to help in any way we can. Money, personnel."

"There might be some projects we could work on together," Thomas told him. "I have one in mind right now."

"I'd like to hear about it."

"Garnet, will you let Dorothy or Marie show you around some more while I talk to Chris about this?"

She nodded. Thomas looked different. For a moment she didn't know why; then she understood. The tension was gone. He looked relaxed and at home. He looked like a powerful man who was once more in control of his life.

He smiled at her, as if he realized what she was thinking. "I'll join you just as soon as we're done," he said. "There's more snow expected, and we've got a long drive home."

Home. Not "back to the Corners." Home! She was comforted by his word choice.

~

That evening Garnet turned on the Christmas tree lights and watched them sparkle joyously. She had spent little money on holiday decorations, but there was no doubting the season in this room. Fat red candles from the grocery store decorated the windowsills. Holly from a parishioner's bush lined a bowl filled with pine cones and seedpods. Loops of gold and silver tinsel hung over the door, and dangling from the door frame was a sprig of mistletoe.

Thomas came up behind her and pulled her under the mistletoe before she could resist. His kiss was long, slow and thoroughly provocative. She clung to him afterward, wishing for more.

"Thank you for going with me this afternoon," he said.

They had talked of other things on the ride home—when they had talked at all. She had wondered when or if he would discuss their visit to the church.

"They loved you, Thomas. They still do."

"I've never doubted that they loved me. I loved myself. That was the problem."

"Can you honestly say that when you were serving that church, you were doing it all for your own glorification? That you didn't feel a sense of commitment to others or maybe, just maybe, to a higher purpose?"

"I'm not sure what I think right now," he said. "Except that it's getting late. It's been a long day."

"And you want to go to bed."

He pulled her closer. "Yes."

Her heart threatened to stop beating. This was a different Thomas, one who was not so torn by his past mistakes. A man looking toward the future. And if the light smoldering in his eyes was any sign, he believed that future included one Garnet Anthony Stonehill.

"I love your hair." He reached up and unclasped the wide gold barrette holding it back from her face. "It has a mind of its own. Like a certain woman I know."

She had always done the seducing. Now she was nearly tongue-tied in her eagerness to see what he would do next. She circled his waist with her arms. "What else do you love?"

"Your eyes. They're a collage of greens, and they change with your moods. When you're angry they're almost gold, the way I imagine a tigress's eyes."

"Grrr..."

"And your skin." He trailed kisses to her neck. "It's the color of wildflower honey, and it tastes as wild and sweet."

She arched her neck to give him better access. "Don't stop."

"Oh, I don't intend to." He sealed his intention by swinging her up into his arms.

He kissed her as he carried her into the bedroom. She felt boneless in his arms, a willing participant in this new chapter in their marriage. She was sure, absolutely sure for the first time, that he wanted her. Not because she had provoked him. Not because she had seduced him. But because he was a man who desired the woman he had married.

He helped her undress, one piece of clothing at a time stripped at an agonizingly slow pace from her willing body. She repaid him in kind, her pace even slower and more provocative, until they were both naked, their bodies flushed with desire.

The evidence of his desire was there for her to see. He was ready for her, proud and indisputably male. She had seen him this way before, then felt his desire disappear in the next moment. But she knew that tonight was going to be different. Tonight Thomas wanted her. Tonight he believed in their future together. Tonight he believed in himself.

They fell to the bed together. Their limbs tangled; their hands collided as they caressed each other. Thomas kissed her as if each kiss was a discovery. She entwined her legs with his as he pulled her on top of him. She looked into his eyes and knew that he was the man she had never believed existed, the man she had given up hope of finding—before hope had even been allowed to grow.

"I love you," she whispered. "The man you were, the man you are, the man you'll be. All the Thomas Stonehills."

He closed his eyes, but not in sorrow. He looked humbled, as if the gift of her love was more than he had ever asked for.

"Make love to me, Thomas," she said, closing her eyes, too. "And let me be your lover now."

She eased herself over him. She could feel the rigid pulsing of his arousal inside her. Pleasure burst through her. He filled her as completely as a dream. *This* was a dream that had been denied them too long. "Oh, yes," she whispered. "Oh, yes, Thomas."

She moved slowly, filling herself with him again. His whole body was rigid beneath her, as if his pleasure was too exquisite to allow him movement.

And then the pleasure was gone for both of them.

At first she was confused. They had conquered the problem. They were victorious. They had truly become one. She moved, but there was no answering pulsing inside her. His body no longer responded to hers. She opened her eyes and saw that his were open, too. And instead of confidence, instead of belief in a future, she saw a bleakness that turned his eyes to ice.

She couldn't tell him it was all right. It wasn't, and she wouldn't patronize him by pretending. She lay against his chest, but his arms didn't come around her in comfort.

Finally she moved to the bed beside him. "This time we're going to talk about it," she said.

He wondered how much pain one person could endure, how much humiliation a man had to experience before he saw the truth. "What is there to say?"

"What happens in your head, Thomas? What memory or thought comes between us?"

"If I knew that, don't you think I could get beyond it?"

"We got farther today."

"As if it made any difference! Sex isn't a climb up Mount Everest. You don't get credit for every hundred yards you go up the side of a cliff."

"Maybe not, but it gives me even more hope that eventually we'll reach the top."

He stared at the ceiling. There was so little he was sure of, but in the last agonizing moments, one thing had become crystal clear. "There won't be any eventually, Garnet. I'm not going to put you through this again. The marriage vows don't apply here. You never signed on for better or worse. You signed on so I could help you through a tough time in your life. That time has ended. You're safe now. No one is going to go after you again now that Demon's in jail."

"And I'm not allowed to stay with you through *your* tough times?"

"You would be bound to me for life."

"That's ridiculous. This will change. It was better tonight-"

"Better?" He sat up and faced her. He could no longer avoid the fact that she was lying there, warm and desirable and completely unattainable beside him. "Do you think this travesty was better? Do you know how tortured I feel every time I fail?"

"I know. Thomas, I *know* it must be terrible. The frustration must tear you apart inside. But you didn't fail, you just weren't as successful—"

"I failed you!" He stood up and reached for his clothes. They were right beside the bed, but he couldn't find them quickly enough to suit him.

"No, you—"

"I can live with the frustration. I have been living with it. But I can't live with you and know that I'm failing you every time we try to make love. You're a sensual, vital woman who needs a man in her life who can perform!"

"You make it sound like I'm looking for a gigolo!"

"You need a man. Not a eunuch. I'm not going to sit by and watch you dedicate your life to someone who can't give you sex, can't give you children—"

"But you will. When the time is right."

For a moment, for just one single moment, he found himself yearning to believe her. Then reality intruded. He was standing beside the most desirable woman he had ever known, and he was incapable of making love to her. Even now, with their relationship coming to an end, his body could not comply with what his heart craved.

He turned away from her. “The time will never be right. I thought tonight it might be. I thought maybe I’d put some of my ghosts to rest today. But it didn’t matter. Not even a little bit. And it’s never going to be better than this. I’m never going to be better! It’s time for you to think about the rest of your life.” He turned away. “But don’t include me in it. Because I’m not going to be there.”

“Do you care anything for me at all? Since you’re being so viciously honest, why not go all the way. Do you? Have you learned to care for me?”

“That doesn’t have anything to do with this.”

“It has everything to do with it.”

“I’ve learned to care enough to let you go.”

She sat up, pulling the sheet around her as she did. “What does that mean?”

“It means that it’s time for you to think about moving out.”

She stared at him. “Moving out?”

“Soon, Garnet. We’re fooling ourselves. We’re just getting deeper into something that’s going to hurt us both. Get out now, while it doesn’t matter so much. You told me your old apartment is almost ready to move back into. Talk to your landlord and tell him you’ll be in after Christmas.”

“I see.” She looked away. The sheet felt cool against her breasts. The wall she stared at was a pale yellow; she had painted it herself one weekend. She was aware of cars passing on the streets below, cautiously, because of the falling snow. She was aware of so much—and so, so little.

“I’m sorry,” he said. The words threatened to choke him. “I never wanted to hurt you.”

“So your intentions were honorable, Thomas. They were

honorable when you were married to Patricia, too. Just exactly what does that say about the patterns in your life?"

He didn't answer. He disappeared into the living room. She could hear sounds, as if he was dressing. Then she heard the front door close.

She wondered why he had given her until Christmas. Was this to be her Christmas present, a few more weeks with the man she claimed to love? A few more weeks of trying to make him see that they could conquer his problem together?

She didn't want those weeks. She stared at the wall and knew that she couldn't stay in Thomas's apartment any longer. She cast around for a place to go until the repairs on her apartment were finished. There were plenty of people who would welcome her. Serena would take her in, despite having only a little space for herself and Chantelle. Tex and Finn would be happy to have her. She considered a dozen other names and discarded them. No place was really right.

No place but home.

Still trailing the sheet, she went into the living room. Thomas was gone, just as she'd thought.

She found her address book and turned the pages. For the first time in the years since she had committed herself to staying in the Corners, she could not imagine staying here any longer.

She called Tex for a brief conversation. Then she dialed her mother's phone number in Florida.

14

There was a light snow on Christmas Eve after a week of no snow at all. The snow crunched softly under the tires of workers rushing home for the coming holiday. It fell over Kensington Park, and the city's Christmas lights glittered brighter against the swirls of white. It fell on the sidewalk in front of the Church of the Samaritan and in front of all of the Corners' churches, where it disappeared under the booted feet of candlelight processions moving toward the Kensington Hotel.

Thomas led the silent procession from the Church of the Samaritan. Behind him, two by two, walked the members of his congregation. There were many more than the thirty who had made their membership official. Some of the men who had helped him repair the building walked behind him. Others in the procession had been brought there by publicity about the coming event.

The publicity had been excellent. With the help of his contacts at Deering Hills Community and media people he had known during his years there, the word had gotten out to the city at large. When the other churches in the community had agreed to participate, even with such short notice, news had spread still farther.

There were representatives from Deering Hills Community in the line behind him. Chris Shallcross and his family planned to come later, after their Christmas Eve service was finished. In the meantime, two dozen Community members walked behind Thomas in support.

He could see the other candlelight processions converging on the hotel. Some had walked for over a mile, lighting and relighting candles, he supposed, as the falling snow extinguished them. Some processions were short, and one that was now nearing the hotel looked to be almost a block long.

His procession walked slowly. They were to converge on the hotel and the abandoned warehouse just beyond it at seven-thirty. The time had been chosen to coordinate with various church services. It fell between the most traditional times of early evening and midnight.

They paused at the stoplight where Thomas had first encountered Garnet. Across the street at Wilford Heights a procession was forming on the sidewalk. The leader was a retired minister who lived in the housing project with his daughter and her family. He had been a friend of Dorothy Brown's, and now he was a friend of Thomas's. He was an old man, and life in the project was particularly hard for the old, who were easy prey for the young and armed. But when Thomas had told him of the plans for Christmas Eve, the Reverend Ray Johnson, bent and wizened, had gone from apartment to apartment throughout the complex recruiting his own volunteers.

By the time everyone gathered on the sidewalk outside the hotel, the count was in the hundreds. Thomas was gratified that so many had turned out. Some of those in attendance were onlookers. The processions had drawn attention, as they had been designed to do. Thomas saw kids flaunting gang colors on the sidelines, along with people who had obviously just returned from work and vagrants who hadn't worked in years.

He also saw the media. He recognized one newscaster, a young man who anchored the earliest local evening news program and probably wished that he was home with his family. There were others from the media who weren't familiar but whom he identified by their equipment.

The crowd parted as the Samaritan procession arrived. Thomas, as prime organizer, was to lead the way. It wasn't an honor he had asked for or even coveted. The idea had been his, but he felt no claim on it. This demonstration of the meaning of Christmas belonged to the community, and he wished someone else would act as spokesman. But the decision had been unanimous. Thomas and his church were to lead.

There was a narrow alley behind the Kensington Hotel. Some of the homeless families who lived temporarily at the hotel watched from windows as the procession turned into the alley. Until this afternoon it had been lined with garbage cans and debris. Now it was cleared of everything except one permanent Dumpster in front of the empty warehouse that stood at the alley's end.

The alley wasn't dark. It was lit by one security beacon from the warehouse roof. It shone on the people walking, two by two, toward the warehouse doors. The people in the procession were silent, but the barking of guard dogs inside the warehouse shattered the reverent hush.

As Thomas and his followers approached the doors, they were pushed open from the inside. The warehouse was dimly lit, empty of almost everything except cobwebs and a few abandoned crates. But in the center, fifty yards from the doors, were two figures kneeling beside another crate, and others standing nearby. This crate hadn't been abandoned. It was open at the top, and inside it, on a bed made of blankets and swaddled from head to toe against the cold, was a child.

The procession parted as they reached the center of the room, surrounding the two lonely figures kneeling beside the child.

Candy, kneeling on one side, was dressed in the colors of the MidKnights, black T-shirt under a dark plaid shirt with a long hoodie dragging the ground at her feet. She wore a blue bandanna over her blond hair, but the reverent look on her face as she gazed at Matty was worthy of any Madonna.

Francis was dressed in Coroner's colors, white shirt, thick parka, and a red hat with the letter C emblazoned on it. He gazed at his son, too, a proud young man who was obviously moved by his participation in this event.

The procession continued to enter the warehouse, and behind them, the onlookers came, followed by the media. When everyone was assembled, Thomas nodded. The dogs, four Dobermans chained near the doors, had barked unceasingly as the procession had filed into the room. Now, with their handlers beside them, they were brought to the front. At a spoken command, the dogs stopped barking and lay, heads on their paws, at the side of the room. They stared silently at the tableau in front of them, but they didn't move.

Men in uniform, who had been waiting as the crowd entered, moved closer to the center of the room, as if to adore the child. There were no shepherds in the Corners. But there were city workers who cleaned the streets and cared for the park. There were firefighters and police. Finn was one of the men who moved in a semicircle around Candy, Francis and Matty, as if to protect them.

No one else moved for a long time. The room was silent. Then the last of the people who had been in the warehouse when the others entered stepped forward. They were three women. One was dressed in the distinctive uniform of the Salvation Army. Another was dressed in a suit and heels. The third wore jeans and a heavy sweater. Separately, one at a time, they approached the kneeling mother.

"I have no frankincense," the woman from the Salvation Army said, "but I have clothes enough for you and your child." She left a bundle in front of the crate where Matty lay.

The second woman stepped forward and left her gift. "I have no gold, but I work for HUD, and I have forms you can fill out to get rental housing."

"I have no myrrh," the third woman said, "but I bring supplies from the emergency food pantry." She put a small box of canned goods beside the other gifts.

The women stepped to one side and stood silently.

Thomas nodded to the choir director of St. Michael's church. A group of nearly a dozen stepped forward, and after one note on the director's pitch pipe, they began to sing "Silent Night." The assembled worshipers took up the song.

Thomas looked around at the faces of those singing. They were all beautiful, old and young, black and white, Hispanic, Mideastern and Asian. He saw people who were singing the carol in a language other than English, people whose lives were so bleak and desperate that only a great faith could have brought them to this place tonight.

He tried to sing, too, but his throat closed around the familiar words. The idea for the manger scene had come to him when he and Garnet had spoken of Candy and Francis's alienation from their own community. It had been a simple idea, but there had been a great deal of planning and coordination needed. He had thrown himself into it, as he had once thrown himself into his ministry at Deering Hills Community. He had ignored everything else, as he had once ignored his personal life in Deering Hills.

He had ignored Garnet's departure.

Now there was no more work. The community had come together for this brief, shining moment. There were still people coming in from the streets. He saw MidKnight's colors and Coroner's colors. He saw someone in the back who might be Andre, and closer to the front he saw Francis's brothers, with their mother between them. No one was pushing or shoving, no one was speaking. Everyone stood together, witnessing a small miracle.

The St. Michael's choir went on to sing more carols. Their voices were fine and strong, and the others joined them when the songs were familiar. The choir from the Church of the Samaritan stepped forward to sing a gospel version of "Go Tell it on the Mountain."

Finally the singing ended and Thomas's own part in the program arrived.

He stepped forward and opened the Bible that he had carried under his arm. The lights were dim, but not too dim to make out the familiar words.

He swallowed. The pages blurred mysteriously in front of his eyes. For a moment he was sure that he wouldn't be heard. He knew he couldn't speak above a whisper.

He began, and his voice wavered, just as he'd feared. He pushed on, reading the familiar, comforting words from the Gospel of Luke, and his voice grew stronger. He told the story of a humble woman and man, caught up in a drama that had changed the world. He told of a baby so beloved, so awaited, that angel choirs and beacon stars had announced His birth, and shepherds and wise men had come to pay tribute.

Finally he closed his Bible. A minister from a church at the far end of the Corners stepped forward for a benediction. He prayed that those gathered there that night would remember that all children were holy.

Thomas looked over the bowed heads, his heart full and yet emptier than it had ever been. He had worked tirelessly for this moment. Both the procession and the reenactment had been more poignant, more memorable than he had dared to hope. But now it had ended. Some people would stay; more would come and go through the evening. Candy, Francis and Matty would leave in a little while to be replaced by another young couple and their child. But his part in the drama had ended.

He would go back to his empty apartment and his empty personal life. He would go back to face the demons that tormented him, the memories of a faith that was no longer his.

He would go home to think of Garnet.

If one thing wasn't perfect about the events of the night, it was that Garnet wasn't there to witness them.

He scanned the crowd again as the benediction ended. Heads lifted, candlelit faces were glowing with faith and hope. And one face toward the door of the warehouse, a face more beautiful to him than any of the others, lifted just as his gaze found it.

The night had been perfect after all.

He couldn't return to his apartment for another hour. The alley outside the warehouse was crowded with people wishing each other Christmas happiness. He was interviewed by the television crew about the meaning of the reenactment. His status as former pastor of Deering Hills Community and the tragic history of Patricia's death were mined by the young anchorman for all they were worth.

But he also had an opportunity to talk about his ministry at the Church of the Samaritan, and what he and his small congregation were trying to build here in the Corners. He talked about hope, about taking back city streets, about providing opportunities for babies like Matty, for families who were struggling against terrible odds and kids who believed their only opportunity for protection and community was joining a gang. When he was finished, he knew that most of what he had said would be edited away, but he hoped that the core of his message, the simple words of a Nazareth carpenter, "Love thy neighbor as thyself," would still shine through.

He went to the church to find people still lingering there, as if reluctant to let go of the evening's experience. Finally he closed and locked the front door of the church when the last well-wisher had gone home. He turned off the lights one by one until the church was dark. Then, because he had no alternative, he went upstairs to his apartment.

He wasn't sure what he wanted to find. Garnet was back in town; he knew that now. The day she had returned from Florida was unknown. She might have been back for a while. She'd had no reason to announce her return. He had told her their marriage was over. He had been the one to sever all ties.

But the thought that she might have come back and been here for days without letting him know filled him with despair. The thought that she might just have returned, that she might be waiting in the apartment for him now, filled him with a different kind of despair.

The door was ajar, and he knew what he was going to find.

Garnet was in the bedroom, folding clothes that she had left behind and stacking them neatly in a suitcase. "I won't be long," she said without looking up. "I just need my warm clothes. I'll be back to get everything else at the beginning of next week."

"There's no hurry."

She tossed her hair from her face and flicked him a quick glance. "Sorry to disagree, but I think there probably is."

"I meant that I don't need the room."

"I'm glad I'm not inconveniencing you."

The words could have been sarcastic, but they hadn't been said that way. She seemed to feel no emotion whatsoever.

"Where will you be living?" he asked.

"With Tex. My apartment will be ready on Monday. It just needs another coat of paint."

"I can help you move."

"Thanks, but I'll manage." She looked up from folding a sweater. "That was very inspirational tonight, Thomas."

He nodded.

"You must have worked hard to pull it off."

"It took some time."

"I'm sure you're proud." She stared at him, then shook her head. "No, I forgot, you wouldn't feel proud, would you? It probably wasn't perfect. You're probably ashamed."

"I *am* proud."

"Well, good." She went back to her packing.

"How was Ema?"

"Happy. And the girls look better than I've ever seen them. She sends her love."

"And your mother?"

"She's happy, too. For the first time ever she's found a decent man. I think she'll be getting married soon."

"I'm glad. I-"

"Thomas, there's no point in polite conversation, is there? We aren't going to survive this as friends, you know. You'll look at me and see your failures. I'll look at you and feel angry that you gave up so easily. We'll be better off just to get this out of the way quickly and be done with it." She turned toward her dresser for an armload of sweaters.

He formed a hundred answers but didn't have time for even one. There was a knock at the front door. Another well-wisher, he supposed, who was coming to share good feelings.

He didn't want to answer the door; he wanted to walk through it and keep on walking. Whatever hope he'd had of salvaging anything from their relationship had died with Garnet's words.

He opened the door anyway to find Andre standing on the threshold. He had never felt less hospitable or patient, but months of work aimed at a moment like this one were too important to destroy now. Andre had come to him. He had to listen, regardless of any personal crises.

"Hello, Andre." Thomas stepped back and gestured him inside, scanning the stairway to see if Andre was alone. "Were you at the warehouse? I thought I saw you there."

"I was there."

Thomas closed the door. "Have a seat. What's on your mind?"

He softened the abruptness of his words by sitting down on the sofa to signal that he planned to give the young man his complete attention.

Andre didn't sit. He had taken off a wool watch cap. He twisted it in his hands as he looked around the room. "You don't have much, do you?"

"No." He was going to have even less in a few minutes when Garnet walked out of his life. Thomas saw that she had closed the bedroom door, although it was still ajar. He could see flashes of her green sweater through the crack as she walked back and forth, packing her clothes.

"Why do you do what you do?"

Thomas's attention was snagged by Andre's tone. "I'm not sure what you're asking."

"Did God call you or something?"

"I thought so once."

"But now you're not sure?"

"There are a lot of things I'm not sure about. But I'm sure that what we're doing in that church down there is good. And I'm sure that what happened tonight is good."

"How do you know?"

It was a fair question. "I feel it inside me, I guess. And I look around and see that no one is hurt by what I do, but that a lot of people claim their lives are better."

"You look around." Andre paced, twisting his hat. "That's all you got to say?"

"Believe me, I'd like to be able to give a better answer."

"You used to believe in God. In Jesus." It wasn't a question. It was definitely a statement.

Thomas nodded. "Yes."

"I did, too, when I was a kid."

Thomas didn't say the obvious, that in many ways Andre was still a kid. "What happened to make you stop believing? Or did you?"

"I grew up."

"On tough streets, in a tough neighborhood. You don't get too much Jesus in a place like this one, do you, Andre?"

"You don't know what it's like, what it do to you living in a place like this."

"I don't know it the way you do, that's true."

"I went to church with my mama when I was a little kid. They told me all about how much God loved me. All that Jesus crap. Then I'd go out and dudes would be prying radios out of people's cars or slinging right there in front of the church."

Thomas knew all too well that slinging dope was a favorite Corners Sunday afternoon pastime. "Go on."

"When I was eleven, my cousin told me I had to be a Knight. There wasn't no way out of it. I didn't be a Knight, they'd make sure I didn't live long enough to be anything else. So I was a wannabe for a few years. I kicked with the MidKnights, but I didn't do it all the time. Just enough to keep them from coming after me."

Thomas's attention wandered. He could still see Garnet moving past the door. He suspected she had slowed her packing. She was too considerate to break in on this conversation. She would wait until Andre left before she left herself.

"Then I got to be sixteen, and it was time for initiation," Andre said. "You know about initiation, Padre?"

"No."

"You got to do something bad. You got to prove you're tough enough to be a Knight."

Thomas tried to pay attention to what Andre was saying. "And so you were forced to do something to show you were man enough to belong?"

"They said I had to be jacked in, and I knew what that meant. I got to steal something." He flopped to the edge of the sofa, as far away from Thomas as he could sit. "Do you think someone can do something bad and then get forgiven for it?"

Thomas knew the beginnings of a confession when he heard one. Andre had his full attention now. "I believe that with all my heart."

"You don't even believe in God."

"I'm not sure of some things, but I am sure that forgiveness exists."

That seemed to satisfy Andre. "That night there was three of us. We was told to get somebody's wallet and bring it back. They took all our money, so we wouldn't have no way home except by walking unless we got a wallet with some money in it. Then one of the brothers drove us out of the city." He stopped.

Thomas tried to prod him on. "Were you afraid?"

Andre didn't look at him. "The place they took us to was Deering Hills."

A cold wind seemed to sweep through the apartment. Thomas sat frozen, afraid to hear what was coming next, and afraid not to.

"You know about Deering Hills. You was living there once," Andre said.

"Yes." Thomas calculated Andre's age. He had been sixteen on the night he spoke of. He was nineteen now. Three years ago. Three years.

"They dropped us off in the middle of town. I went one way, the other two went off somewheres else, I never did hear where. It was a cold night, and I wasn't wearing much warm clothes. I started to walk. All I wanted was to grab a wallet and get out of there. Deering Hill's the kind of place where cops follow you around if you black."

"Yes."

"I saw a church sitting on a hill."

Thomas leaned forward and put his head in his hands. He felt the sofa move beneath him, and he knew Andre was pacing again. "Go on," he said in a low voice.

"I saw a church, and I wasn't going to bother with going there, because it was late at night and there wasn't any cars I could see in the parking lot. Then a car turned in from the road. I saw a woman was driving, and I knew I'd found my mark."

"You didn't mean to kill her, did you?" Thomas squeezed the question out of some sane part of himself. The only part that could still speak.

"I got to the door before she did. All I wanted was her purse. Just her wallet. I told her that, but she didn't listen. She tried to push me away, then she made like she was going to scream. I couldn't let her scream. I knew the cops'd be all over me. I pushed her hard to shut her up. She fell back, like she didn't know I was going to push her."

"And she hit her head and died."

"I didn't know that till the next day. I got her wallet, and I ran real fast. I walked for a long time, then I got a bus into the city. When I got back to the Corners I gave the wallet to the main man. He threw away all the ID and kept the money. I got to be a Knight."

Thomas looked up.

"And the next day I found out she was dead and I'd killed her." Andre twisted the hat in his hands.

Thomas stared at him. Patricia's killer was standing an arm's length away. He had come of his own accord, the first real step in a life that could someday be filled with meaning.

Andre had killed Patricia.

Thomas was filled with such fury he could hardly breathe. Every instinct he possessed told him to take justice into his own hands. Andre deserved punishment. He was larger than the boy, larger and stronger. Thomas could feel the blood rushing to his fingertips. His hands tingled with the desire to hurt Andre.

Andre stood there as if he expected punishment. He stood regal and tall and indefinably different.

"How could you come to me this way?" Thomas asked.

"I don't know where else to go."

Thomas shut his eyes. Anger was a red cloud tinting the room, tinting the very darkness that should have helped him grow calmer. It suffused his very being, threatened to shut off the air he breathed.

He saw Patricia on their wedding day, a glowing young bride with her whole life ahead of her. He saw her at the window of a country inn at Christmastime, her face serene with happiness. He saw her in a million different ways, some that he didn't want to remember and other, happier ways that he had allowed himself to forget.

And he saw her at prayer, a bishop's daughter, whose religion had been lived and not spoken. She had believed in God. Her faith had never wavered.

His faith in God had wavered. But he had told Andre that he believed in forgiveness. Patricia had believed in forgiveness, too. He opened his eyes, not sure how much time had passed. Andre still stood before him. Waiting. A young man poised on the brink of a life that could be filled with meaning. A young man with so much to give.

Thomas extended his hand. Andre swallowed hard; then he grasped it. As Thomas watched, tears filled the young man's eyes. Answering tears filled his own. Andre joined him on the sofa, and they sat together in silence.

In the bedroom Garnet sat on the edge of the bed. Tears slid down her cheeks. There was no privacy in the small apartment. She had heard Andre's confession, and she knew the woman he had killed must be Patricia. She knew her own anger and sorrow must be only a small fraction of what Thomas felt. She wished that she could go to him when Andre left and soothe his pain, but that was no longer a possibility.

By the time the front door had closed and Andre was gone, she had washed her face and finished her packing. She gave Thomas a few moments alone, then opened the bedroom door.

He was sitting with his face in his hands. Her heart twisted painfully at the sight, but she lifted her suitcases and carried them toward the front door.

"I heard it all," she said quietly.

"He killed Patricia."

"I know." She set down the suitcases. "Are you going to turn him in to the police?"

Thomas looked up wearily. "No."

"No?"

"Andre isn't Demon. He's suffered for three years because of what he did."

"A woman died."

"He never meant to kill her, not even to hurt her. He was caught up in something that got out of control." He got to his feet. "He came to me, knowing I would probably go to the police. I think he was ready to be punished by somebody else. He's been punishing himself since that night. But if he was sent to jail, and I think he probably would be, no one would ever have a chance to reach him again. He's vulnerable now, and he's made the first step toward a new life. I'm not going to cut him off before it begins."

"Then he just walks away?"

"No. I'll talk to him when I'm under control again. We'll decide together what he should do. Community service, maybe, or going back to school. Something that assures me he's on the right track."

She nodded. Thomas was being fairer, kinder than anyone should ever have to be. He moved to her side, and when she looked in his eyes, she saw that neither fairness nor kindness had come easily. And she saw something else.

"You've forgiven him, haven't you?"

Thomas looked inside himself. He was still angry and filled with unspeakable pain. Patricia's death would always be an empty space inside him, an empty space in a world that had needed her sweetness, her gentleness. But Garnet's question had been a different one.

"I've forgiven him," Thomas said, and knew, deep in his heart, that he was telling the truth.

She stared at him, and tears glazed her eyes. She saw a man in conflict. A good man, heroic in all ways.

Except one.

"So, that makes you better than God, doesn't it?" She opened the door and picked up her suitcases.

He was so filled with emotions, a spectrum of emotions, that he could hardly speak. He clamped his hand on her shoulder to stop her. "What in the hell does that mean?" he asked softly, fiercely.

She turned back to look at him. "You can forgive Andre, but you don't believe God can forgive you. That makes you better than Him, doesn't it? You always said you were arrogant. I just never understood how far it reached."

He dropped his hand. She saw powerful emotions cross his face. Then she saw nothing more of him at all. She found her way to the stairs and left the building.

15

Sometime on the Wednesday before Easter, the homeless man broke into the church again. In the morning when Thomas walked through on his way to a meeting, he found him standing in front of Ferdinand's mural.

The mural was illuminated by springtime sunshine. In the strong light the old man looked dirtier and more destitute. "Do you like this better than you like the picture in front?" Thomas asked, crossing to stand beside him.

"Still don't understand what you're doin' here in the Corners."

Thomas crossed his arms. "I've asked myself that a time or two."

"Who asked you to come here, anyway?"

Thomas contemplated that question. "I think I came here because I needed what the Corners could give me."

The old man humphed. "No one needs this place."

"I did," Thomas said.

"You're as crazy as the person who painted that."

"I hope so." Thomas smiled at his uninvited guest. "I know you don't take charity, but we have sharing suppers on Wednesday night—"

"You told me that last time."

"I know. But I'm hoping that *this* time you'll join us. You've lived on these streets for a long time. I think there are things you could tell us about it."

The old man's eyes narrowed. "What things?"

"First and most of all, what needs to be done for the Corners, I guess. You'd know better than anyone."

"I'm just a sick old man who drinks himself blind every night. Remember?"

"Has that changed?"

The old man didn't answer.

"At one time I drank myself blind every night, too. And even when I stopped drinking, I was still blind. Then one day I was lucky enough to have someone open my eyes."

The old man spat on the floor Thomas had swept the night before. "God?" he said.

"No. A woman. But she opened my eyes so I could see God again."

"Doesn't sound like any woman I've ever heard of."

Thomas didn't know how to respond to that. Garnet was not like anyone else in the world. But the world was filled with people who cared enough about each other to stretch out a hand when a hand was needed.

She had taught him that.

It was time to tell her. At that moment, after months of waiting and praying, after surges of hope and lapses into doubt, after the gray, remorseful weeks of Lent, he knew it was finally time.

"Sunday is Easter," he said. "It's a time of new beginnings. Come join us. You're always welcome here, even when the door *isn't* locked."

The old man chuckled. Thomas hadn't thought it was possible. But in the last months he had come to believe in the impossible. Nowadays he called it faith.

The rubber band pinged off the side of the wastepaper basket and fell to the floor.

"You've really lost your touch." Tex dropped a file on Garnet's desk. "You should have retired a winner."

"Long, long day." Garnet stood and stretched. "And I just got a call. Mary Ann had her baby."

"So what's the verdict?"

"A boy, almost six pounds. A seven on the Apgar scale. No obvious signs of addiction, but they've put him under constant watch for the next forty-eight hours."

"I think Mary Ann cleaned up her act toward the end."

"She says she did, but we'll know better in a day or so, I guess."

Tex folded her arms. "We've got four free days coming up. What's planned for the weekend?"

Garnet tapped her fingernails on her desk. "You don't have to take care of me. I'll be fine. It's just a long weekend."

"It's Easter. Come over for dinner on Sunday. Finn's going to smoke a leg of lamb."

"Can I let you know?"

"Can I give you some advice?"

Garnet stopped tapping. "Since when did you need permission?"

"Don't spend the holiday alone. Get out and see people."

"Do what? Go to church services? Did you know that Thomas is slaying dragons again? He and the other local pastors are sponsoring a sunrise service at Kensington Park. They're going to take over the park because the city refuses to, plant flowers, pick up litter, trim shrubs—"

"I'll expect you for dinner. Three o'clock sharp."

Garnet sighed. "I'm sorry."

"And no excuses." Tex gave her a hug before she left the room.

Garnet stared after her. She knew that in the months since Christmas she hadn't been herself. She had done her job, gone through the motions of keeping in touch with her friends, but she had craved silence and space to lick her wounds. Tex, and others who cared about her, were tired of standing back. They wanted her to feel better, to be the old Garnet.

She wasn't that woman anymore. That Garnet hadn't expected or wanted anything from the world, and every good thing that had come along had been a surprise and a pleasure. Then something had come along that she *had* wanted, and her life had changed.

But not for the better.

The day had been long; she knew she could make it longer. There was always more work to do and no one to stop her from doing it. But more work wasn't an antidote for what she was feeling, which was why she had agreed to close the clinic from Friday through Monday. Everyone on staff needed a break, and all the physicians were going out of town, anyway. Maybe Tex was right. Maybe what she needed was to call a friend and go out for the evening.

Halfway up the stairs to her apartment she knew she wasn't going to bother. She wanted to spend another evening alone, with her familiar possessions, her music. She would make dinner and read the novel she'd bought last week. And she wouldn't let herself think about Thomas. Because in the months since Christmas, Thomas obviously hadn't been thinking about her.

In the hall outside Serena's apartment she paused and considered knocking. But the apartment was quiet, which meant Serena and Chantelle probably weren't there. Lately a young man from the neighborhood—a young man with definite possibilities—had been showing up a lot to take Serena and the baby out for the evening. Serena just smiled when Garnet asked about him. She wasn't getting serious about anybody, she claimed, not until she was finished with school. The young man in question was just coming to see Chantelle.

Inside her apartment Garnet promised herself a good dinner. For too long making complicated meals had reminded her of evenings with Thomas. Evenings had been the best part of their days together, quiet, intimate times when they had worked side by side and talked about their jobs. Tonight she would cook something special, and she wouldn't remember those nights and the hope that had stirred in her heart with each brush of a hip, each quiet laugh, each warmly assessing look.

She had already prepared the sauce and grated two kinds of cheese for lasagna when there was a knock at her door. She didn't even jump at the sound. Nowadays she was in no more danger than anyone else living in the Corners. No longer was she marked for retribution.

The Coroners and the MidKnights hadn't suddenly become buddies; that might be asking the impossible. But a truce of sorts was in force. Until another Demon came along to stir up trouble, they coexisted warily. Candy and Francis came and went freely now. Andre was working at a center for the elderly and studying for his G.E.D. so he could start community college in the fall. Rumor had it that Thomas had been successful in having the gangs meet together at the church to discuss their differences.

Rumor was her only source of information about Thomas.

She washed her hands before she answered the door. The apartment smelled like garlic and herbs, and her favorite tape of Billie Holiday songs was resonating from her new stereo. Quite possibly she was on the up side of down now. Quite possibly she was going to put Thomas out of her life.

Four seconds of staring at Thomas, who was standing on the threshold, proved just how wrong one person could be.

"You look well," he said.

"What did you expect? Weight loss? Weight gain? Scars on my wrists?" She stepped back so he could come in if he wanted.

"It smells like I'm interrupting dinner."

"Not yet."

"I could come back another time."

"But the question is, would you bother?" She gestured toward the apartment. "Come in. Or the hall's going to smell like garlic."

"It already does." He stepped inside. The apartment was hardly the same sad place he recalled from his last visit. Then it had been a burned-out shell, and most of her belongings had been damaged by water or smoke. Now there were no signs that anything had ever been wrong here. The paint was fresh and the carpet new. Garnet's possessions, an eclectic mixture of things she had brought to his apartment and new purchases, were tastefully arranged to fill the room.

Why, then, did something seem out of order? He took another moment to scan the room, even though he knew Garnet was watching him. The apartment was pleasant, tidy and... dull.

For the first moment in a long, long time he wondered if things were really going to be all right, if *they* were finally, irrevocably going to be all right.

"What's wrong, Padre? Doesn't it meet with your approval? Think I should have put the sofa where the stereo is? I was still a little gun-shy there for a while. I kept thinking someone might use the back of my head for target practice if I sat too close to a window."

"Padre again? I've been a lot of things, Garnet. But never your father."

"True. You were around longer than he was. Not much longer, but longer." She gestured to the kitchen. "Want something to drink? I've got mineral water, juice—"

"This place doesn't look like it belongs to you."

"I'll have to talk to my decorator."

"There should be plants, funny little things on the shelves, a stuffed giraffe in the corner."

"My ceilings would have to be taller."

He swept the room with his hand. "The woman I knew wouldn't be happy living here."

"The woman you knew? I don't know who that is, Thomas. But the woman who moved back in here is satisfied with things the way they are."

"Is she? The man you knew isn't."

She looked away. "Feel free to take a seat. I've only put in a ten-hour day, and I'm in the middle of making dinner."

"At least the sense of humor hasn't changed."

She felt herself go cold with anger. Icy, aching cold. "Don't you think so? Well, who the hell are you to worry about it? You find this situation humorous? I don't. Not one little bit. Why are you even here? One of your pastoral calls? Haven't I been at church often enough for you?"

"You haven't been at church at all."

"And that's the way it's going to stay. If I want church on a Sunday, I'll visit St. Michael's or Second Baptist or the temple at the end of Wilford."

"Better try the temple on a Saturday or you'll be disappointed."

She stared at him. "What are you doing here?"

"Right now I'm trying to warm you up a little."

She couldn't believe him. This was not the Thomas she had known. His blue eyes were sympathetic as they searched for clues to her feelings. He looked both tormented and confident, a combination no one else could have managed. The torment? She couldn't speak for its source, but the confidence was easier to pinpoint. It seemed to exude from him, to be a very part of his being.

"Why?" she asked. "Why do you care whether I'm warm or cold as a glacier? Why should it matter to you? You're here to talk about a divorce, aren't you? You're too considerate to have me served with papers without a warning."

"That's not why I'm here."

"I'm a little tired of guessing games."

"*May* I sit down? Or would it really be better if I came back later?"

She sighed. "Sit."

He sprawled at the edge of her new sofa. It was something she'd bought without much thought. She'd needed a place to sit. The sofa had been in the front of the first and only furniture store she'd visited, which had cinched the decision for her. Now she noticed that it was too low to the ground and narrow. Thomas made it look as if it had been designed for a children's playhouse.

"Will you sit, too?"

Reluctantly she chose to sit beside him. The only other seat had been placed so far away that sitting there would look as if she was afraid of him. And fear was one of the few emotions she wasn't experiencing.

"I don't know how to start," he said.

"Then I guess this is going to be a long evening."

"Make this a little easier for me. Be polite." He softened his words with a smile that cut heavily into her defenses.

She leaned back and settled in a little. "I'm sorry." She shrugged. "I'm listening."

"I've wanted to see you for months now. I've wanted to talk to you every day since you left."

"You know where I live."

"I've been afraid I'd get here and do what I'm doing now."

"Ramble? Avoid the issues?"

He smiled again; then he leaned back, too, and slipped his arm along the back of the sofa. He wasn't touching her, but he was closer. Their positions were almost intimate.

She felt herself respond. Her analysis of it was clinical. Her heart beat faster; her temperature rose. Her immune system refused to cooperate with her brain and reject the foreign body beside her. She still wanted Thomas. God help her, despite the most crushing rejection, she still undeniably wanted him.

"I've done a lot of thinking since you left," he said. "I've had lots of time. I never knew an apartment could feel so empty."

She knew just how empty an apartment could feel. She gave a noncommittal nod.

"Do you remember the last thing you said to me?" He didn't wait for an answer. "You told me I thought I was better than God, because I could forgive Andre, but I didn't believe God could forgive me. I felt like you'd slugged me in the gut."

"If you've come for an apology, I'll say I'm sorry. I had no right."

"Don't be sorry. You changed my life." He wanted to touch her hair. It was restrained in a tight braid, as restrained as her apartment, as the tight line of her mouth. He wanted to release her hair, to see it fall over the back of the sofa and bounce against her shoulders, to send its electric tendrils curling around his fingers.

Garnet wanted to demand that he get to the point, but she knew how revealing that would be. She had already revealed far too much emotion. She waited, and the atmosphere in the room grew more charged.

"You were right," he said at last. "You made me face the truth. I never lost my faith in God, but I believed God had lost His faith in me. If I, with all my sins, all my fallibility, could forgive Andre, then surely God, the infallible, could forgive me. But in my arrogance, I believed that my sins were too terrible for God to forgive. I'd failed to be a god myself, but I still thought I was above God's forgiveness. So I shut Him out of my life."

Despite all her efforts, she was moved by the expression in his eyes, an expression almost of wonder. "And that's changed?"

"Yes." He smiled again, such a different smile than she remembered, but somehow a hundred times more captivating. She could feel more of her defenses being whittled away. Quite obviously this war was to be won with smiles and warm, sensitive looks.

She looked away, but the damage was already done. "I'm glad for you, Thomas."

"You've given me back my life," he said.

"No, I didn't give you anything. I was angry. I wanted to hurt you. That's all."

He touched her shoulder. She couldn't avoid looking at him any longer. "You gave me back my life. You were the only person who would stand up to me and make me face the truth. Not only because you were angry. Because you saw my arrogance, and you cared enough to make *me* see it, too."

"However it happened, I'm glad for you."

As the rest of her defenses crumbled, she faced the fact that she had never stopped loving him, never stopped caring what happened to him. Despite what she knew was coming, a divorce, a complete and final severing of all their ties, she could not protect herself from loving him.

"I'd lost the most essential part of myself, Garnet. It's taken months to put it in perspective."

Months when he hadn't called her or come to see her. She was happy for him, genuinely happy, but she knew that those months were proof that she, Garnet Anthony Stonehill, had never really mattered to him. If she had mattered, he would have come to her sooner and shared his battle with her.

She told herself that the final thing she could do for him was to make this easy. "Now you want to get on with your life. Both of us deserve that much. Our marriage was never intended to be real. I was upset when I left, but afterward I realized I'd never thanked you for what you'd done for me. Maybe it didn't turn out exactly the way either of us planned, but you tried to protect me. And that was the reason you married me."

"No, it wasn't." He gave in to the impulse to touch her hair. The solid mass of the braid was unsatisfying against his fingertips. "I married you because I needed you in my life. You were everything I wasn't—warm, vital, alive. I'd been a dead man for more than two years. I couldn't bear to think that something might happen to you, that you might die and I'd lose the one glimpse of life I'd had. Even then, even in those first hours together, I loved you."

She couldn't look away again. He had captured her. She made a noise low in her throat, a protest, a moan. He wove his fingers into the braid and slowly, giving her all the time she needed to move away, brought her lips to his.

She'd had both no time and all the time in the world to resist, but only when his lips touched hers did she realize how final her defeat was. Kissing Thomas was a door into the world, into emotion, sorrow and despair. She didn't believe they could start where they'd left off and build something new together. She didn't believe he really loved her. He was an honorable man, a man who believed in standing by vows, even vows made for the wrong reasons.

Yet she kissed him anyway. His mouth slanted over hers, and she drank in the moist warmth of his kiss as if she were dying and he could keep her alive. Her hands crept to his neck. His skin was warm, and she could feel the rapid thrum of his pulse against her fingertips. Her lips parted, and the invitation was accepted. The kiss deepened, and he moved closer; she moved closer, too, until her breasts pressed gently against his chest.

At last he cradled her head against his shoulder. He had loosened her hair and spread it like a cape around them both.

"The attraction has always been there," she said, giving him one last chance to retreat, "but that doesn't mean the marriage can work. You don't have to stay married to me. Your obligations are over, and you're alive again."

"Will you marry me?" he asked against her hair. "A real marriage? I couldn't come to you before. I wasn't sure I could be the husband you needed."

"Sex is only a part of marriage. We could have worked it out if we'd tried."

"I'm not talking about sex. I'm talking about all the ways I failed Patricia. I was ambitious and shortsighted and selfish. I never let Patricia be a real wife, and then she was gone and I didn't have a chance to try anymore."

"But you understood how you'd failed her."

"I still questioned my ability to be a real husband to you. Can you see that? I was afraid I hadn't learned enough from what had happened, but even worse, I was afraid there was something vital missing inside me. I couldn't trust myself, and I didn't trust God. I was sure I'd sinned so terribly that I was beyond His love. I couldn't be a real husband to you before, not in any way that mattered. I wouldn't let myself. Now, I can be."

She knew he was talking about more than days spent building a marriage. He was talking about nights together in each other's arms. "And what will happen if you try to be a husband, if you try to make love to me, and you still can't?"

"Then we try again. And if that doesn't succeed after a while, we go for help." He smiled tenderly, confidently. "But I don't think we'll need to save our pennies for counseling. I don't think we'll need to worry about counseling at all."

She knew what he was offering. A lifetime together. This was not to be a marriage of convenience. Nothing would be held back now. From this moment on, if she said yes, they would share their days and nights, share their anger and sorrows, and most of all—and most frightening—share their love. It would hurt. There would be times when they both would wish they had never married, times when life in the Corners would make love painful.

She knew what she was getting into. But she knew, even better, what life was like without him. "I think I've said it before. I've always lived dangerously."

She could feel him sag against her, as if he had doubted that she would accept. He squeezed her tightly, exuberantly. "You can't know how much I've missed you. I just had to be sure I could give you what you needed. I love you too much to shortchange you."

This time she surrendered her doubts that he loved her. He had told her twice. But she didn't know where to go from here. This was nearly perfect. She was afraid to breathe, afraid to move, because she was afraid that if she did, she would find she had dreamed it all.

Then he kissed her again, and she knew it wasn't a dream. He was warm and real and determined. The patience it had taken to explain himself was gone. His hands trembled slightly against her neck, but not, she thought, from fear. From desire. From longing.

Months of repressed feelings welled inside her. She couldn't touch him enough. Later she would take her time, explore him slowly and thoroughly, indulge herself in the feel of his broad shoulders under her palms, his heartbeat under her fingertips. Now she swept him with her hands, touching everywhere and nowhere, filling her senses with the whole man.

She couldn't separate one kiss from another, one warm, intimate caress from the next. Her clothes disappeared, and she didn't know how they were removed. His followed the same path, and she had only the vaguest sense of helping him undress. Passion was a haze that both sped and slowed time. Words blurred one into the next in her head. She only realized that she had told him out loud that she loved him when he responded in kind.

On her bed, their bodies entwined, she was too overcome with happier emotions to have any room for fear. Sometime between one burst of sensation and another she had pushed away all doubts. She had to believe Thomas's promise that if he was still unable to make love to her, it wouldn't matter. They would find a way to conquer this, as they had conquered their emotional barriers. Surely this, too, could be theirs. He wouldn't withdraw ashamed, tortured into silence once more. He wouldn't sacrifice their marriage on the altar of his pride. The marriage would be real, no matter what happened here.

While they were entwined, he rolled to his back, bringing her over him as he kissed her. She could feel the stretch of his legs, the breadth of his chest, the cradle of his hips, the proof of his longing for her. She knew he was ready for lovemaking. He had branded her with his kisses, left indelible impressions in her heart. Now he had only to claim her.

She slid her hands between them, but he grasped them before she could possess him. He turned her to her back, covering her with his body as he did. Then, gazing into her eyes, he made them one.

He didn't take his eyes from hers as he made love to her. Every emotion he felt was there for her to see, the joy, the love, the pride. In seconds she was lost, consumed by what she saw. She could feel his love inside her, like dawn after the darkest night.

He struggled for patience, murmuring love words and kissing her as he filled her again and again. He seemed to understand her deepest needs and doubts, showing her with his body, his lips, the emotion in his eyes, that she was his very heart. His love was sunlight, blazing through her to warm the coldest parts of her soul.

She had not known that lovemaking could be this way, that each movement, each caress, could be an awakening and a renewal. Now she was sure that he needed her in the most elemental way, just as she needed him.

When fulfillment was no longer an impossible dream but a reality neither of them could resist, she gave herself to the heat and the radiant burst that encompassed them both.

She gave herself to him.

~

Time passed before they spoke. She didn't know how much time. She had drifted into sleep, exhausted. Complete satisfaction was more draining than she had ever imagined.

"Are you awake?" he asked.

"Mmm..." She tried to cuddle closer and found it was impossible.

"Does this mean you're going to give our marriage another try?" he asked.

"And another and another." She brushed a lock of hair off his forehead. "I'll have to lengthen my skirts, won't I? And scoop ice cream at Wednesday night sharing suppers."

"Your skirts are fine, and you can leave the ice cream to somebody else. Just be there for me, and I'll be there for you. It will be simple."

She knew that being together would never be simple. They both had dragons to slay, both inside themselves and in the small world of the Corners where they had chosen to stand and fight. But she wasn't going to remind him of that. Not now. Because, simple or not, it was possible. It was necessary. It was as vital as the air they breathed.

"I'll be there," she said. "You can count on it."

He smiled the warm, confident smile that was completely new and one hundred and ten percent seductive. "And I'll be there, too," he said.

She gave herself up to the promise in his voice, his eyes, his hands. They had months to make up for and a lifetime ahead of them.

A real marriage had begun.

ABOUT THE AUTHOR

Emilie Richards is the author of seventy plus novels, which have been published in more than twenty-one countries and sixteen languages. Emilie has won the RITA from Romance Writers of America, and multiple awards from RT Book Reviews, including one for career achievement. She regularly appears on bestseller lists, and ten of her books have been made into television movies in Germany. Emilie lives in Southwest Florida with her husband in the winter and western New York in the summer.

Join Emilie and her readers at her website.

To learn more about upcoming books, giveaways and special content for subscribers, sign up for Emilie's mailing list at www.emilierichards.com.

AUTHOR'S NOTE

Some years ago I was happily writing romances for Silhouette Books when my editor tapped me for a new promotion. Did I have a profession I would like to explore? I immediately volunteered to write about a minister.

Be careful what you volunteer for. It's rarely as easy as it sounds.

At the time–and still--I was a big fan of ministers, having been married to one for years. Churches are microcosms of the world around them, with the same problems and possibilities. And the men and women who serve them professionally are saints *and* sinners, sometimes in the very same day. Like the rest of us, they get discouraged, angry, depressed, but they also find inspiration and sustenance not only from their relationship with the holy, but also by trying to make the world around them a better place.

I didn't want to preach, and I wasn't interested in writing about anybody who had all the answers. In fact the more I got to know the Reverend Thomas Stonehill, the more I realized he had few. The answers he'd found earlier in life had all been destroyed by a personal tragedy, leaving him an empty shell. Then in walked Garnet Anthony, a maternal health nurse as different from the women he'd known, as fire and ice. Put them together in the inner city where gangs roamed the streets and opportunities for a better life were few, and the book, which was then titled *Dragonslayer,* came into being.

The year after publication, the book won the Romance Writers of America RITA award, and just as thrilling, one of Romantic Times magazine's extremely rare 5 Star reviews.

In the words of Melinda Helfer, one of RT's top reviewers: "*Innovative plots can often open gateways for an author, but they can never take the place of the gifts of the human experience that the very best books bring to our hearts. Every reader has their own set of 5s, books that have significantly influenced the way they look at the world. Without question, Dragonslayer (5) is one of mine.*"

I hope that you, too, find this story compelling, and that the characters' struggles will resonate with your own, as different as they may be. I've made only a few revisions to help make the details more relevant for today's readers. But the story is the same, and all these years later, I'm still delighted I wrote it.

The biggest revision of all is the title. *Hold Back the Night* represents the story so much better I couldn't resist.

In the years since I've written two more novels with ministers as major characters. *Endless Chain*, the second novel of my five book Shenandoah Album series, and *The Color of Light*, the fourth novel of my Goddesses Anonymous series. You can discover more about both of them by following this link to my book pages.

~

If you would like to share your thoughts about *Hold Back the Night*, please take a moment to share your review online. Reviews are always appreciated by authors and other readers.

To learn more about upcoming books, giveaways and special content for subscribers, sign up for Emilie's monthly newsletter at www.emilierichards.com.

ONCE UPON A FEELING CHAPTER 1

If you enjoyed *Hold Back the Night* I think you'll enjoy some other earlier romances. You can find the list of available books at my website at emilierichards.com under ebook exclusives. Here are two of my favorites, though, written about the same time as *Hold Back the Night*. They are connected stories meant to be read together. I hope you enjoy this excerpt from *Once Upon A Feeling.*

Elisabeth Whitfield is having a doozy of a midlife crisis, but that midlife is about to take an extraordinary turn. Following a near-fatal car wreck, the Elisabeth who awakens in the hospital is a new woman, in someone else's younger, sexier body. Now she has a second chance at the exciting life she gave up to marry and be a full-time mother. But "be careful what you wish for" could be more than a cliche. Getting everything she wanted might cost her everything that matters.

Publisher's Weekly said: "Richards guides Elisabeth through this seductive women's daydream with skill, humor and an iron morality."

Purchase *Once More With Feeling at emilierichards.com.*

ONCE MORE WITH FEELING: Chapter 1

Sometime during the restless eternity of Thursday night, Elisabeth Whitfield dreamed that Owen, her husband of twenty-five years, was having an affair. She woke up Friday morning, as she had every morning for the past month, afraid it wasn't a dream at all. As Friday afternoon waned she completed preparations for the dinner party that might give her the proof she needed.

Elisabeth's parties were always elegant, tasteful, and ultimately forgettable, too much like their hostess to be truly memorable. She had learned to give a party from her mother Katherine Brookshire Vanderhoff, who had insisted that God and the American flag came in a poor third and fourth behind an eternally pleasant expression and a flair with canapés. She had learned to choose wines and menus, caterers and florists. She had learned how to set a congenial atmosphere.

But she had never learned to like any of it.

This afternoon Elisabeth was enjoying the fine art of hostessing even less than usual. Weeks before, when she had seen the party only as a chance to socialize with old friends, she had rashly decided to hire younger, fashionable, and totally unfamiliar staff. Now, with her enthusiasm at a historically low ebb, she was paying the price.

The new caterer, a sleek young redhead in Ralph Lauren khaki, had furtively examined every visible room of the Whitfield residence as she and her assistant marched in and out carrying platters and equipment. Elisabeth's own kitchen had not yielded the proper number of copper bowls and marble pastry slabs. She had carefully evaluated the neoclassical furniture, Owen's prized collection of Barbizon landscapes, the octagonal skylights and the white granite floor of the entrance hall.

"You have an absolutely spectacular home," the caterer pronounced at last, when Elisabeth's kitchen no longer looked as if it belonged to her.

Elisabeth acknowledged the compliment with the smile she had learned from her mother. "It's kind of you to say so."

"I've catered parties all over the Gold Coast, and I've never seen anything quite like this. Everything's . . . perfect." The young woman dragged out the last word like a feline with an exceptional vocabulary.

"My husband is the architect."

"I know."

Elisabeth suspected that the caterer also knew what clients Owen had designed for, the international competitions he had won, and his income to the nearest hundred thousand. She obviously had her sights set on more than the kitchens of Long Island.

The florist was new, as well. The old man who had faithfully provided Elizabeth with pastel tulips in the spring and pastel chrysanthemums in the fall had died quietly at Christmas, knee deep in pink and white poinsettias. Rick With-No-Last Name, his ponytailed and fashionable replacement, was a different breed entirely.

Elisabeth found the young man in the first floor powder room, assembling an arrangement of leafless twigs and excrement-hued cinnamon fern in three upturned rolls of toilet paper. As she watched he stood back to observe what he'd done, then leaned forward and artistically unwound a foot of one of the rolls and draped it over the edge of the counter.

It was good toilet paper. Elisabeth had to give him that much. A squeezable roll of ecological white. He turned and grinned infectiously. "Sm. . .oking!"

Blinded by white teeth and shining expectations, she lowered her eyes and found an arrangement of brightly colored bowl brushes in a stainless steel urinal on the floor beside the commode. The brushes were interspersed with long stems of bottlebrush buckeye.

"I can't wait to see what you'll do in the dining room." She added a gentle, vaguely regretful warning. "Just remember, there are going to be some terribly staid old fogies here tonight. And there are only so many Nassau County paramedics on call at any given moment."

He laughed conspiratorially. "I thought an aquatic theme since you're serving fish . . ."

She pictured mermaids impaled on skewers and belly-up dolphins with arugula and radicchio in what passed for their navels. "Remember the first arrangement you did as a very young man. That's what I want."

"Can't do it. I didn't bring my skulls today."

Elisabeth could see that this conversation, like too many aspects of her life, had spun out of control. Rick had quickly guessed the truth about the woman who had hired him. She was the eternal peacemaker, a doormat who would always back down rather than cause a fight. She was so nauseatingly gracious, so intrinsically diplomatic, that one time or another every charity on Long Island had asked her to oversee a fund-raiser.

She was a woman on whom a man could easily cheat, assured that she would be too dignified to call the matter to his attention.

She swept methodically through the rest of the house to consult with the cleaning crew, examine the linens and reprimand Owen's bookend golden retrievers, who lolled on a Savonnerie carpet and refused to move as much as a tail for Georgina, the gray-haired matron in a fifties housedress who was attempting to vacuum around them.

Today Elisabeth found no comfort in familiar rituals. She probably needed hormones. She definitely needed a drink.

Instead, upstairs in the master suite bath she fished aspirin from a plastic vial and swallowed it without water. In the mirror with a museum-quality gilded frame, she saw an ash-blond, forty-something woman with a serene expression and pale blue eyes that were as untroubled as the May sky.

Behind the eyes was a fishwife clawing her way to freedom.

She washed her hands and automatically massaged lotion over them. At thirty she had been able to pretend that she would age gracefully. She had dieted and exercised, and the flat plane of her abdomen had fueled the lie. But now, at forty-eight, the truth was always in view. Hands with prominent veins, hips that had blossomed to their full genetic potential, feet in shoes that were designed primarily for comfort.

The telephone rang, but she ignored it. It would be Owen's secretary Marsha, checking to see if Elisabeth needed any last- minute assistance before the party. If there were errands, Owen wouldn't do them himself, of course. His staff was motivated to help by personal loyalty and generous salaries. Owen would smile his warmest smile and extend his hands in a little-boy-lost gesture. They would respond with whatever was needed. Scottish salmon from Fraser Morris? Consider it done, Mr. Whitfield. Three bottles of Chateau Haut-Brion? I'll make the calls.

Owen could design and oversee every detail of the construction of award-winning houses or entire developments, but he could not locate a case of Bordeaux if he were standing in a Paris wine cellar. Everyone understood that.

She had understood it once upon a time.

Elisabeth had one blessed hour before she had to reassemble the worst of the florist's masterpieces, an hour before she had to give last-minute instructions to the caterer. She forced everything out of her mind: the fact that she was growing older with nothing substantial to show for it, the fact that she was married to a man who looked at her and didn't see her anymore, the fact that she was giving an intimate dinner party for her closest friends and was no longer looking forward to being with any of them.

The fact that one of her guests might well be sleeping with her husband.

She did what she had been doing for more than a year to forget the shackles that bound her to her outwardly enviable life.

She turned on the television.

On her bed, snuggled against Irish lace pillows, she watched a familiar crystal globe materialize on the screen. Once she had counted the globe's facets by taping the opening of the show, then pausing frame by frame as the globe turned full circle. There were twenty-four, each with a different scene reflected on its surface. She knew each image, although the effect was meant to be subliminal. A soaring eagle, the convertible that had carried Jack and Jackie Kennedy on their final ride together, the mushroom cloud of a nuclear bomb, Hopi kachina dancers, Bill and Hillary.

That scene dissolved into the next. A gavel fell against a polished wood surface, once, twice, three times. And before the sound could die away, a man began to speak.

"What you are about to hear is the truth, the whole truth, and nothing but the truth." Elisabeth mouthed the words in sync with the announcer. As the final truth was uttered, a woman appeared on the screen.

"Hello. This is *The Whole Truth*, and I'm Gypsy Dugan."

Before she had married Owen, in the days when she was still young and filled with confidence and spirit, Elisabeth had worked in television news, too. She had briefly tasted the joys that Gypsy probably took for granted, and she had relished them.

She didn't know when Gypsy Dugan had become her alter-ego. She didn't know when the sexy news anchor had begun to represent all the things that were missing in her own life. She did know that no one suspected her fascination with the woman or the show, and that she intended to keep it that way.

She was Elisabeth Whitfield, scion of a family as old as the thirteen colonies, wife of the revered Owen Whitfield, mother of a grown, beloved son. She appeared to have everything, but she was only just discovering how little she had settled for.

On the screen Gypsy Dugan shook back her short dark hair. There was nothing warm or sympathetic about her smile. It was as erotic as an X-rated film and every bit as cynical. She was Scarlett O'Hara with a mission. No matter how maudlin the subject matter, how shocking the feature story of the day, her dimples flirted dangerously with her ripe, full lips. She was every man's fantasy and every woman's nightmare. She was Gypsy Dugan.

And she was a living reminder that Elisabeth Whitfield might have been somebody, too, if she had just tried harder.

TWICE UPON A TIME CHAPTER 1

Mary Kate McKenzie has pledged herself to a life of service, but a knock on the head shatters her rose-colored glasses. She awakens, a stranger in her own mysteriously pregnant body. The starry-eyed young woman, who planned to devote her life to the Eden's Gate religious community, is now a take-no-prisoners dynamo who avoids sentiment and religion.

Despite this, or because of it, she manages to capture the attention of the wayward teens she works with in the center's community garden. But when former broadcast journalist Charles Casey arrives to do a newspaper article, his presence begins to unlock memories of someone else's life. Whose? And who is the father of the baby she carries?

Romantic Times said: "*Emilie Richards gives her fans a wonderful companion book to her first reincarnation novel,* Once More With Feeling. *You will smile and root for the indomitable Mary Kate, as she faces her uncertain voyage of self discovery.*"

Purchase *Twice Upon A Time at emilierichards.com.*

~

TWICE UPON A TIME: Chapter One

"Hey man, you got a cigarette?"

Charles Casey got out of his car and faced the boy who had asked the question. The teenager wore a Cavaliers' starter jacket and a sneer, one as well-worn as the other. "Nope," Casey said. "Not even a stub."

The kid shoved his thumbs in the pockets of his jeans in a stance Casey recognized from childhood street corners. "I bet."

"Sorry, but those things can kill you."

"Yeah? Something else'll get me first." The kid spit on the ground before he sauntered off.

Casey watched for a moment before he realized he ought to lock the car. This was rural mid-America, where "delinquent" was a word the gas company stamped on an overdue bill. In the month since he had left the Big Apple, Casey's street smarts had already gotten rusty. "Welcome to Eden's Gate," he said under his breath.

He twisted his key in the lock and started toward the house where the Sisters of Redemption lived and administered the Eden's Gate Ecology Center. It was a hulking Victorian monstrosity--Second Empire, if his memory of old college lectures served him correctly. He didn't have to knock. Two more teenagers, a boy and a girl, came out the side door with a middle-aged woman between them. She smiled and held the door, and Casey entered the house through a warm, fragrant kitchen.

By the time someone showed him to the administrator's study, Casey had already gotten a feel for the house. The rooms were spacious, the furniture simple and comfortable. The atmosphere was serene, with a subtle character all its own.

As he waited for Sarah Bradshaw he went to the window to contemplate the winter-brown landscape stretching beyond the house. Contemplation was becoming Casey's closest friend. Every night when he was supposed to be sleeping, he questioned the events that had brought him so far from his home in New York. Every morning when he thought about the day stretching in front of him, he considered the decisions he had made.

In between he had plenty of time to ask himself if he had lost his mind.

"Mr. Casey? I'm sorry I've kept you waiting."

Casey turned to see an attractive woman somewhere in her late forties coming through the open door, her right hand extended. He had prepared himself to discover that the Sisters of Redemption were nothing like the nuns that had taught in the Hell's Kitchen parochial school he had attended as a boy. But Sarah Bradshaw was still a surprise. She was dressed in a dark plum skirt with a blouse of palest lilac, and the colors perfectly complemented her ivory complexion and straight black hair with its wide silver streak.

He shook her hand. "I'm pleased to meet you, Sister." He paused at her grimace. "I'm sorry. Isn't that correct?"

"We're an informal bunch here. Just call me Sarah."

Casey stepped around a coffee table as she ushered him to a couch that sat at an angle from a massive rosewood desk.

The office had provided a number of clues to the woman, if he had cared to look for them. Despite the carved walnut paneling and twelve foot ceiling with its ornate plaster frieze, the room had a no-nonsense appearance. The paired triple hung windows were unembellished, so that the countryside view seemed to come right into the room. Books and photographs were the only adornments on the shelves, and the desk was uncluttered.

Sarah seated herself beside him, which was another surprise, and fluffed the cushions behind her. "You know, you're an answer to a prayer," she said, as she settled back.

He barely suppressed a snort. "That has to be a first."

"Not a religious man, I take it?"

Since adolescence Casey had been much too busy and much too guilty to risk crossing the threshold of a church. "Not so that anyone would notice."

She lifted a brow. "But raised a Catholic."

His surprise must have been obvious, because she nodded. "I can tell. No one knows what to do in the presence of a nun. Catholics think we're judging them for every sin they've committed, and non-Catholics remember the terrible jokes they've heard. But you definitely look like a man hoping to escape a thousand Hail Marys."

He liked Sarah Bradshaw already. "A thousand might not cover it. Anyway, I'm not here for confession. I want to find out if we can come to an agreement about a feature article for the paper."

"And that's the prayer that was answered," she said, going back to her first statement. "Some decent publicity for Eden's Gate."

"How do you know it'll be decent?"

"Do you mean considering the publicity we've already had? Or your background?"

He whistled softly. "Not pulling any punches, are we?"

"Sorry, but I never seem to have time for tact. Someday I'm going to resurrect my social skills, but for now, I have to cut to the chase. Keeping the center going is a big job."

"Some would say a big, futile job."

"Oh, absolutely. Most of the town of Shandley Falls would say so."

A knock sounded, followed closely by the same woman he'd seen coming out of the house. "I have tea and coffee, Sarah, and some of my shortbread."

"Wonderful." Sarah leaned forward and made a place for the tray on a table between symmetrical stacks of Sierra and Utne Reader. "Marie Bennett, this is Charles Casey."

As he murmured a polite greeting, Marie, a sandy-haired blonde, peered at Casey through thick glasses of a trendy oval design. "Better in person," she said calmly.

"Nicer, too," Sarah agreed.

"Glad to meet you, Mr. Casey." Marie turned her gaze back to Sarah. "If you want anything else, let me know. I'm on patrol this morning."

Sarah glanced at her watch. "Any problems yet?"

"Nothing worth noting."

Casey wondered if Marie meant that there was nothing worth noting in front of him. He listened with interest.

"No more destruction by the pond?" Sarah said.

"Everything looks peaceful. Most of the kids are washing windows in the greenhouse now." The door closed behind Marie, and Sarah bent to peek inside a white china teapot. "Coffee or tea, Mr. Casey?"

"Just Casey, please. And coffee." He didn't pause. "Tell me about the kids."

"During the school year we have a dozen or so teenagers assigned here for weekends by the juvenile court. In the summer they live and work here full-time. But I bet you knew that already." Sarah poured a cup from a taller pot and held it out to him. "I'll bet this coffee beats anything you had when you were working on *The Whole Truth*."

"The coffee at the paper's not much better." He took the cup and then a sip. "This is excellent."

"Well, we believe in quality." Sarah poured herself tea. "I hope you do, too."

"My reputation has preceded me." He tried not to smile. He was dark-haired and dark-eyed. He had been told by the only woman he'd ever loved that he had the black-hearted grin of a pirate.

"Your reputation would be hard to hide, wouldn't it? Until just a few months ago I could turn on my television five nights a week and watch you making your reputation."

"Or destroying it."

She watched him intently, as if trying to read his thoughts. "It all depends on perspective, doesn't it? You were very good at what you did."

"I don't do it any more. I left *The Whole Truth* forever."

"And moved well down the career ladder to a weekly paper in Ohio where the most exciting story you'll ever encounter will be the one about this center."

Casey, who didn't want to talk about his reasons for leaving New York, realized they were back at the beginning of their conversation. "Let's talk about that."

She didn't probe any further. "We've had more than our share of bad publicity since our center was established. No, it goes even further back than that. It began when the Sisters of Redemption inherited Eden's Gate. Right from the beginning people in Shandley Falls felt our presence could only detract from progress in the community. I'm not sure what they expected, but they did seem to feel we would change the character of the town, and they were right, of course. Because we have."

He pulled a notebook from the inside pocket of his sports coat. "You've been here one year?"

"One and a half. We spent the first six months assessing the property, improving the buildings and working with the local zoning board, the city council." She shrugged to show that the list went on and on.

She didn't seem at all perturbed by the experience. "And then?"

"We began to put together our programs. We made arrangements to work with the local hospice. We built dormitories and opened our program for juvenile offenders during our first summer. We spent that summer fine tuning it and publicizing our goals. And this year we've doubled the number of teens we're working with."

"As I understand it, that means you've gone from nine kids to eighteen, which is still surprisingly few considering how many troubled kids roam the streets of Ohio. Just from glancing around the estate and the facilities, you appear to have room for many more than that."

"Oh, we do. We hope to have up to sixty kids in the next two years, maybe more after we build new dormitories and renovate the barn as a meeting center."

"Has that program remained small because you're still feeling your way?"

"We've remained small because we haven't yet proven ourselves."

Casey's instincts were still intact, despite his career change. He leaned in for the kill. "In fact, haven't you proven that there are good reasons to be concerned about safety here?"

"I suppose if we were on television, this is where you'd zoom in to find me sweating and shaking."

Casey set down his cup, surprised to see that he'd already finished the contents. "Are you?"

"No." She looked absolutely calm. "We've had our share of trouble at Eden's Gate. That's a matter of record."

He opened the notebook. "Let's see. Last summer while camp was in session you had a fire in the girl's dormitory--"

"Which was immediately extinguished."

He continued. "A boy found with a knife on a field trip to the Cleveland zoo, a girl who accused a male counselor of attempted rape--"

"A charge she dropped immediately because it wasn't true."

"And finally, on a Saturday in December a nearly fatal attack on one of your sisters which resulted in permanent brain damage." He flipped through his notebook until he found a fresh page and pulled out a pen. "Am I wrong?"

"Not about the things that really matter, although some of your assumptions are incorrect." Sarah sipped her tea a moment, then she set down her cup. "First, Mary Kate, the woman who was injured, was--and is--on staff, but she's not one of the sisters."

"Really? I was told the teenagers called her Sister Sunshine."

"Their name. Not ours. Mary Kate had been working with us for some time before she was attacked, but she'd never taken vows. As for the brain damage. . ." Sarah looked up. "Her recovery has been astonishing. There was a time, at the very beginning, when we were told she would never walk, talk, laugh, pray. Her heart stopped on the trip to the hospital."

She shook her head. "It was a very difficult time for all of us. We were advised to put her in a nursing home, but no one was willing. So we undertook her rehabilitation here, following instructions and working with her constantly. No one in the medical community was hopeful, but one day. . ." Her voice trailed off.

"She's better, then?"

"Better?" Her eyes widened. "No, Casey. Nothing that mundane. Quite simply, Mary Kate is a miracle."

Originally published as *Dragonslayer* by Silhouette Books in 1993

Cover by Tina McGee

Ebook Creation by Michael McGee

CPSIA information can be obtained
at www.ICGtesting.com
Printed in the USA
BVHW031835101220
595394BV00024B/221

9 781950 365005